15 99

In the Same Space

To order additional copies, please contact us.
BookSurge, LLC
www.booksurge.com
1-866-308-6235
orders@booksurge.com

In the Same Space

Charles E. Soule

2007

In the Same Space

My sincere thanks to the following for their encouragement, for taking the time to read my manuscript and for making suggestions for its improvement. It has been a labor of love for me, but would not have been completed without the love of friends and family. They include:

Lori Boivin, Joe Boivin, Ann LaBrie, Andrew Lang, Kim Lang, Marc Lang, Chuck Soule, Jr., Elna Soule, Jared Soule, Jon Soule, Lori Soule, Pam Soule, Peter Soule.

And, to the editorial staff at Booksurge, Inc. for their careful and constructive editing of the manuscript, my sincere gratitude.

Dedication: To the Grey Lady, for inspiration.

I

PROLOGUE

The steamship ferry was cruising along toward its distant island destination. The man stood alone at the stern porthole, a large open oval one used for docking the ship, and he peered out at the gently rolling waves against the evening horizon. He appeared to be relaxed, perhaps contemplating the future or revisiting the past. A second man crept between the parked vehicles, and when he was as close as he could get without being heard, he moved silently from behind the nearest truck and quickly ran to the man at the porthole. He took the tire iron in his right hand and violently struck the first man on the side of his skull. Just as quickly, he stooped down, and as the now unconscious man fell against the porthole opening, the assailant picked up his legs and pushed him through the porthole. The body fell the seven feet to the ocean surface and drifted away from the ferry, unseen by anyone but the killer.

2

FRIDAY

Jack Kendrick sat in his car along with his yellow Lab, waiting for the ferry to complete the docking procedure so that he could get to his island vacation home and get settled in for the night.

The docking always seemed to take a little longer for the large ferry than he thought it should, his normal impatience showing. At first it struck the end of the docking pier gently, then floated back a short distance—a reaction to the initial bump. The captain then slowly moved the ship into its final position so it could be firmly locked to the dock. The ferry on this trip carried perhaps ten large trucks bringing freight to the island, and some twenty-five autos—just about a full load. The trucks were parked in the center of the vessel in four rows from front to back, or more nautically correct, from bow to stern. There were two more rows for vehicles on each side under an overhang that held cars alone. Jack Kendrick's car was on one of these side aisles, where he could not move forward until the car in front of him moved.

Jack was thinking about the chores he had to do over the next twenty-four hours to get the house ready for winter. He had finished work in Boston this Friday afternoon in early October, went quickly home, said a quick good-bye to his wife, Amy, and his two children as he rushed to catch the last ferry. Then he whistled to his dog, Jessie, who was only too willing to join him wherever and whenever he went. The quick one-day trip to Nantucket Island to close up the summer cottage was one Jack had taken for at least the last twelve years since he had married Amy, and the responsibility for care of the summer house fell to him. It wasn't really a problem or a chore, though, as he loved the island getaway as much as Amy and her family had for two generations.

He thought about how lucky he was to have this getaway, something that he could never have dreamed of before he met Amy. Neither his family, nor the income he made from his own job, would have ever supported the vacation home on what had become one of the most sought-after and expensive islands in the country. He enjoyed it mostly in the off-season when the crowds were gone and when you could walk the beaches or the moors and take in all the open beauty of nature and the expansiveness of the ocean. He even enjoyed the storms that, with the change in seasons, often brought thunder that seemed to echo louder than on the mainland, and the lightning that seemed so much more brilliant without buildings or hills to interfere with the spectacle.

The tasks to close up the cottage would be completed easily over the next day, and he mentally made a list of the things that needed to be done—putting away lawn and deck furniture, removing the flower boxes, putting on the storm windows, a final clean-out of the refrigerator, double-checking the windows to see that they were closed and locked, draining the water system, and finally turning off the electricity. Normally Amy and the two kids, Jeremy and Natalie, would have come along for a long weekend, but his work demands at WBOS allowed him to take only one day off this year—an unusually busy time for a TV cameraman.

As he drifted back from his daydreaming about the next twenty-four hours, Jack realized that his row of cars had not yet begun to move. Subconsciously he had heard the trucks and cars from the center aisles leave the ship, and he fumed a little that his own row was the last one to leave the boat. It sometimes seemed that he was always one of the last ones to exit the ferry, no matter when he drove his car on—his impatience showing again.

As he concentrated more on the sounds in the ship he noticed that while the car immediately in front of his had not moved, all of the cars in front of that one had left the ship.

Where is the damn driver of that car anyway? he wondered, almost speaking out loud. *He's holding up everyone behind him. Some people are so inconsiderate of others and live by their own timetable! There was plenty of time for that driver to have made his way from the passenger lounge upstairs down to the vehicle deck.*

Then Jack remembered that the driver who was causing his anxiety was the one he had visited in the passenger area during the two-hour crossing. *Why isn't he here? On the other hand, it's his first trip to the island, but he must have heard the announcement over the loudspeaker for all drivers to return to their vehicles. He must have known he has to drive his own car off the ferry, just as he drove it on.*

His thoughts were interrupted at that moment by a knock on his side window. As he rolled down the window, one of the ship's crew asked him, "Have you seen the driver of the Ford in front of you? That's what's holding up everyone in this line."

"I saw him in the lounge upstairs some time ago," Jack replied, "but I haven't seen him in the past hour or so." The crewman said they were bringing on a small tractor to move the car so that the remaining cars could leave. Apparently this had happened before, and they were prepared to promptly remove driverless vehicles and get on with the ferry's schedule.

3

Bill Andrews didn't know whether or not this trip was a wild goose chase. It had been a long time since he had become so involved in a drug case, but this one, still unsolved, had a special meaning for him. He had brought Ed Proctor into the agency and had worked with him for twelve years. His disappearance five months ago had been like the loss of a son, and the fact that no one had yet solved the mystery of his whereabouts kept the wound open and festering, even growing.

How could he retire from the DEA and take the chance that Proctor's disappearance would perhaps never be solved? And so, several weeks ago, Bill had taken it upon himself to personally dig into Proctor's files to try to reconstruct what might have happened, to find something that may have been missed in the previous investigation. He was scheduled to retire at year's end, after more than thirty years of service with the government, and he had convinced the director of the northeast region in Boston to let him pursue the mystery of Ed's disappearance. His years of service gave him some latitude in how he would spend his time during his last few weeks on the job.

Bill had spent all of his government years within the Justice Department, first with the FBI and for the last twenty years with the Drug Enforcement Administration. After several years in the field doing investigative work for both agencies, he had been assigned to the director's office in Boston. As deputy director he had seen the agency grow as the nation's drug problem grew, and he was aware of all of the outstanding agency investigations—more frustrations than successes. Although most of the nation's drug traffic came into the country through the southern borders, some came in through seaport cities like Boston.

Ed Proctor had been working on a case that had frustrated the DEA for many months. There was a steady source of heroin that was coming into southern New England that could not be traced. The DEA had determined that the supply of high-quality heroin was being significantly replenished every couple of weeks. The normal routes for drug trafficking had been watched, examined, and pursued, but there hadn't been any productive results. Ed had chased down dozens of leads—each one leading to a blank wall.

Bill remembered several casual discussions with Ed over coffee or lunch about the case. The file Ed kept had left a lot of gaps that Bill had tried to fill in from memories of those conversations. As Bill went through the notes he realized that Ed had clearly not been as disciplined and careful about recording the details as he himself would have been.

Ed had disappeared in May, and his notes for the month before his disappearance had unfortunately been especially brief. Bill recalled that Ed had mentioned a new lead that had pointed to Nantucket Island, just south of Cape Cod, as a possible source of the heroin flow. He remembered Ed mentioning something about fishing boats possibly bringing the drugs to the island. During the last lunch he had with Ed, he recalled that Ed had thought he might have an idea as to how the drugs were getting from Nantucket to the Boston area. But Bill couldn't recall any details, except that perhaps a trucking firm might be involved.

Bill had decided to make this trip to Nantucket in order to poke around for more information on the fishing boats. The ferry ride of thirty miles took a little more than two hours, and during the first hour he had sat in the passenger lounge and read a novel. A friendly young man had invited him to sit at his table in the lounge and they had talked briefly about mystery writers that they both enjoyed. The seats were not very comfortable, and after an hour or so Bill became restless and walked around the ship before deciding to check on his car on the lower vehicle deck. As he was walking around the vehicles to his own car, his thoughts returned to Ed's comment about a trucking company possibly being involved in transporting drugs to the mainland. He decided to take a closer look at the trucks on the ferry to see if anything helped him recall something more from his conversations with Ed. He had casually looked at some of the freight trucks while waiting to board the ferry in Hyannis. Most of the trucks were from various trucking companies delivering supplies, including food, building materials, and general merchandise, to the island. He was somewhat amazed at how many large tractor-trailers were carrying building materials, and then he recalled that Nantucket had been experiencing a building boom over the past several years. There was even one truck pulling a trailer with a pre-fabricated house on it. He thought he recalled that Ed had mentioned a general freight delivery line, like UPS, Federal Express, or some other express company, and he decided to concentrate on those kinds of trucks alone. After spending some time wandering down one aisle after another, he found four express-type trucks.

The first was a UPS truck, another was Federal Express, then a New England Express, and finally one called Island Delivery. While there were more than a dozen other trucks, of all shapes and sizes, these were the only ones that looked like they belonged to express delivery concerns. He wrote down the names and license plate numbers of each of them. Then, realizing that he appeared to be alone on the vehicle deck, he took a look inside the cab of each truck, but that didn't reveal anything. He wanted to look in the cargo area of each, but that was too risky and required a search warrant anyway. Even though he had no concrete reason at this stage to suspect anyone, he decided to try to identify each of the drivers before he left the ship. He felt better at least trying to put some pieces of a vague puzzle together, even though he might pursue an entirely different course of action once he arrived on the island. The best way to see the drivers was to find a good observation point and be as inconspicuous as possible.

With about thirty minutes to go before the ferry arrived, he walked to the stern of the boat, where he had a pretty good view of the stairs coming down from the passenger deck and where he might be able to pick out some of the drivers. He stood beside a large porthole—one used by the crew to throw out lines when the boat was being docked. As he looked through the porthole he could see a flashing light off to the east, and he assumed it was the Great Point Lighthouse, which he had noticed on the map. He knew that Nantucket was surrounded by shoals and shallow water that made for treacherous sailing, unless you knew the area and followed the charts. Many shipwrecks over the past three hundred years had occurred at different points around the island. The lighthouses, placed strategically around the island, were to help mariners avoid the shoals. It was a clear night and the stars were particularly numerous and brilliant. It always startled him to see the sky from the ocean on a clear night as the moon was brighter and the stars were much more numerous—not just a few hundred, but thousands across the heavens. It made him realize how small and insignificant one human being was, and indeed how small the earth was in comparison to the heavens. Although Bill had never done any sailing or navigating, he could appreciate how sailors could navigate by the stars on a clear night like this one.

The very last thought Bill Andrews had was suddenly becoming aware of a movement and a rustle behind him. As he was about to turn to identify the noise, his conscious thinking process ceased to function forever.

4

As Jack Kendrick sat in his car waiting for the car blocking him to move, he tried to recall more about its driver.

He had been in his late fifties or early sixties, and Jack remembered that he had said something about working for the government. He had said he had some kind of government business on the island for a couple of days, but Jack didn't want to be nosey and hadn't asked any questions. However, it had occurred to Jack that it was odd for anyone, never mind a government employee, to be going over to the island on a Friday to do "a couple of days' business." *Oh well,* he had thought to himself somewhat cynically, *it's probably an example of a civil service employee taking a weekend in a popular vacation spot at the expense of the taxpayer.* He also remembered the driver had said he would be retiring in a few months.

Jack had first met the man as they got out of their cars on the vehicle deck, and he had shown him the stairwell up to the passenger lounge. They had sat at the table together, and both of them became engrossed for a while reading novels. Somewhere partway through the trip, perhaps halfway across Nantucket Sound, the other man had apparently finished his book and then said he was going to "stretch his legs."

He never did come back to the table, and in fact had left his paperback there for Jack to read, since they had agreed to exchange their books. Jack finished his book just before the ferry arrived and took it with him as he left the lounge to give to the man. When he got to the vehicle deck he tried the door of the man's car, found it was unlocked, and tossed the book in the front seat on top of a folder that was left there.

Where the hell is he and where is the goddamn tractor to pull the car out of the way? Once again, his impatience was showing. In spite of his many attempts to get a little better control of it, Jack had never really gotten there. Amy was patient, and even patient with his impatience. He probably, subconsciously, took advantage of Amy's good nature. Well, opposite personalities did seem to balance out in marriage and in his case had led to a successful one; undoubtedly most of the credit should go to Amy.

Just as Jack was about to get out of his car and find out what was going on, a small tractor backed in, quickly hooked onto the car in front of him, lifted up the front end, and pulled it from the ferry. As Jack began to move his own car, the same crewmember he had seen before motioned for him to lower his window.

"What can you tell me about the driver of that car?" he asked. "I've got to make a report, and it would help to know what he looked like."

Jack was really in no mood to be delayed longer, but gave him a brief description of the man's age, height, and build. "I really didn't pay a lot of attention to how he looked or how he was dressed," Jack replied. "He was just an ordinary-looking older guy." Jack's description was at best rough—his best recollection of the man's appearance.

"OK," the crewman replied, "but could I have your name and telephone number in case the authorities have some questions?"

Jack gave him the information but told him he would be leaving the island on the late boat the next day. Finally the man thanked Jack and told him to go ahead and leave.

Jack and Amy's summer home was just on the outskirts

of the town, only about a mile from the dock, and Jack drove there with no further delays. The first thing he did upon arriving was to let Jessie out in the yard to relieve herself after the long ferry ride. Upon entering the house he went immediately to the thermostat to bring up the heat; the outside temperature was in the mid-forties and the house was not much warmer. He then grabbed a leash and took Jessie for a walk while the house warmed up.

When he returned a half hour later the heat had begun to take the chill from the house and he readied himself for bed. As he lay in bed his thoughts went back to the events on the ferry and the man who had never showed up to drive his car off. He tried to remember more about him, but their conversation had been very brief. He didn't seem to be the type of person who wouldn't realize he had to get down to the vehicle deck and be ready to drive his car off as soon as the ferry arrived. Just before he slipped off to sleep he thought, *Maybe he ran across someone he knew and got engrossed in a conversation, or perhaps he became ill up in the passenger cabin and was in the bathroom! Well, there had to be some logical explanation.*

5

Joe Hinkle left the ferry as inconspicuously as he could, considering he was driving a large delivery truck. He didn't want anything in the way he drove off the ferry to draw attention to himself. He was perspiring and his hands were slippery on the wheel. He wiped them against his trousers, pulled away from the dock, and drove to the inn where he had a reservation.

Shit, how could this same thing happen again? He had figured that after five months he had nothing to worry about. He had been really nervous and edgy for the first several weeks after that ferry crossing in May, when that first nosy DEA officer stumbled on him. He really hadn't had any choice but to get rid of him—to push him overboard. Luckily they had never found his body, and Joe had become convinced after a while that his own life would return to normal and the body would never be found. Well, as normal as anyone's life who was trafficking in drugs.

But here it was five months later, in October, with yet another DEA spook poking around where he had no business. On that first occasion in May, the government agent had made a point of sitting down with him on the boat and asking him questions. He had been just a little too friendly and too obvious in inquiring about how many trips Joe made to the island per month. What company was he with? What kind of things did he deliver and pick up? How long was he going to be here, and what boat was he taking back? At first Joe had joined in the conversation, but after awhile he had become suspicious. Finally Joe had said he really had to get some sleep because it had been a long day, and the man had left him alone. Sometime later, when the man went to get a cup of coffee, Joe had noticed a luggage tag on his overnight bag that said, "Justice Dept., DEA." *Did he purposely leave that there to try to intimidate me?* Joe had wondered back then.

Joe knew well what the DEA was, and was sure it was no coincidence that this guy had sat down with him and started to ask questions. Joe had decided that he had to do something about this dangerous character if he was going to be able to continue making the lucrative deliveries from the island to the mainland. He had finally decided to be a little friendly with Agent Proctor, engaged him in conversation, and inquired as to his stay on the island. He had learned that Proctor hadn't made any hotel reservations but was open to suggestions. Joe had offered to drive him to the Nantucket Inn, out near the airport, where he was going to stay himself. That's when Joe's plan had begun to take shape.

He had then encouraged Proctor to come down to the vehicle deck well before others were returning to their cars and trucks. As he was climbing into Joe's truck, Joe had struck him sharply—a karate-type blow—on the side of the neck. It had knocked him unconscious immediately, and Joe had quickly dragged the body to a large porthole nearby and dumped him overboard. He had then thrown the man's overnight bag in the truck and disposed of it when he returned to the mainland. With the help of the currents and the ocean sea life, the body itself had never been found. Ed Proctor's bag had contained a folder with rough notes on his DEA investigation into the flow of heroin from Nantucket to Boston. Somehow he had become suspicious of New England Express as a possible source for the transport of the drugs, and even though he hadn't had Joe's name anywhere, it was obvious to Joe that he had been getting too close.

Joe had wondered then who else had known of Proctor's investigation, of his suspicions about New England Express, and of Joe himself? After five months, however, he had convinced himself that he was really in the clear. The first couple of months Joe was fearful that someone else would pick up where Proctor had left off, but nothing had occurred to alarm him. He hadn't seen or heard or read anything that would be a tip-off that the feds were getting close.

But now, for a second time in just a few months, he had left the ferry having just killed a man—another DEA agent at that. This one hadn't tried to engage him in conversation, but he had been a little too obvious back in Hyannis looking at his truck and looking at him. Then he had found him on the vehicle deck when they were about halfway across looking into the cab of Joe's truck. There was no reason for this man to be down on the vehicle deck with an hour left in the crossing.

After becoming uneasy back in Hyannis, Hinkle had kept an eye on this nosy passenger and had followed him when he had gone downstairs to the vehicle deck. He had been sitting in the passenger area with another man, but Joe didn't think they were together. The agent had first circled his truck and then checked both the passenger and driver doors. Good thing he had locked them both! By this time Joe was certain this was another government agent. The man had finally looked into the cab, obviously trying to see something—anything! He had written down the license plate number and had then looked at some other freight trucks, also writing down their numbers; but Joe didn't think he had spent as much time looking them over. The spook had then returned to his own car briefly before walking to the stern of the ship.

Joe had taken the opportunity to do a little snooping of his own, and when the man was out of sight he had gone to look into his vehicle. He had opened the door cautiously and there, right on the front seat, was a similar folder to the one he had found in the first agent's overnight bag. The DEA—Justice Department logo was clearly stamped in silver on the blue background. He had opened the folder, taken out the papers inside, and stuffed them in his shirt.

That had clinched it! No more doubts that this too was a DEA agent who was getting close and looking for him. Joe had been lucky after the first killing, sure that he already would have been arrested if the DEA had had any clue. It looked like this agent was just poking around and didn't know even as much as the first agent. Otherwise, why had he been looking at several other trucks and not his alone?

Well, Joe had gotten away with the first one and the body had never been found. Could he be that lucky again? Would the sea and the currents be his allies in another crime? He couldn't afford to let this guy follow him around on the island! So Joe had returned to his truck, grabbed a tire iron, and crept to the rear of the vessel to find the agent. There was probably no better place for another murder and for getting rid of the body.

j

6

Albert Collins, senior detective in the Nantucket Police Department, would be through his shift in about fifteen minutes, at 11 p.m. His normal hours were much more civil—7 a.m. to 3 p.m. each day—but he was pinch-hitting for another officer who was on vacation. No one was given vacation time during the busy weeks of the summer; so now that the summer tourist season was over, the department's vacation schedule was just beginning in earnest.

Al Collins had the weekend off and it was time to get serious about scalloping. The season always began on the first Wednesday of October and he was usually one of the first out to get his catch before everything was picked over. This year, however, he had been too busy with overtime at the station and had not been out even once. He had heard that the Madaket Harbor area was supposed to be especially plentiful this season, and this was really great news, since the last few years the catch all over the island had been on the low side. Some people blamed it on the global warming effect of the ocean, some said it was pollution in the harbors and inlets where the scallops were normally found, and others said it was lack of conservation in the past—too many people taking too many scallops. The natives, however, said that the size of the crop ran in cycles, and a few bad years meant nothing. Well, maybe they were right, Al thought. In any event, he was going to get his maximum this weekend. He had to make up for lost time. Who knew when he'd have time to get out again?

The telephone rang and after a short conversation the switchboard clerk asked Al to pick up.

It was the steamship office explaining that they had pulled a car off the ferry that had been driven on in Hyannis by a passenger; but that the passenger hadn't turned up to drive it off in Nantucket. They had searched the ferry—bathrooms, dark corners, stairwells, and other out-of-the-way places—but with no luck.

Occasionally over the years, incidents had occurred on the ferry ride from Hyannis, usually the result of too much alcohol, and a passenger had to be arrested for disturbing the peace. On a few occasions passengers had fallen overboard, but usually someone had seen them fall or jump, and the rescue had been successful. There had been a few instances of successful suicides or suspected suicides from people jumping overboard on the high seas, but the last one of these had been some seven years ago.

Al put on his jacket and hat and drove the two short blocks to the steamship wharf. It was now ten minutes before his shift was to end, and there was no way he would be done before 11:30 p.m. It sure sounded like another suicide, and he would just have to wrap it up quickly.

He made a quick examination of the exterior of the car and found no marks or dents of any particular significance. It was a nondescript Saturn—nondescript in color as well as in its features. He opened the door, careful not to disturb fingerprints, and looked inside. There was a small overnight bag in the back seat and a thin folder and a book on the front seat. No marks or signs of a struggle or violence in the interior of the car.

He called over a couple of the crew who were standing nearby.

"OK, what can you tell me? Do you know anything about the driver? Did anyone see him or talk to him?"

One crewman said, "I guess I was the first one to notice that the driver was missing, but I don't know what he looked like or whether there was more than one person. I did talk to the driver of the car in back of this one, and he said he remembered the driver and had talked to him when they drove their cars on in Hyannis."

"Are you sure this wasn't a 'drive-on' in Hyannis and that one of the crew forgot to drive it off?" Al asked. It was possible to arrange to have steamship personnel drive a car on and off the ferry and for the car's owner to pick it up later.

"No, this wasn't a drive-on," the same crewman said, "and I also told you, another passenger visited with this driver after they got on board."

"You didn't say 'they visited!' You said another driver had simply talked to him. What do you mean, 'visited?'" Al's irritation and arrogance began to show through in the tone of his voice.

"Well," said the crewman, "he said he had seen the driver up in the passenger lounge, and it sounded like they had talked to each other. He gave me a description of the guy." The crewman handed over a piece of paper with the brief notes he had taken when talking with Jack Kendrick.

"Well, that's not a hell of a lot to go on," Al said, looking over the paper. "OK, I guess that's about all we can do here tonight!"

Detective Collins officially impounded the vehicle until it could be examined in the morning. Unless the driver showed up, he would have someone go over it carefully—take fingerprints, vacuum the interior, examine all of the contents. In the meantime, he would have the 11 p.m. to 7 a.m. shift people check on the vehicle registration and see if they could ID the missing passenger. There was no urgency to stay around longer this evening. There would be time enough when he called in tomorrow morning—his Saturday off! Chances were that the driver would show up, having left the ship with too much alcohol in his bloodstream. *What a goddamn nuisance!* he thought. *Things had better go smoothly or my weekend plans will be screwed up.* He put the contents from the car's interior into a plastic evidence bag and returned to the station.

By this time his replacement for the night shift had arrived and Al filled him in briefly and gave him the vehicle registration number to run through the identity check before rushing out the door.

7

On a clear fall day Nantucket Island can be seen about halfway across Nantucket Sound from Cape Cod. The first object that comes into view is the Great Point Lighthouse that sits on the northeastern-most arm of the island, isolated from the main part by some four miles of sand and accessible only with a four-wheel-drive vehicle. It is a spot that attracts many local fishermen early in the morning, especially when the bluefish are running. In the fall and spring many seals can be found bathing in the sun, most of them curious enough to stay close to shore even when humans show up. There are many shoals around the island that make it difficult for navigating boats with a deep keel, but the shoal running out from Great Point is an especially abundant area for fishing. This is a popular area for the charter fishing boats to bring their eager customers during the summer months—sometimes so many that it's a wonder there are enough bluefish to go around.

As the ferry draws closer to the island, the taller structures begin to come into view—the water tower at the end of Cliff Road, the white steeple of the First Congregational Church, and finally the gold dome of the Unitarian Church. Both churches are closely intertwined with the island's history, the Congregational Church and its Old North Vestry dating back to the early 1700s, when the town was first settled. It was later that the Quakers became a strong influence on the island's development, and later still in the 1840s that some of the members of the Congregational Church split off and formed the Unitarian

Church—a movement that took place in many other New England communities at that time.

The whaling industry grew from the late 1700s through most of the 1800s and was responsible for Nantucket's prosperity. Many sea captains and ship owners became very wealthy and built many large homes that still exist today. The island economy, however, began to decline sharply in the late 1800s with the advent of electricity and the fact that the Nantucket harbor was too shallow to accommodate the larger whaling ships that were being built.

The economic decline continued well into the twentieth century until tourism began to take hold following World War II. Today that tourism trend continues, and the Nantucket community is bustling, especially during the summer months when the population on a weekend may quadruple to more than 50,000.

As the ferry nears the island, it passes between the stone jetties that thrust out from the harbor, past Jetties Beach and the Brant Point Lighthouse that marks the entrance to the inner harbor. The auto and truck ferry docks are close to downtown Nantucket, the only true commercial center on the island. Actually, the island of Nantucket is also the County of Nantucket as well as the Township of Nantucket. There is one other small village on the eastern end of the island called Siasconset, but it is still part of Nantucket Township proper and has a small general store and a few restaurants that are open only during the summer months.

The island's growth during the last quarter of the twentieth century continues into the new century, a building boom that has made it one of the fastest growing towns in the state. The current year-round population includes many retirees, while the seclusion of the island has attracted many wealthy people as summer vacationers, many of whom have built large second homes.

During the off-season from September to June, the island becomes a relatively small and close-knit community of some 12,000 residents who are brought even closer together during the cold winter months.

8

SATURDAY

Jack Kendrick woke a little before 7 a.m. with Jessie standing next to the bed and breathing heavily in his face. He knew that the next step would escalate to face lapping, and then nudging, and finally barking—all sending the same urgent message that she needed to go outside and relieve herself.

Now well awake, he put on his jogging clothes—a long shirt and shorts would be OK once he got moving. The slow jog on the beach was really something he looked forward to, especially in the summer, but this time of year wasn't so bad either. Jessie knew the routine, and Jack expected that if he could get inside his four-legged friend's mind he'd find that the dog enjoyed the run at least as much as he did. Although for Jack it was the exercise that was paramount, Jessie was sure that the companionship was what really excited her—a common characteristic of "man's best friend."

They jogged about a quarter mile to Step Beach, down the stairs, all thirty-nine of them, to the sand dunes leading to the shore. Some parts of the beach were really too soft to run on, but once Jack reached the high tide area he found firmer footing. They ran west toward Dionis Beach and Eel Point, with Jessie jumping in the water and sniffing at various things and places on the beach. What a wonderful exploration of smells for a dog! After about half a mile Jessie picked up a cap that had either been left there by a sunbather or floated ashore from a boater who had lost it overboard. The hat said "Drexel University," was in pretty decent shape, and Jack saw no harm in letting Jessie follow her retriever instinct and continue to carry the hat on their jog. They reversed direction and ran back, past the entrance to Step Beach toward the largest beach on the island, Jetties Beach. Jessie continued to sniff at mounds of seaweed and an occasional dead fish, but always moved on after picking up the hat again.

Some dogs, especially retrievers, have to always have something in their mouths—usually a stick or some piece of wood—and sometimes look very silly and awkward. Jessie seemed to be particularly attached to this blue and gold hat. After reaching Jetties Beach, Jack ran past the jetty that was built out into the water, and then ran down the protected inside of the harbor to the beginning of the houses on Hulbert Avenue. He then reversed direction again and ran the mile back to Step Beach.

As he and his running pal were leaving the beach, Jack noticed several people standing on the edge of the shore a couple of hundred yards away, near the area where he had first run. It looked as though at least one person was standing in the water, and he thought to himself, *It's pretty cold to get wet, except for dogs.* They continued their run, about three miles in total, he estimated.

Back at the house, Jack took a shower, gave Jessie some water, and felt refreshed enough to begin his chores. After a light breakfast of juice, cereal, and milk he brewed himself a good-sized pot of decaf coffee. It was now a little after eight o'clock, plenty of time to finish what had to be done and still catch the 5:45 p.m. boat back to Hyannis.

First the storm windows! Thank God the entire window didn't need to be washed in the fall—just the storms themselves. They had been in the cellar since last spring and had collected the inevitable amount of dust and grime. The washing took more time than removing the screens and putting in the storm windows. The other big task was getting all the outdoor furniture into the cellar—chairs, lounges, tables, etc. He needed to save some time before 3 p.m. to make a trip to the dump before it closed. If he was lucky and had planned his time right, he might be finished early enough to take a late lunch downtown. He didn't particularly like eating out alone, but a bowl of chowder at the Brotherhood Restaurant would really hit the spot. That was something to look forward to, an incentive to get serious about completing his chores and to stop daydreaming. The Brotherhood was his and Amy's favorite eating spot, a pub-type place in the cellar of an older building with good food and a great atmosphere.

By 11:15 a.m. the windows were all in place, the screens put away, half of the lawn furniture was in the cellar; and Jessie remained sleeping off the morning exercise with the hat close by. The telephone rang and Jack rushed upstairs to answer it; but by the time he got there, the person had hung up. It must have started ringing while he was still outside, and he hadn't heard it until he got into the cellar. Well, it was undoubtedly Amy, and she would call back. No sooner had he returned to the cellar than the phone rang again. This time he made it before the fourth ring.

He was a little startled to hear a man's voice ask, "Is this John Kendrick?"

"Yes, it is!" Jack replied. "Can I help you?"

"This is Detective Lt. Albert Collins of the Nantucket Police."

"Yes?" Jack replied.

"You came over on the late ferry last night from Hyannis, and you were delayed leaving the ship because of a car in front of you?"

"Yeah, that's right! The driver in the car in front of me

never showed up to drive it off. I had to sit there for some time until the car was finally towed off the boat."

"We're trying to figure out just what happened last night and would like to talk with you. I understand you saw the driver of the car at some point on the trip and may have talked with him."

"Yes, that's correct. We chatted for a while on the boat, but I'm afraid I don't remember his name. I'm not even sure he ever told me what it was."

"Well," said the detective, "we know who he is, Mr. Kendrick, but we'd still like to talk with you."

Jack hesitated. Obviously he would cooperate with the police, but he didn't want to be tied up and either not complete his chores or miss the boat. *They obviously haven't found the driver of the car yet*, he thought. *I wonder if they think he may have fallen overboard.*

"Is this something we can handle over the phone?" Jack asked.

"No, we need to see you in person," Detective Collins replied quickly, with impatience in his voice.

"When would you like to see me?" Jack asked.

"Well, I'm here at the station now," Detective Collins said, "and this would be an ideal time for me."

Jack thought to himself, *Well, not so ideal for me!* but said, "Give me a few minutes to clean up and I'll be right down. No more than a half-hour."

Collins thanked him and hung up the phone.

"Well," Jack said aloud, "there goes my lunch and chowder at the Brotherhood."

9

Friday night, after the incident at the steamship, Al Collins had gone home, immediately to bed, slept soundly, and dreamed about the largest scallop bed on the island he was going to discover during the next couple of weeks. On Saturday morning, his supposed day off, he was up by 7:30 a.m. By that time his wife was already up and he could smell the breakfast being made—the aroma seemed to be one of bacon and pancakes. Saturday always began with a more leisurely meal because it was his day off.

As he was in the middle of a stack of pancakes, with an ample amount of maple syrup and butter, the phone rang. His wife, Alice, answered it and said, "Al, it's the station!"

What now? he thought. *I was going to call in a few minutes and check on that car on the ferry last night. What's the big rush?*

"What's up?" he asked, without saying hello or asking who was calling.

"Al, its Dick," said the weekend detective on duty, Dick Hines. "I'm afraid we've got a problem here and need you to come down." Dick spoke a little hesitantly, having experienced Al Collins' temper in the past.

"Jesus Christ, what kind of a problem, Dick? This is my day off, and I didn't get home until after midnight last night because of some stupid drunken idiot who forgot to drive his car off the ferry. Can't you handle it?"

"Al, this *is* about the car incident last night. We've ID'd the car, and it belongs to a DEA official out of Boston. We've also just had a call that a body's washed up on the north shore near Step Beach. I think—"

"Aw, shit! There goes this day! Give me a chance to finish my breakfast and I'll be down."

10

Joe Hinkle was up with the alarm clock at 7 a.m. He could have used more sleep after the late ferry arrival, but if he was going to catch the 5:45 p.m. boat back to Hyannis he had to complete his deliveries, make his pickups, and especially leave time for the "special" pickup that would put real money in his pocket.

The Nantucket Inn was out by the airport, away from town, and his company had special rates. The room was OK—the cable TV picked up some of the stations he was used to in Boston—but most of his favorite sports stations were missing. Also, the selection of movie channels was really limited—nothing that really appealed to him.

He packed his bag and went across the street to Hutch's Restaurant at the airport for breakfast around 7:30 a.m. His truck was about two-thirds full and he had to pick up some additional items that were being flown over from Boston this morning. The plane was to arrive a little after eight, and he could start his deliveries after that, once people were up and businesses were open.

That meant he had time enough for a good heavy breakfast, especially since he wouldn't be sitting down for a real meal until late this evening. The restaurant was a well-known eatery on the island for locals and offered the kind of generous helpings that any truck driver would appreciate. Around the walls were several pictures of the cast of the TV sitcom "Wings," which was centered around the airport on Nantucket. Joe ordered a double ham and cheese omelet with plenty of onions and peppers, along with several pieces of sourdough toast.

That should hold me until I get a sandwich for lunch! he thought.

After picking up the additional items at the airport, he began his deliveries. New England Express made two deliveries to the island each week, on Tuesday and Saturday. Its business was picking up small and medium-sized parcels, usually from retail or wholesale stores, and delivering them to customers. Almost all of its pickups and deliveries were in the six New England states, with a few stops along the New York border. NEEx advertised that it covered every town and village in New England, and that's why it made the long ferry trip to Nantucket, as well as Martha's Vineyard and Block Island. Many other truckers covered the mainland and large metropolitan areas but left it to smaller local companies to deliver to the more remote areas, especially in northern Maine. If the package was routed out of New England, then NEEx either passed it onto another trucking company, or more likely it was handled from the start by another trucking firm. Its rates tended to be less than some of its larger competitors; its delivery time was a little longer than other companies; but it attracted regional retail stores whose margins were thin and where overnight or two-day delivery wasn't essential.

The last few packages Joe picked up at the airport were some that had come into the Waltham, Massachusetts, terminal after he had left the mainland yesterday afternoon. His company flew them down on a small cargo plane for him to deliver this Saturday; otherwise their next delivery wouldn't be until the following Tuesday.

Joe had worked for NEEx for four years, the longest he had ever worked for anyone. The pay was OK, but not as much as the longer-haul truckers made, nor were the benefits as good.

But there were certainly some "extra benefits!" His hours were usually fewer than other truckers, since he could end his day as soon as the last delivery was made. He tended to be a faster worker than others, who he thought wasted too much time talking and visiting with customers along the way. NEEx didn't mind his leaving early as long as he had finished his route. His every-other-week trip to Nantucket was the exception. Both Friday and Saturday were long days—twelve to fifteen hours each—but some of the mainland drivers took turns with these trips, alternating with each other. Joe not only didn't mind the longer hours, but this was truly the highlight of his job, because it was this trip where he made his real money from those "extra benefits."

Joe Hinkle had had what many would consider a truly disturbing life almost from the outset. Born in the South End of Boston, he had found from an early age that physical size and strength gave someone a dominating presence over others. His father had left home when Joe was about nine years old, leaving Joe, his younger sister, and his mother, who had had to struggle to provide for the family throughout Joe's growing-up years. The only clear recollections of his father were the too-frequent physical beatings when he had misbehaved; and these occurred usually after his father had been drinking. His mother had allowed as how lucky he was that his father hadn't been around as he got into his teenage years.

When Joe was thirteen, he had joined a local gang, even though his mother had continually cautioned him to "stay away from those punks." He grew up in a tough neighborhood and learned to fight at a young age, if only to survive. As he grew, bigger and stronger than most kids his age, his fighting and quick temper became increasingly more aggressive, not defensive. He had been arrested three times as a youth, and although he hadn't had to spend time in a youth detention center, he had been on probation for many months. Two of the arrests had been for stealing and one for beating up a member of a rival gang. After the third offense, when he was threatened with being sent away—and with his mother's increasing pressure—he had gradually drifted away from the gang.

He had dropped out of high school at age seventeen and picked up odd jobs for a few years. Never one to "laze around," he had always seemed to be able to find some work, even though most of his jobs were menial. However, in his early twenties he had made contact with some of the old gang members and participated in several burglaries. He was caught after an armed burglary of a local liquor store and served six months at the Suffolk County Jail.

That had been the worst experience of his life, and he had vowed upon being released that he'd never return. However, after only about a year he had again found himself back in prison following another failed robbery—one that his buddies had told him was an "easy job with no risk." After his release from prison the second time, he had made a point to stay away from the old gang and had thus avoided any further trouble with the law.

Joe had been fortunate to meet Penny a few months after he got of prison the second time. She had been exactly what he needed as he tried to right himself, and over the next several months he had experienced what was to be the happiest period of his life. He went to work for NEEx on their loading platform and seemed to be settling down to a stable job. Penny became pregnant and they were married. Their relationship continued to grow as a young couple and, with the birth of their daughter, Joe found he even enjoyed the playful affection of his baby.

After a couple of years he was offered a job as a truck driver for NEEx and got a good jump in pay; however, by that time things had begun to deteriorate in his marriage. Two years later Joe and Penny divorced, and Joe had even cut off contact with his infant daughter, except for the monthly child support payments, which he greatly resented making.

The further he got away from the experience of his imprisonment, the more the temptation for "easy money" began to overcome his fear of being caught again. He had been ready to leave NEEx for a higher-paying truck driver job when Bennie Haas, a friend from his old neighborhood, approached him with a deal. Joe knew that Bennie had been into drugs going back to their days in high school, and there were rumors that he was now making really "big bucks." Bennie had been arrested a couple of times in the past and had spent a few months in prison for a drug offense, although a plea bargain had lowered the charges from dealing to possession of drugs.

Joe had immediately jumped at Bennie Haas' proposition. He was told all he had to do was pick up a package or two at the waterfront in Nantucket at the end of each of his routine trips for NEEx, and then drop them off with Bennie on his way back into Boston. Bennie never said, but Joe guessed it was some kind of drugs, probably cocaine. Actually, he didn't really care to know, since the price was right—$1,000 for each trip. That put an additional $25,000 a year into Joe's pocket—all non-taxable. Easy money!

Joe had asked Bennie about the risks and was assured that they were almost nonexistent. After Bennie described exactly how the pickup would work he felt more relieved; and after all, he was being paid good money for each trip to simply make a pickup and delivery. Wasn't that what trucking companies did anyway? A great cover for drug trafficking!

Everything had gone without a hitch for the past two years until the DEA snoop appeared last May, and now, a second one last evening. Joe had a great fear of going back to prison, and now the issue was murder, not burglary or even drug trafficking.

How close are they to finding me? Joe asked himself. *Should I quit while I'm ahead? On the other hand, if they were sure I was involved, wouldn't I have already been arrested? And how can I replace the extra $25,000 a year of easy money that allows me to do the things I really want to?*

Since he had agreed to Haas' offer two years ago he had become really dependent on the additional money that made it easier to make the child support payments—although not without his continued resentment. He didn't want to think about going back to breaking and entering in order to make some extra money, and he wanted even less to think about spending more time in prison. This time it would be for a long stretch—probably a life sentence!

Bennie had told him yesterday that there was an additional "special" pickup coming in the next month, and there'd be an extra $5,000 in it for him. Bennie hadn't told him what it was, and Joe decided he'd simply wait until after that special trip to make up his mind about giving up this drug pickup deal altogether.

The breakfast was delivered and his worries disappeared into the welcome aroma of the omelet.

II

It was almost noon and Jack had been at the Nantucket police station for more than an hour. First, he had waited for close to thirty minutes for Detective Collins to show his face, and since then he had wished he'd never shown up. Collins' manner was surly and overbearing, as if Jack was to blame for him having to come in on Saturday. As soon as they sat down Collins had mentioned that this should have been his day off.

"Well, my day's plans are all screwed up with this problem," Collins said. "Now what can you tell me that will shed some light on this damn fool that jumped overboard last night?"

"Well," As Jack was about to answer, he was startled as Collins interrupted him.

"We've found a body we think is the missing man, and we've ID'd the car and know that the owner worked for the government. Now, let's hear what you know!"

After Jack recovered a little from the shock of learning that the man he had seen last night was now dead, he said, "Well, I can't tell you much of anything. I first ran into the guy right after I parked my car on the ferry last night."

Collins began to take some notes.

"His car was in front of mine, and when I got out to head up the stairs to the passenger lounge, I saw this man standing around, obviously unsure where to go. I asked him if he was looking for the passenger area, and he said yes. We walked up the stairs together, and then I think he went toward the snack bar."

"Was that the first time you saw him, or did you see him before you drove your car onto the boat?"

"I don't remember seeing him while we were waiting at the dock, but I suppose his car must have been in front of me there also."

"What was he wearing?" Collins asked, somewhat impatiently.

"His clothes were sort of nondescript, I guess," Jack replied. "He had on dark slacks, a windbreaker jacket, and I think he was wearing a sweater—red or maroon."

"How tall, how big, how old?" asked Collins, continuing to show his irritation.

"I'd say he was about my height, maybe a little shorter—say around five feet ten inches—and I'd say he was around sixty years old. Maybe a little heavy for his height, but he looked to be in pretty good shape. He went up the two flights of stairs to the passenger area easily and quickly."

"What else can you tell me?"

"After the boat was underway, I saw this same man walking toward me, looking around for a place to sit," Jack went on. "There were plenty of seats left on the boat, but the seats with tables where I was sitting had a great view and more room, so I asked him if he would like to sit with me. The table can hold six people."

"I know what the boat looks like!" said Collins impatiently. "What happened then?"

"Well, he slid into the other side of the table and pulled out a paperback to read."

Collins sat up a little more interested. "Did he tell you his name or did you have any conversation?"

Kendrick thought for a minute and said, "I guess we each

introduced ourselves, but I don't remember his name. He said he was coming to the island for a couple of days on business. He worked for the government, I think he said, and was going to be retiring in the near future."

"What else did you talk about?"

Jack tried to remember. "We really didn't talk much further. We both were reading mystery novels by David Baldacci, and we talked about other books we had read by the same author. We then turned to reading our books, and after a while he got up and never returned. It was probably about halfway across Nantucket Sound when he got up. He said he was going to stretch his legs. I didn't see him again after that."

"What was his mood? Was he negative or depressed?"

"No, he seemed sort of relaxed. We both were reading books, and I really didn't sense anything unusual about his mood."

Collins asked, "Do you think you would recognize him if you saw him again?"

"Oh, I'm sure I would," Jack said. "I just remembered that he had a pretty obvious previous injury to his head, sort of a depression in his forehead that you couldn't miss. It really stood out after he took his cap off."

"I want you to take a look at the body we found on the beach this morning. We're pretty sure it's the same man you met on the boat last night."

Jack hesitated, uncomfortable about looking at a corpse and still concerned about completing his work in order to make the boat back that afternoon. But he recognized his civic duty regardless of how much he might be delayed. He just wished this cop was a little more friendly and understanding.

"OK, where do I go, and when?"

"I'll take you to the hospital—that's our morgue, so to speak, on the island. I'm ready to go right now, and it shouldn't take us more that fifteen minutes or so." Collins got up, took his jacket, and left the room with Jack Kendrick following.

12

Joe Hinkle's day was busier than usual—more stops, more waiting, and more miles to cover. Nantucket Island from east to west was no more than thirteen miles long, and at its widest point only four miles. The center of the town was halfway down the island on the north coast, and Joe had to make deliveries at both ends of the island, although the majority of the stops were within two miles of the town center. The island had grown more in year-round residents, and the deliveries took much longer than when Joe had made his first trip here a few years before.

One somewhat difficult task for Joe was making the "pick-ups" at the same time he was delivering parcels. He couldn't wait until all the deliveries were made before starting to pick up the outgoing parcels, because this would mean chasing all over the island a second time. Having made more than one hundred trips in the past, he was now very familiar with the island and made certain that he coordinated his deliveries and pickups so that he didn't have to retrace his steps and lose time. When he had first made trips to the island he was constantly confused with one-way and narrow streets that slowed him down and on a few occasions had resulted in his missing the boat back to the mainland. The island still had many unpaved roads, and some of them had deep ruts that prevented vehicles from traveling at normal speeds. Fortunately most of the residents in these more secluded parts were summer people, and at this time of the year Joe had only a few of these stops.

He was done with all of the deliveries on his scheduled route a little after 4 p.m. He had to be at Steamship Wharf around 5 p.m. to get in line for the ferry, which would begin loading around 5:15 p.m. Actually the ferry ticket stated that vehicles had to be in line, ready to board, one hour before sailing time; but the Nantucket Steamship Authority was not strict about this, especially for regular travelers like the NEEx trucks.

Plenty of time for my last and most important pickup, Joe thought.

He drove back through downtown to the town pier, over the cobblestones, which always gave him a real jarring in his truck. An automobile wasn't much better over these round rocks that never seemed to wear down even after many decades of traffic. The stones had supposedly arrived in Nantucket as ballast in ships carrying goods back and forth from Europe. Joe's arrangement was to meet Ed Gatious, a fishing boat captain, at the dock between 4:30 and 4:45 p.m. every other Saturday. Although Joe had never had problems on the island, he was more than a little nervous because of the incident with the second "government snoop" last night. He had not told Bennie Haas or Ed Gatious about the first incident last May, since he was sure he had taken care of it, and he feared that Bennie would cut him off from further deliveries. Joe needed that $1,000 extra he earned each trip. It kept his head above water financially, and he wasn't about to tell them about last night's problem either.

Every time he made the pickup, Gatious gave him two boxes, each weighing about thirty pounds. Their size and shape wasn't different from other parcels he was carrying, and they were always addressed to a business in Springfield, Massachusetts, although Joe knew this was a fictitious location and was only printed on the label in the event the police stopped him. Joe could claim this was a normal pickup for him, and the address would lead them nowhere. Joe's actual delivery would be made later that evening to a warehouse in South Boston, only a few miles from where the NEEx terminal was located.

He didn't know much about Ed Gatious, even though he had met him every other week for two years. Their meetings were always brief, and Gatious was always gruff and abrupt. He dressed in the kind of clothing you'd expect a professional fisherman to wear—heavy and worn, yellow, foul-weather gear and boots. Joe knew his job was deep-sea fishing, but didn't know the name of his boat or what it looked like. On occasion he had toyed with the idea of trying to find the boat, but he had been told initially to meet Ed only at the end of the dock and not to go looking for him. Ed had once told him that they came into Nantucket every weekend but were out at sea during the rest of the week. Well, as long as the money kept coming he wasn't about to run the risk of screwing things up.

Today Joe took the two boxes from Gatious, put them in the back of the truck with all the other parcel pickups, and left for the ferryboat. It didn't make sense to linger any longer with Gatious than with any of his other pickups. They tried to avoid anything that would look suspicious, and Gatious always appeared somewhat nervous.

As Hinkle was leaving, Gatious said, "See you in two weeks, and remember, we'll have a special pickup for you!"

Joe hadn't forgotten, especially the fact that there would be "extra bucks" for him. He wondered what this "special pickup" was all about; but again, as long as the money was right he wasn't going to ask any questions.

A good day, and good bucks! Joe thought to himself. *If only that goddamn government agent hadn't showed up last night!*

Someone a little more intelligent would have been more alarmed that this was the second incident, and that Joe had in fact killed two people, both government agents. He pushed his concern quickly out of his mind.

13

Jack Kendrick was in a hurry. It was after 5:15 p.m. and he was supposed to have been at the steamship much sooner. He had just barely been able to finish the rest of his chores after returning from the morgue. The little things always took the longest—moving the flower boxes and flowerpots into the cellar, cleaning out the refrigerator, making a quick trip to the town dump, draining the water pipes, and doing about a dozen other minor things along the way.

No time for a real lunch—just some leftover crackers and somewhat stale peanut butter, but enough to hold him till he could eat on the boat. He really hated to rush through all the chores for fear that he might miss something really important. If Amy were with him they would be reminding each other of those little things.

The morgue visit was still occupying most of his thoughts. He had learned that the dead man was named William Andrews and that he worked for the U.S. Department of Justice. The body had been in the water for some ten hours before it was found and was terribly bloated. It was truly gruesome to look at, and Jack found his stomach had really become very queasy. Except for the indented skull it would not have been as easy for Jack to be sure of the identification. They had also showed him the dead man's clothes, still soaked, and he had told the police they looked like what the man on the boat had been wearing the previous night.

Detective Collins had taken him back to his car at the police station and asked for Jack's off-island address and telephone number. By the time he got back to the summer cottage it was well after one o'clock.

What a grisly experience! Jack thought. *What caused this man, Andrews, to take his own life? He couldn't have fallen overboard accidentally; there just aren't open places on the boat where that could happen. He certainly didn't seem depressed or upset when he talked with me. I wonder if he had a family or children. I wonder just what his job with the government was, and what he was going to do in Nantucket.*

Jack decided he'd have to make certain to check the papers tomorrow for more information. Perhaps it might even make the TV news on WBOS. He should be able to get the details from his contacts in the newsroom.

He and Jessie arrived at the boat as some of the cars and trucks were already being loaded. The steamship attendant looked at his ticket and told him to get in line. Jack was more than a little nervous, since it was well after five o'clock, and he wondered if they would be strict about when he was supposed to be in line as there were always some cars on "standby" waiting to see if there would be any openings.

As the second attendant checked his ticket and waved him on, Jack thought in relief, *Well, at least one thing is going right for me today.*

The steamship was quite full again—more people closing up their summer homes and returning to the mainland for the winter. Jack grabbed a hot dog and some chips from the snack bar on the boat, as well as a Coke to wash them down. Jessie lay down as soon as they got on board and welcomed the chance to sleep after a busy day, while Jack took the time to stretch out on one of the benches and snooze for a little while during the two-hour crossing. The trip back was calm and they arrived at the dock in Hyannis on time, a little before eight o'clock in the evening.

Jack wouldn't be back home in Quincy until almost 9:30 p.m. He really would have liked to stay in Nantucket longer, to have a chance to enjoy the relaxed atmosphere on a quiet fall weekend. In other years the whole family would have come along and made it the last vacation weekend of the year.

Well, Jack thought, *it's just not possible this year with all of the extra duty at WBOS. It's getting to be a little too much, but it's a job and I know that most people have things about their jobs they have to put up with.*

His hours as a TV cameraman, covering news events all over the city and sometimes beyond, had really increased this fall. Two of the experienced cameramen had left to go to other stations, and their replacements were not yet fully trained. He was now assigned to the premier reporting team, and that had meant a raise in his pay but also more overtime. But his chores to close up the summerhouse were now done, and hopefully things at work would settle down over the next few weeks.

He drove off the ferry behind a delivery truck with bright red and yellow markings and the logo and name of New England Express—NEEx.

14

Detective Collins never did get to enjoy his Saturday off. By the time he returned to the station after ID'ing the body at the morgue, "all hell was breaking loose" at the station.

As he walked in the door, the chief, who never appeared on weekends unless there was some kind of an emergency, met him. He went into the chief's office and was told that they were dealing with a probable homicide—not a suicide or accidental death.

"Al," said Chief Campbell, "it looks like we've got a real mess on our hands. That guy you just ID'd was a DEA agent in Boston; actually he was the deputy director of the Boston office, and he was down here investigating a possible drug smuggling ring. I've been on the phone with the DEA director in Boston, and he believes this guy, Bill Andrews, was probably murdered. Andrews was on the case because another agent who he was very close to disappeared last May while investigating the same drug ring. They think this first agent who disappeared was murdered somewhere on the Cape and his body hasn't been found."

Al Collins began to run back through his mind the series of events since the first call he had received from the steamship office last night. *Did I follow all of the required procedures and cover all the bases? There's always something you missed or might have done differently. Certainly if I had suspected it to be a homicide I would have approached the case much differently.*

"Al, we've got to kick this into high gear," the chief continued. "We've got the feds involved, and they'll be breathing down our necks. Here's what we've got to do, right now! First, get hold of the state police and tell them we need their help in a murder investigation. We need to go over the dead man's car with a fine-tooth comb. You need to look through the items you took from the car last night. We need the state forensics people to look for any kind of evidence from the car. Get a list of the passengers on that boat last night and—"

"Chief," Al interrupted, "they don't keep a passenger list."

"I know that, Al, but they do have a list of all the vehicles, their owners, and hopefully the vehicle registration numbers," said the chief impatiently. "Finally, make sure that autopsy is thorough and done right. A DEA official will be down here to-morrow and I don't want him to take over the investigation. I want him to see that we're on top of this and have everything un-der control. No stone left unturned! No bases uncovered! Our reputation is on the line here, and this will be a very visible case. We don't have many homicides to deal with here, but I don't want that to be an excuse for sloppy police work. Do you think you can handle this, Al?"

"Chief, of course I can do it, but I'm going to need some help. Can I use Dick Hines? We work pretty well together."

"Yeah, sure," said Campbell, "and get back to me here at six o'clock tonight with an update. If anything really important comes up in the meantime, call me at home."

"OK, Chief."

"See you at six, Al, and don't let me down on this one!"

15

At thirty-three, Amy Kendrick had made the self-determined transition from career woman to "stay-at-home mom" with her two pre-school children. The decision to take a leave of absence from her teaching career had not been a difficult one, since she had strong feelings as a teacher about the importance of early childhood development and the belief that the mother could provide that education better than a day care program or even a nanny.

There had been a struggle with the financial transition from two incomes to one, but Jack had continued to get modest pay increases at the TV station, and she planned to return to work once the children, Jeremy and Natalie, were in school full-time. She knew that when that occurred, in some three or four years, she would be facing another period of adjustment to yet another new lifestyle.

Jack did not leave all the parenting to her. He loved the children, and she enjoyed watching him play with them and being a part of this important developmental period. He provided the physical challenge in his roughhousing with the kids, but he also exhibited a soft and compassionate side that she knew was an important characteristic for their children to see in their father. It was that sensitive side of Jack that had attracted her to him—so different from other men who were too fearful of showing any crack in their masculinity.

She had been raised in a family with much more financial security than Jack, but they shared similar values in the way they looked at life, and more importantly in the way they were raising their children. Even though her parents had helped with the down payment on their house and freely offered the use of the Nantucket cottage, Jack did not see this as a threat to his own position as the principal provider for the family.

Amy enjoyed the times when they dreamed about Jack having his own photography studio, and she was confident this would happen. Her parents had even offered to help them financially start the business, and Jack would probably accept this as long as it was done as a strict business transaction—an investment by her parents with a fixed schedule to pay back the loan. She knew there would be some risk involved but felt that Jack's special photography skills and his personal commitment would overcome any serious problems.

She still found time in her busy life for jogging and occasional biking on evenings and weekends. She enjoyed the special feeling of physical stress when extending herself while running along the back roads near their home. The chance to be alone and enjoy the rush of the outdoor air was always invigorating. She especially looked forward to the summer months on Nantucket, where she could jog on one of the bike paths and smell and feel the salt air.

She still looked back on her college and graduate school years as a very special time in her life. Although she had done well academically, there were times when she felt there were opportunities she had missed in college, a feeling that some of her friends shared as they looked back on their college years. She anticipated a time in the future when she might be able to continue her education at one of Boston's many universities. She dreamed a little of taking some writing courses, an endeavor she now wished she had pursued more of in college. She had begun keeping a daily journal since the children were born. When she was first pregnant she had read about the value of recording the little things that happen in the daily life development of children—something that could be looked back on later to recall events that otherwise would have slipped away.

She thought that with some writing training she might even be able to provide the necessary narrative to the photography book that Jack dreamed about publishing some day. She continued to encourage him to pursue this dream and felt that his unique and special talents and sensitivity as a photographer came through sharply in most of his pictures.

Her life was truly full and she looked forward to the future with enthusiasm and expectation. For the time being, though, her primary focus was on the two children. Jeremy, at age three, a handful at times; and Natalie, who was not quite one, occupied her waking hours almost fully. Jeremy was a true boy, always seeming to test her to see how far he could go. She especially enjoyed watching his affection for his younger sister, in many ways an early expression of the sensitivity she saw in Jack. It continued to amaze Amy how evident personality traits appeared in children at an early age. Even Natalie, less than one, showed different traits than her brother had at that age. She was playful with Jeremy but would clearly make her own displeasure known when he teased her. She seemed to really enjoy the physical play with both her father and brother.

The telephone rang and Amy was taken away from her daydreaming. Jack was calling from Nantucket. "I've just got on the boat, and it's supposed to get to Hyannis around quarter to eight," he said, "so I should be home by nine-thirty, even with traffic."

"OK, honey, I'll be looking for you."

"I've had a little excitement since I arrived. You won't believe this, but a man went overboard last night on the ferry and

I had to identify his body today. You may hear about it on the news."

Amy gasped. "What happened? How did you get involved?"

"Well, I sat with this man for a while on the boat and the police wanted me to look at the body to see if it was the same person. It was the same guy, and I guess he jumped overboard."

"Are you OK? That doesn't sound very pleasant."

"I'm fine. The viewing of the body was pretty gruesome, but I'm OK. Look, the ferry's about ready to leave and I need to find a seat. I'll fill you in when I get home. Give the kids a hug and a kiss and tell them I'll be there when they wake up tomorrow morning."

"OK, I love you."

"Me too!"

16

In spite of all of the crazy things that had happened on Saturday, Jack Kendrick slept pretty well that night. He had to work the four-to-midnight shift on Sunday, usually a very quiet one from a news point of view, but you could never predict what events would occupy a TV news crew. At least he would have most of the day at home with Amy and the children before going to work. He and Amy had spent Saturday evening talking about his quick trip to Nantucket, the closing up of the cottage, and the man who had died on the ferry trip.

As soon as he woke up on Sunday morning Jack checked the newspaper to see if there was any mention of the man's death. He found it on the second page of the *Boston Globe*. The headline read, "DEA OFFICIAL FOUND DEAD."

Nantucket, Mass.—William G. Andrews, age 64, of Marblehead, Deputy Director of the Boston office of the U.S. Drug Enforcement Administration (DEA), was found dead yesterday morning on a Nantucket beach. His body washed ashore about one mile from the center of town on the north side of the island. Officials say he apparently was a passenger on the steamship that left Hyannis at 8:30 p.m. on Friday evening and arrived in Nantucket at 10:45 p.m. There is no information at this time as to how Andrews died, or whether the death was accidental; however, he allegedly fell, jumped, or was pushed overboard as the steamship was approaching the island. Nantucket police officials state that a full investigation has been initiated with the complete cooperation of state and federal authorities. They declined to say whether the investigation is focusing primarily on an accident, suicide, or homicide. Andrews leaves his wife, Barbara, three children, and five grandchildren. Funeral arrangements at this time are incomplete.

Jack read the article a second time. They hadn't told him yesterday that this man, Andrews, worked for the Drug Enforcement Administration or that he had been a deputy director of the agency.

What was he doing "on business" in Nantucket? Jack wondered. *Was he working on some drug investigation? It's funny that the police aren't saying it was either a suicide or an accident. Inspector Collins gave me every indication it could have been either one. Could it be something more than that? Why didn't they rule out homicide in the article? Well, I'm letting my imagination run away from me now! The article is probably just the routine language that police officials use early in an investigation.*

Jack decided he would check the news wires when he got into work later on. They'd probably have more detailed information, and he was fortunate to be in a position where he had easy access to news as it happened.

17

Ahmed Khalil packed his bag with only a few personal be-longings. He had been told that Western clothes would be pro-vided for him before he boarded the plane for Canada. He carried with him only his own personal care items—razor, toothbrush, deodorant, hair cream, and underwear. He was excited and yet apprehensive. This had all happened so quickly! And yet, it was what he had hoped would happen when he had joined Hamas almost two years ago. More than anything he was committed to the goals of this radical Islamic resistance movement—the destruction of the State of Israel.

He thought about that day four years ago that was the turn-ing point in his young life—that horrible event that changed forever the things that were really important to him. He had loved his older brother Hassim! Hassim had been like a sec-ond father to him—always bigger, always stronger, always more knowledgeable, always able to do things that Ahmed, six years younger, could not yet do. Their life growing up had been rela-tively peaceful—more so than most Arab families in Israel.

The city of Nazareth, where Ahmed's family lived, was, for the most part, away from the real hotspots of the Arab-Israeli conflicts. During the Lebanon-based Hezbollah rocket attacks on northern Israel in 2006, one rocket had in fact landed in the city, but such violence was an unusual occurrence. Nazareth was not located in the occupied territories where most of the violence occurred. It was a city that was about fifty percent Arab Muslim, fifty percent Arab Christian, and had only a small Jewish population. Most of its citizens had been relatively content to be citizens of the State of Israel.

Ahmed's family lived in one of the better sections of Nazareth, and his father owned his own pharmacy. His family's standard of living was much better than most Palestinians, many of whom were unemployed and living in poverty. One of the boys in Ahmed's neighborhood was the son of a Jewish doctor, and this doctor and Ahmed's father had a close business/medical relationship. The doctor's son, David Mier, was the same age as Ahmed, and up until David went away to private school when he was fourteen, the two boys had played almost daily and were close friends. Soccer games were a frequent activity for both Ahmed and David after school, and even more so during school vacations. Their religious differences were secondary to their common interests as young boys; however, as they grew older they gradually became aware of the historical and traditional distinctions between their families. Still their friendship overshadowed their differences in heritage. Each boy would say that the other was truly his closest friend, even though they were sometimes ridiculed by other boys.

After David went away to school, their relationship began to cool. At first they would be eager to get together as soon as David returned for a holiday, but as time passed their contact became less frequent. David's experiences in the private school began to spur interests that were different from Ahmed's, and Ahmed had made new Arab friends in Nazareth.

Ahmed's older brother, Hassim, had grown to become somewhat of a militant in supporting and championing the Palestinian causes in Israel. Ahmed had always listened to his brother talk about his strong beliefs, even though he was uneasy with Hassim's growing anger and was cautioned by his parents not to "listen to or believe everything his brother said." However, many of Ahmed's teenage Arab friends were increasingly influenced and enthralled with the more militant Palestinian activities and causes around them. They had been further energized by the Hezbollah attacks on Israel and felt that it demonstrated Israel was vulnerable. Most of them came from families that were struggling financially and believed the Israeli government was the source of their problems.

His father would say, "Wait until you're older and then make the decisions for yourself, after you've had a chance to learn more and truly understand all of the issues. Some of what Hassim says is true, but he goes too far for me, and some of his friends are dangerous people to be with. These extremists have been at war with the Jews for more than fifty years, and where has it gotten us? I don't think any of these extremist groups will make life any better for our people, and more likely worse. I think we must find a way of working with the Jews to form a separate Palestinian state, but do it peacefully. These extremists who want to turn the clock back and push the Jews into the Mediterranean Sea are not being realistic. They're so caught up in their own hatred that they can't listen to reasonable people."

Although Nazareth was relatively free of the acts of terror and violence that were a constant threat in other parts of Israel, it was located only some twenty miles to the north of the West Bank, where demonstrations and confrontations with the Israeli authorities were commonplace. and where there had been great violence and bloodshed during the intifada after the year 2000. Ahmed's brother had participated in some of these demonstrations, and Ahmed was sure he had also been a part of the violence. The West Bank experienced frequent clashes and confrontations between Palestinian demonstrators and the Israeli militia.

For several weeks prior to that awful day four years ago the demonstrations in the occupied territories had grown in number and frequency and were becoming increasingly more violent. Ahmed remembered his parents urging his brother to stay away from the West Bank and the volatile areas. Ahmed knew his brother would not and could not! Hassim even bragged to Ahmed about his bravery in challenging the Israeli soldiers. Ahmed's parents and Hassim regularly got into arguments, sometimes very heated ones, about the danger, the risks he was taking, and the circle of friends he had made. Hassim would even talk admiringly and emotionally about the young Palestinian men and boys who were taking their own lives as suicide bombers in the name of Allah. Hassim had finished school two years before and had not been able to find employment and this idleness had only added to his anger. Ahmed would listen to these arguments and found that his younger friends were increasingly making statements that sounded like Hassim's.

It was late in the evening of that awful day, and Ahmed and his parents were anxiously waiting for his brother to come home. Hassim was much later than usual and he almost always came home for dinner. They had heard on the radio two hours before that a demonstration in the West Bank town of Nablus had become violent, that some shots had been fired, and some demonstrators had been injured. Their concern grew that Hassim might have been injured or arrested. Then they received the frantic call from a friend of Hassim's that he had been shot and taken to a hospital. By the time they arrived, Ahmed's brother was dead.

The Israeli papers said the demonstrators had provoked the incident, and that they had fired the first shots. The Nazareth Arab newspaper clearly felt that the Israeli militia had overreacted. The West Bank Palestinian papers were clear and harsh in their vilification of the Israeli militia and charged that it had used "unnecessary violence and brutality."

After the funeral and the period of mourning, Ahmed tried to return to his normal school life, but more and more he listened to and grew sympathetic with the more radical Palestinian beliefs. Many of his friends openly espoused their belief that:

> An independent Palestine is not enough! The Jews must be driven out of all land that rightfully belongs to the Palestinians, land that was taken away from them illegally by force. There can be no peace until what is ours is given back!

Ahmed had done very well in school, especially in electronics and computers. He had also excelled in English language courses, thanks to his close friendship with David Mier and his family. David's mother had grown up in America and English was the language spoken around the house. Over several years Ahmed had learned to understand and speak English fluently, although with a decided American accent. In school he had taken several English courses and he was much more proficient than any of his Arab friends in both speaking and writing the language.

Ahmed's growing anger and support for the Palestinian causes continued to be fueled after his graduation from high school. He went to a two-year trade school in electronics and earned a certificate as a computer and electronics technician. At age twenty-one he secured a job with a small electronics firm, something that earned him enough to satisfy his financial needs; but his heart was not in looking or planning for his long-term future.

Meanwhile he had become more and more indoctrinated in the Hamas beliefs and soon found himself fully embracing their militant philosophy. This was the case with many of his Arab friends as the violence and killing on both sides increased during the intifada. He began attending some meetings with Palestinian and Arab extremists. More and more he came to understand and believe in their goals. He was looked upon as somewhat of a hero in the Palestinian cause because his brother had died defending their rights. In the summer after his twenty-second birthday he spent his vacation at a Hamas training and indoctrination camp. The two weeks brought him into daily contact with men and women who had committed their lives to the destruction of Israel. He learned some basic skills in handling explosive devises and weapons. His electronics background made this training easier for him than for others. He understood how explosives and bombs could be electronically designed to fit special situations.

At the end of the two-week period he was asked to meet with the official in charge. After a few pleasantries he was told that Hamas had a special interest in him. His knowledge of electronics and his fluent English made him an ideal candidate for special assignments outside of Israel. The official told him—he did not ask—that they would like him to come to a longer and more intensive training school in about three months. Ahmed at first hesitated but then agreed, even though he had obvious questions and concerns about what kind of activities or terrorism might be involved.

The course took three weeks in a remote area of the West Bank and not only demonstrated how bombs and explosive devices were made, but actually had the trainees personally make and explode them. Some were triggered by pressure (someone stepping on them) or were rigged to explode when a car was started. Some were to be detonated by suicide bombers.

Ahmed apparently did well. He was told to go home and when the right time came he would be called. That had been almost a year ago, and during that time he had continued to attend meetings, but had heard nothing more from the official or others at the training camp until three days ago.

The telephone call had instructed him to prepare for a trip of more than a month outside of Israel. He was not to tell his family or anyone that he would be leaving the country.

18

Al Collins was on the hot seat. The Boston media were breathing down the chief's back, and the chief was leaning on Al in a way he'd never seen before. He wanted answers right away! He wanted the names of some suspects! He wanted an arrest!

For Christ's sake, the chief knows this kind of investigation takes time, Al thought. *It can't be done overnight! It's a complicated case! Hell, the coroner isn't even 100% sure it was a murder, and not a suicide!*

Even so, Al himself knew that the odds were pretty slim that it was an accident or suicide.

When Detective Collins had called the coroner yesterday to suggest that it could be a homicide, the coroner had said, "I was about to call you. There's a deep wound on the back of the skull that I don't think was caused by a fall. It looks like he was hit with a blunt object, knocked unconscious, and then pushed overboard. I can't be absolutely positive, but that's the way it looks to me. The wound on the head definitely happened before he drowned, not after. The body was in pretty bad shape after several hours in the water, but I've seen a lot of drownings before, and this one is different."

Collins had followed the chief's orders—he had asked the state police for help in the investigation. The forensics people had gone over Bill Andrews' car and his personal belongings but wouldn't have a report for him for a few days. They had said that if they found anything really significant they would inform him immediately. He wished they had a stronger sense of urgency on this case that meant so much to him. The arrogance of the state police when dealing with local police departments always angered him.

He recalled his initial visit to the steamship the evening that the man had gone overboard.

Could there be any additional important forensic information there? he wondered. *Since Friday night, when Andrews went overboard, the steamship has made four roundtrips and is on its way back to Nantucket now. Could I have missed something? What else should I be doing now? Who can I get to do the work? I'll really be criticized if I don't make a full-bore attempt, even though it may be a wild goose chase.*

He called his partner Dick Hines and told him to take one of the forensics people and get down to the boat when it arrived back in Nantucket. He couldn't impound the boat or even stop it from making its next trip, but at least he could have the forensics people take another look.

They'll have to do their investigation while the ferry is underway on its next roundtrip to Hyannis. Probably any evidence that might have been there is long gone or contaminated, but they'd better have another look to be on the safe side and avoid criticism.

Hines sailed on the ferry's next trip to Hyannis and then called Al from his cell phone when the boat was almost to Hyannis. "We've found something that the forensics guy is pretty sure is blood," he said. "It was on the vehicle deck near one of the large docking portholes. We've taken some samples."

Like any good cop, Hines had been smart and had taken the time to think where or how a body might go overboard. Except for the open area around the passenger decks, he had realized that the four large docking portholes on the vehicle deck were the only likely places to look. The open passenger areas were almost too large to cover and find anything, were always visible to other passengers, and would likely have been contaminated during the four subsequent round-trips. The docking portholes, on the other hand, were the only openings on the vehicle deck that were big enough for a person to fit through, except for the large cargo doors on each end of the boat, which were always closed until just before docking.

Hines and the forensics specialist had looked at two of the docking portholes and found nothing. On the third one they had found blood, or something that had looked like blood, on the metal edge and on the deck floor. The forensics man thought he had enough of a sample to do the necessary testing.

If this is Andrews' blood, thought Collins, *it will prove conclusively that it was murder. You don't knock yourself out and then jump overboard.*

He told Hines to continue to look around on the trip back.

"See if one of the crew members can tell you where Andrews' car was parked. There's probably nothing there, but I don't want to be second-guessed by anyone. Make sure you take any fingerprint samples around the area and look for a weapon that might have been hidden."

The preliminary blood test later that day matched the blood type of the dead man, but it would take several days to get an accurate DNA match. In the meantime Collins would continue to check and interview those passengers he was able to find who had been on the steamship that night. So far no one had seen or heard anything. Hines had found nothing further on the return ferry trip, but Collins knew he'd better continue to slog away even though they weren't likely to turn up anything.

19

Joe Hinkle had made the return trip on the ferry Saturday afternoon, still feeling nervous and edgy over the events of the day before. He hadn't noticed anything unusual as he sat waiting to board the ferry, and he was especially alert for any evidence of police presence on the steamship and at the dock in Hyannis. On a Saturday afternoon at this time of year there were only a few passengers, and he didn't see anyone who was taking an unusual interest in him or his truck. He had driven the ninety minutes up the Massachusetts coast and made the drop-off of the two boxes at the same place as usual in South Boston and then returned the truck to the NEEx terminal in Waltham. He had checked his rearview mirror periodically on the drive up to Boston to see if he was being followed. He was pretty sure he would have picked out any vehicle that showed too much of an interest in his truck, and as he got closer to Boston he became more and more convinced that he was again home free.

Sunday morning he was relaxing in his apartment reading the sports page of the *Boston Herald* when he heard the news on the radio.

"The body of a United States Drug Enforcement Administration official has washed up on the shore of Nantucket Island," the reporter said. "The body of a senior official of the Drug Enforcement Administration in Boston was found yesterday morning on the beach in Nantucket. William G. Andrews was the deputy director of the local DEA office and apparently boarded the Steamship Authority ferry Friday evening in Hyannis for the two-hour ride to the island. His body was found around 9 a.m. Saturday morning, having washed ashore on the north side of the island.

"State and local officials said an autopsy was being performed to determine the cause of death. They refused to speculate as to whether the death was accidental, but said a full investigation was underway that would consider all possibilities. They declined to say whether Andrews was on vacation or on official DEA business."

The reporter concluded by saying, "He leaves a wife and three grown children."

"Shit!" Hinkle said out loud. "This guy was a big shot government agent—a director of some kind. Why didn't the body simply disappear at sea? The other one did! Now there'll be a full investigation and I'll have to be extra careful. Jesus Christ, I don't need this kind of trouble, especially when I'm close to calling it quits with this drug business!"

He began to run over in his mind the details of what had happened on Friday night. Had he forgotten anything? Had he left anything that could be traced back to him? He had thrown the tire iron overboard. No one would ever find it several miles at sea on the ocean bottom! Had anyone seen him around the porthole or on the vehicle deck around the time he had killed this guy Andrews? He was pretty sure he had been alone on that end of the deck and that nobody could have seen him. Still he was uncomfortable.

What did the feds have that made them suspect something was going on in Nantucket? Do they have my name? Did someone see the NEEx truck making the pickup in Nantucket or the drop-off in Boston? If they had definitely tied me or the truck to the drugs, wouldn't they have picked me up already? Or were they following me to learn the source? Wouldn't I have noticed someone following me?

Still, they had to have something that caused them to have two different agents take the ferry to the island. I guess I'd better call Bennie Haas and let him know what happened. He's going to hear about the DEA guy's death and put two and two together. On the other hand, maybe the police will think the death was an accident or a suicide, that he somehow banged his head as he was leaping from the boat, or hit it on some object when the body was in the water.

Goddamn it, why didn't the body just sink or float out to sea? Of all the goddamn luck!

20

When Jack Kendrick left for work on Monday morning, the events of the weekend were still dominating all of his thoughts. After reading the newspaper story, he had turned on the radio and later watched the TV news, hoping to get additional information from the twenty-four-hour all-news stations, but he hadn't learned anything new.

He had talked with Amy about the whole affair, and she thought he would more than likely be interviewed again by the police, or maybe the DEA, since the dead man was a senior drug official in Boston. The thought that it might not have been an accident or a suicide had crossed Jack's mind, but he discounted it, figuring it was his imagination running a little wild. After all, it seemed to him that the police in Nantucket were handling the investigation as sort of a "routine" death, and the police officer in Nantucket hadn't even hinted that there might be foul play involved.

He speculated with Amy about whether it was an accident or a suicide. He really couldn't see how anyone could accidentally fall off the boat. Most people in October stayed inside during the two-hour ride, and the open deck areas were surrounded with fairly high fencing and guard rails. He had never noticed any areas without barriers of some kind, and down on the vehicle deck the large entry and exit doors were always kept closed tight until just before the ship docked.

Jack was an avid reader of mysteries and spy novels and couldn't help but play the game in his mind of "What if?" If it wasn't an accident, then a suicide seemed most likely. If a person was determined to end his or her life, a leap off the boat, in the dark, miles out at sea, would certainly do the trick. Anyone had to be truly desperate and depressed to end his or her life in that way.

"But why go to all the way to the Cape to commit suicide?" he asked Amy. "It just doesn't make much sense! There are plenty of other ways and places to end your life. This guy said he'd never been on the ferry before, had never been to Nantucket before, and was only there for a couple of days on business! Why would he pick this place at random to end his life? Nothing about him seemed unusual! He didn't seem uneasy or tense! He was perhaps a little serious, but not upset. He was casually reading a book and was friendly and easy in his conversation with me."

"Jack, don't go overboard on this with your imagination until you learn more," Amy cautioned. "All the reports say they don't yet know the cause of death. Maybe he had a heart attack or some kind of a spell and fell overboard. Stranger things have happened. It's too bad you had to get involved in this thing and especially that you had to identify the body. That must have been terrible."

Jack's thoughts went back to the morgue at the Nantucket Hospital and to the body lying there—a body that had been a living, breathing human being only a few hours before. He had never seen a body laid out like that before, and the appearance of the corpse after hours in the ocean water was truly gruesome. He wasn't one to be squeamish about blood or unpleasant sights or smells, but that whole scene had brought him as close to vomiting as he'd ever been. He thought the police officer had noticed his unease and had sort of enjoyed it.

How had he died? What were his last thoughts? Was it a suicide? Jack wondered. *Was he so depressed that he took his own life? Could it have been something else? Could the guy have been pushed overboard? Could he have been murdered?*

"Amy, I sat with this guy for almost an hour," Jack continued. "He wasn't loony! He was like you and me! I just can't believe he sat there with me one minute, talking and reading a book and then got up and jumped overboard! He told me he was going to the island on business, even though he didn't say anything about being a government drug official. I just can't believe he was the kind of guy who would commit suicide. Do you suppose this has something to do with a drug investigation?"

"Jack, you're really jumping to conclusions! You've been reading too many of your mysteries! There's no indication of anything like that. Let's be patient and see what happens. There's probably a reasonable explanation and then the whole incident will blow over."

Amy was a good rudder and a calming influence on Jack. She was the practical one in the family. Jack tended to overreact and sometimes jump into situations or to conclusions too quickly. But that quality to think and move quickly was also what made him a good photographer: He could see things that others couldn't. He saw things differently from others. He often felt he could sense things before they actually happened, and had his camera in position to catch the event. He found this sixth sense often put him in a position where he was able to capture pictures that others would miss. He had been told he had a natural talent and knack that few professional photographers had. But it was also true that he was indeed impatient, and even tended to over-exaggerate at times.

Thank God for Amy. She was the best decision of his life, but sometimes he wondered whether she was truly as happy with him as he was with her. He looked at her and silently thought how lucky he was to have her as his wife and the mother of his children. She came from a social background and family wealth that was much different than his. Although her family wasn't filthy rich, they were well enough off to have a home in a nice Boston suburb as well as the house in Nantucket. Amy had gone to a private school that must have cost at least four times as much as the state school Jack had attended. She had been a much better student than he was and she liked to read novels that were historical and biographical, ones that he found a little heavy, while he stuck to his mysteries and spy novels. His grades had always been OK, but he had tended to spend his academic energies on those courses that truly interested him, like the photography courses where he really honed his skills. Amy, on the other hand, had graduated with honors and had had no difficulty being accepted into the graduate program that she desired.

They had met at a party one summer when both of them were in college. He had gone along with a high school buddy of his who had been invited. Amy and Jack had hit it off right away, and before the evening was over Jack had invited her out on a date. They had dated casually over the next couple of years until they both finished college. Amy went on to graduate school and got her master's in education, while Jack went to work for the television station right out of college. It wasn't until they were in their late twenties that things really got serious. There were many ways they were different from each other. Jack had always been active in team sports, while Amy was more of an individual athlete. She loved to get out and jog by herself several times a week, while Jack preferred team sports and, depending on the season of the year, participated in local league teams—basketball, baseball, and touch football. With their young family, however, it was becoming increasingly difficult to find the time to satisfy their physical exercise needs. He looked forward to the time when his children were old enough to give him a physical challenge at the sports he loved.

Perhaps it's really true that opposites do attract each other, and that opposites complement each other and make for a good marriage, he thought.

They both shared other, somewhat conservative views, especially for their generation. Neither of them had ever gotten involved with drugs or alcohol, although Jack had fooled around with marijuana a few times in college. It had never really "turned him on," and the crowd he had hung around with was not into the drug scene. It was ironic, but hadn't been funny at the time, that he had once found himself at a party where drugs were being heavily used and there had been a police raid. Everyone had been arrested, including Jack, but no charges had ever been filed. Looking back, it had been one of those dumb things where you found yourself in a situation that you never would have been in on your own, but you were with a friend and hadn't wanted to make a scene. Sort of similar to being in a car with someone who is driving too fast and you have to decide whether or not to speak up. His parents had really been upset with him and he had vowed never to be in a situation again where he might be accused of something simply for being in the wrong place at the wrong time.

Jack had loved photography even as a teenager. He had taken a couple of courses in college that had helped improve his knowledge and techniques, and he had really enjoyed being the staff photographer on the school newspaper. The problem was that there weren't many attractive jobs in photography that paid well. Most people in the field were there for the love of it, not for the money. One important reason he had taken the job with the TV station was because it gave him an opportunity to get some candid shots with his own camera, while at the same time doing his job running the TV camera. He had been working on a collection of human interest photographs that he hoped he could someday publish. They were an accumulation of pictures that went back to his high school and college years, but more recently he had really begun to focus on a theme for a book involving a study of people in the city from various human perspectives and experiences. He found this hobby a real escape from his everyday work, and he increasingly found himself dreaming about pursuing a photography career on his own.

Amy was his greatest inspiration and encouragement in this project, this dream. She understood how important it was to him. She could sense, sometimes more than himself, how happy and captivated he was when he was talking or thinking about his book. He loved her as much for her understanding of his needs as for anything else. He hoped her needs and dreams were being satisfied in the marriage as much as his. He knew that the children, at this point in her life, were the most important things for her. He also knew that a time would come when she would want to follow her career dreams, and he made a pledge to himself to be as understanding and supportive of her as she was of him.

As he drove toward the city on the Southeast Expressway, his mind wandered as it often did to his dream of leaving the TV station and opening up a retail photography store in Boston. He was sure he had the talent to make a success out of this avocation that he so loved. But with the expenses of a young family he had the natural financial fears of leaving a job that provided a steady income for one that would be a new venture.

When he got to the station Jack checked the newswire for more news. It was right there without having to search very far.

NANTUCKET, Mass.—DEA OFFICIAL'S DEATH SUSPICIOUS

Sources close to the investigation of the death of William G. Andrews, deputy director of the Boston office of the Drug Enforcement Administration (DEA), indicate that the death may not be either an accident or suicide. These sources have revealed that Andrews was on official business investigating the disappearance of another DEA official last spring. These same sources would not comment on whether or not the body showed any evidence of violence. Both the DEA and the Massachusetts State Police have been brought into the investigation. The autopsy is to be completed today (Sunday), but the results will not be released until later, and it was announced that there will be a news conference sometime on Monday.

Andrews left his Boston office on Friday afternoon and drove his own car to the Cape. His car was reportedly on the ferry that left Hyannis at 8:30 p.m. and arrived in Nantucket about 10:45 p.m. He had recently been investigating the death of Edwin Proctor of Quincy, a DEA agent who has been missing since May. Until now there had been no indication from either the DEA or the police of foul play in Proctor's disappearance. It is not known whether Proctor was on official business at the time.

Sources close to the scene report that although the preliminary autopsy shows that Andrews probably died from drowning, authorities are still suspicious of the circumstances surrounding his death. The body had reportedly been in the water about ten hours before it was discovered on a Nantucket beach Saturday morning.

The same source indicated that the DEA has been pursuing various leads and information on the increased flow of illegal drugs into the state and particularly the Boston area during the past two years. However, DEA officials refused to confirm if they suspect that these deaths might be related to drug investigations.

Jack read the report a second time and then called Amy and read it to her. Wow! It looked like he was right in the middle of a murder investigation—the murder of a government drug official! Amy was upset. She didn't see the excitement in this at all, sensing that Jack might be dragged into an investigation.

"Jack, after listening to that, I guess you'd better be ready for another call from the police or the DEA."

"Why? I've told them everything I know."

"But it's now a murder investigation, the murder of a government official," Amy said, bringing things into focus. "Don't you think it's going to be a high-profile case, the press all over the place? The police are probably going to be under a lot of pressure and won't want to leave any detail, no matter how small, uncovered. You're the last one who saw him alive and they're going to want to make sure there isn't anything else that you saw or anything more that this guy said to you!"

"Yeah, I guess you're right. Well, I'll just wait for their call and hope they don't need to involve me further. I've got too much to do, between overtime at work and what we're trying to do around the house." As Jack and Amy's family had grown from two to four, they had needed more space for the growing family, and Jack had started to renovate the cellar as a playroom for the kids.

Should I call the Nantucket police or the DEA and let them know where I live? Jack asked himself after he said goodbye to Amy and hung up the phone. But then he remembered that while he was at the morgue he had filled out a police form that gave his address and telephone number.

There's nothing more I can tell them, even though it now may be a murder, he thought.

Holy shit, if he was murdered, then the murderer was one of the people on the ferry that night! Boy, that's spooky! To think I spent more than two hours on the same boat with a killer!

Jack's interest in mysteries made him begin to play around in his mind with different possibilities. *Could this guy Andrews have been the random victim of a mugging? Perhaps they were after his money and he gave them some resistance. I wonder if his wallet was stolen. It's more likely, though, that this has something to do with a drug investigation and with the other DEA official who was missing. Maybe the first agent, the one they've never found, was also murdered. Is it possible that Andrews found the killer, and then that killer also murdered him? How and where could this have happened on the boat without someone seeing him? Stranger things have happened and it does make some sense. The DEA must be on top of something like this and be looking at all kinds of possibilities. On the other hand, I suppose it's still possible that it really was a freak accident and that Andrews had somehow fallen overboard. Not really likely. The police officer in Nantucket seemed to indicate he thought it was probably a suicide, but I just don't believe it. He wasn't that kind of a guy.*

The more Jack thought about it, the more uncomfortable he became with his own involvement in the whole situation. Maybe Amy was right and he was letting his vivid imagination run away with him.

21

Ahmed Khalil tried to relax in the coach section of the Boeing 747. It was his first international flight, and he was amazed at the size of the airplane. He had seen them flying overhead, of course, and had even seen them sitting at airports, but to be inside of one with more than three hundred other passengers made him wonder at the marvels of modern technology. He had many anxieties as he sat there, not really about the safety of the flight but what awaited him on the other end of the trip.

He had been driven from Nazareth to the international airport in Jerusalem. His Hamas contact had given him a large suitcase, suitably worn to show previous use, and all the Western-style clothes he would need for the trip, which might last a month or more. The forged passport, identification papers, and credit cards showed him to be an Israeli citizen, and that his religion was Jewish. He had been truly nervous when he went through the security at the airport, but everything had gone without a hitch. For the first part of the flight he was uneasy about the people around him in the cabin, but no one seemed to pay him any unusual attention. The first leg of his flight was to Paris on the Israeli airline El Al, and from there he took an Air France flight to Montreal, Quebec, in Canada. Once there, he was to use the forged United Kingdom passport that had been given to him. The names on the two passports were different and he was nervous about making a mistake when someone talked to him.

The total flying time was more than twelve hours, giving Ahmed a lot of time to think about what lay ahead of him. Would all of the arrangements work out? Would all of his contacts be waiting for him? Would the materials he needed to complete the job be waiting for him? How long would it be before he saw his home and family again? It bothered him that he had left home without being able to tell his parents. There was a chance that he would never see them again, and the risks to him were big ones, but he knew they were worth it if only to avenge the death of his brother. Was his English good enough to pass the test of living in another country? When it was time for the big event, would he be able to go through with it? He must always remember that when he arrived at his destination he was supposed to be English if the question came up, since England and English-speaking people came from all over the world with different skin coloring and many different dialects. His alias when he got to his destination, Art Cahill, would also pass for an English name.

He knew his training over the past several months had given him the knowledge and skills he needed to assemble the bomb. His own electronics education and experience had made him very comfortable in working with the electrical timing mechanisms necessary to make the device work the way they wanted it to. The explosives were dangerous, of course, but most people who got into trouble assembling explosive devices didn't understand the electronic complexity. If everything went as planned, then he would have a significant impact on Palestine's future. The time was right for the final steps to declare a Palestinian state, but only on terms that made sense and were fair. The uprising that had begun in 2001, where so many young Palestinians had been killed, had solidified the resolve of most Palestinians.

Ahmed thought about his strong beliefs. *The proposed peace treaty gives Israel too much. The importance of Jerusalem itself to the Muslim faith precludes any compromise with the Jews on who should control the city. It should be clear to anyone that the historical significance of Jerusalem is more important to Muslims than other religious faiths. Up until the formation of the state of Israel in 1948 and the illegal wars against the Arab states, the Jews had not controlled Jerusalem for almost two thousand years. Even before then the Jews' control was sporadic. History is on the Palestinian side, and this is not the time to give up Arab heritage in order to get the world's blessing for a state of Palestine that is really only a token. In addition, all of the Jewish settlements on the West Bank must be abandoned. In order to be a viable state, the new Palestine must include complete control of Jerusalem. Anything else is unacceptable and would mean continual violence and war.*

When he arrived in Montreal, exhausted from a trip that had totaled more than eighteen hours from the time he had left Nazareth, Ahmed went to the hotel connected to the airport and took a room for the night. He was too tired to do any sightseeing, especially in a city where French was the official language, and his mind was solely focused on his final destination. He gave his fake passport at the hotel and casually mentioned that he was in Canada on a holiday and would be going on to visit relatives in Toronto. He had given a previously agreed upon fictitious address as to where he would be staying in Toronto when he cleared Canadian customs.

The next morning he went back to the airport and boarded an Air Canada flight to Halifax, Nova Scotia, using another alias. His superiors had made him feel quite confident that the frequent changes in identity would make it almost impossible for anyone to reconstruct his travel route. He certainly hoped they were right, and so far everything had gone according to plan. Halifax was a small seaport on the North Atlantic and an important center for the Canadian fishing industry. He quickly noticed that the buildings and surroundings looked so different from his home in Israel. There were many evergreen forests that seemed to stretch forever as the plane landed, and on the ride from the airport most of the buildings were constructed of wood. The other thing that struck him was that the temperature in early October was much cooler than what he was used to. He had been given a heavier jacket than he'd ever had to wear back home.

Upon arriving in Halifax, Ahmed went to the previously arranged small cheap hotel on the waterfront and waited for the Silver Wave.

22

David Mier relaxed in the first-class section of the El Al stretch 747 on its way to Washington, D.C., but try as he might he could not hold down the excitement of this trip. At twenty-eight, he had progressed at an unusually rapid rate in the Israeli Foreign Service. Although he was not directly involved in the negotiations or the writing of the treaty to establish a Palestinian state, he had been present for many of the discussions, and as an aide to the foreign secretary, he was really privy to the details. He was well aware of how fortunate he was to be on the front line in this historic process.

Even though he was a native-born Israeli citizen he found himself in the enviable position of speaking fluent English, Arabic, and Hebrew. Furthermore, he had learned his English from his mother, who had been an American citizen. In addition, he had gone to university in the United States, and consequently he had a decided American accent. His being fluent in Arabic was an important reason for his being selected for this assignment, and his American accent and fluent English brought together a combination of linguistic skills that few Israelis possessed. He had learned his Arabic in Nazareth, the city where he had grown up and gone to school. Many of his friends had been Arab, and their language was often the one used when they played, not to mention that since most of the population of Nazareth was Arab, all of its citizens naturally became fluent in their language. David's father had been a doctor in the city and most of his patients were Arab, and in spite of the differences in religion his father got along very well with the Arab community. During David's youth Nazareth had been a relatively peaceful community, perhaps because it was primarily made up of Muslim Arabs and Christian Arabs. David's family was one of the few Jewish families, but for the most part his city was free of the violence that had occurred in other Israeli towns and cities.

David had been an excellent student and his undergraduate education at Brandeis University, just outside of Boston, had prepared him well for his graduate program in international relations at Tel Aviv University. He dreamed that his Foreign Service career would some day lead to an ambassador's position in one of those important countries that supported Israel, a goal that he shared with every other young trainee in the Foreign Service. This special assignment to the team working on the peace treaty with the Palestinians would clearly help to boost his career. He knew that his language skills, both spoken and written, were the reason why he had been chosen, not because he had demonstrated any great promise yet as a Foreign Service official. Many individuals in the service with more experience would have done anything for this opportunity, and he relished his good fortune.

The treaty was not one that was universally embraced by all Israelis, and indeed many Palestinians also opposed it, some with strong words and threats of violence. But in the Middle East it was never possible to reach complete agreement on any issue, especially among Arabs; and within Israel itself the historic tensions and hatred between Arabs and Jews made agreement increasingly more difficult. Previous attempts to reach agreement had failed in spite of the work and dedication of many leaders. The deep-seated animosity and mistrust between the parties always trumped the desire of those people who wished for peace. It was surprising to many that this time negotiations had come this far and that a treaty recognizing a Palestinian state and guaranteeing peace between the two countries was about to be signed. With the death of Palestinian leader Yasser Arafat, the door had opened enough for the two sides to begin to move toward a political settlement. Both the Palestinian and the Israeli leadership had had to reach beyond their political comfort zone to come to the point of this agreement. The Israeli withdrawal from the Gaza Strip, although initially a hopeful event, had itself resulted in more violence. And the Israeli war in 2006 with the Hezbollah in Lebanon had further fueled historic suspicion, fear and anger. The road so far had indeed not been easy and there had been several setbacks, but finally the path to the actual signing of the agreement seemed almost assured.

There had been recent demonstrations, some of them violent. They were not only between Arabs and Jews but also between moderate and militant Jews and between the various Arab factions, who always seemed to have difficulty agreeing on anything. The signing of the peace treaty was to be the culmination of the Bush administration's road map for resolving the Arab-Israeli dispute of more than fifty years.

It would be good to get back to Boston, even if only for a few days. It had been six years since David's graduation, and although none of his close friends were still in the area, he longed to visit places that had been such an important part of his life for four years. He hoped he would find the time, in a schedule over which he really had little control, to visit the Brandeis campus and to run along the Charles River. The choice of Boston as the place for the treaty signing was one of the many compromises that had made up almost all of the treaty discussions. Neither side wanted the signing to take place in Washington, since it might indicate to some that the terms of the treaty were being dictated by the United States. Washington had brokered the treaty, but neither the Israeli nor the Arab factions wanted their constituents to believe that the treaty was being imposed on them by the world's only superpower. The United Nations headquarters in New York had also been rejected, primarily because the Israelis believed this would send a negative message to some of its most militant factions, who harbored many misgivings and mistrust of the world organization. To many the city of Jerusalem seemed to be the logical choice; however, the decision over who would control the city had left deep wounds on both sides, and to hold the ceremony there would have inflamed the extremists on both sides. Boston was finally agreed to, primarily because no one had a serious objection and since it had the added significance of being a location that was historically linked to independence and freedom.

Although the extreme elements on both sides opposed the treaty, the leaders of both the Israeli and Palestinian governments had finally agreed that it was an important first step, and shared the belief that the violence and bloodshed had to cease. It was a delicate political line for each government to walk because of the natural fears on each side. Also, past peace discussions had come close to reaching agreement and a meaningful treaty, but had fallen apart at the last moment, the last time being the Clinton initiatives in the last year of his presidency. Each side was so suspicious of the other; and, of course, the history of violence gave good reason for fear. Although David's Israeli negotiators were confident that the final details could be easily worked out, there still existed the concern that there could be an unforeseen event complicating or compromising the ultimate objective. The negotiators on each side had worked extremely hard over several months and had reached the point where they believed that the final technical details would not cause major problems. The world was looking on and anxiously waiting for the final result, and both sides had carefully managed the expectations in the press to the point where they were now confident of the outcome.

David's tasks during the next few weeks would be to help coordinate some of the physical logistics that led up to the actual signing. There were dignitaries who had to be cared for in the manner they had come to expect, travel arrangements, hotel rooms, meals, etc. There was the very sensitive area of protocols which could raise sensitivities if not handled properly. He knew he must concentrate on his specific assignment and ignore all of the excitement that surrounded this historic event.

23

His closest friends called Al Collins, "Pudge," a nickname he had been labeled with while in elementary school because he had tended to carry an excess amount of baby fat, even though he was taller than most kids his age. He had been offended at first, but most everyone had a nickname, and his had been given in good humor. It had stuck with him throughout his school years, and it sort of became a badge of honor to him as a high school athlete, especially since many sports fans remembered the great years of Carlton "Pudge" Fisk with the Boston Red Sox. Perhaps it was his earlier reaction to the nickname that had molded his temperament at an early age. Many people saw Al as having a gigantic ego problem, but others said his overbearing and surly personality went along with his large physical size that grew with him into adulthood.

As a high school athlete he was better than average, a football lineman who weighed more than 220 pounds in his senior year, way more than other players his age. His intimidating physical size was an asset in his early years as a police officer, although as a detective he often lacked the patience and personal skills necessary to conduct and develop an investigation. In a police department as small as Nantucket's, however, there was not a large pool of candidates to choose from when a detective opening occurred. There was a great deal of turnover in the department, and the year-round staff numbered only about twenty. When the opening for detective had occurred five years ago, Al had taken the state exam and applied for the position. Even though he had been the only candidate, he had barely passed the exam. When the senior detective had retired last year, Al was again the only choice available to Chief Campbell. The chief could have tried to locate someone off island, but that would not have gone down well with the local folks, and his experience with off-island people had taught him that they did not tend to stay very long. They developed a bad case of "island fever," a condition known to the year-round residents as meaning someone who became uneasy with living on an island thirty miles from the malls and other facilities available on the mainland. It was especially difficult to retain young police officers because the social life on the island was truly limited in the off-season.

It was the Tuesday morning following the death of the DEA official, and the pressure to unravel the mystery seemed to grow with each passing hour. If the pressure from the press was not bad enough, the chief continued breathing down Al Collins' neck, in addition to the fact that Al also had to deal with state police, the DEA, and even the FBI. He was smart enough to know that all of the outsiders were suspicious of his department's ability to handle the case. He also knew that Chief Campbell was not entirely happy with him as senior detective and wished that his predecessor was still on the job. Well, this was the first murder case on the island in more than ten years, and Al saw it as an opportunity to really show his expertise. In the back of his mind he also knew that Campbell would have to retire in a few years, and Al wanted that position. From where he sat, the chief's job was the cushiest one in the department, flexible hours, no extra duty, he would give the orders rather than having to take them, and most important of all, along with the title came a big salary. If he didn't stay on top of this case the DEA, FBI, or the press would clamor for his head, and he might be out of the running for the top job in the department.

He couldn't let that happen, and the way to do that was to stay way ahead of the hounds who would like nothing better than to embarrass him.

Al sat at his desk looking over his notes and the reports he had received. The coroner's printed report was among them and didn't add much to what he had heard from him over the telephone.

> The deceased, a Caucasian male, 5'9" in height and 185 pounds, appears to be between 60 and 65 years of age, and from all indications was in relatively good health. His death occurred as the result of drowning, somewhere between 9:30 and 10:15 p.m. on Saturday evening. I estimate that the body had been in the water approximately eight to ten hours before being washed up on the beach. The presence of ocean water in his lungs and respiratory system are consistent with those of a drowning victim. An examination of his heart, circulatory system, and major blood vessels showed no evidence of occlusion or blockage; and there is no evidence of cerebral vascular disease that might have caused unconsciousness before falling into the water.
>
> There is a visible depression of the skull that occurred from some injury in the distant past. The only other significant finding on the exterior examination of the body is a deep open wound to the back of the skull. It is four inches long and caused a fracture of the skull and a slight skull depression. It was made by a blunt object, very likely steel, and was done with some significant force. It would have rendered him unconscious, although it was not severe enough to have caused his death if there had been normal emergency care available.
>
> The swelling around the wound and the seawater in the lungs and respiratory system indicate that the deceased was alive when he entered the water and subsequently drowned, probably without regaining consciousness.

The severity of the wound is not consistent with an accidental fall or the deceased running into an object. Rather, the location and severity of the wound causes me to conclude that the deceased was struck on the back of the skull with a hard object delivered by another human being. He was then probably pushed or fell overboard.

The report from the FBI forensics examiner on the contents of the automobile had revealed little additional concrete information. The book and folder on the front seat of the car both had multiple fingerprints, and in each instance the deceased's prints were by far the most common. It would not be unusual to have multiple prints on a paperback book, the bookstore clerk's prints in particular. The folder could have picked up many prints from being handled by other individuals at the deceased's office, but Al would have to check that out and obtain prints from the deceased's coworkers. It was odd, however, that the folder was empty and that it had no label other than the DEA logo.

The most interesting piece of information to Al was that the book had had a piece of paper in it used as a bookmark that had had Jack Kendrick's name and his apparent address handwritten on it.

Jack Kendrick
392 Plymouth Road
Quincy, MA 02170

Kendrick had told Al that he had had only a brief conversation with Andrews, but why then did Andrews have his address? Was it in Andrews' or Kendrick's handwriting, or someone else's? *Well,* Al thought, *there's probably a logical explanation, but I'll have to check it out anyway.*

The overnight bag revealed nothing surprising whatsoever. There was a change of underwear, socks, a sport shirt, a pair of slacks, a sweater, and a toiletry kit—the minimum one would expect for a one-day stay away from home.

Al's assistant, Dick Hines, had checked with the Steamship Authority and found that Andrews had made reservations to return on Saturday on the 5:45 p.m. ferry. He would have to check around town and see where Andrews had planned to stay that evening. He must have made a reservation. A stay of one night was unusual on Nantucket, especially over a weekend, even in the late fall. Visitors usually stayed at least two days, and people didn't normally come to the island to do business on a Saturday. If Andrews had been coming here on some kind of a drug investigation, he must have had plans to see someone. However, Andrews had not contacted anyone in the police department, and the small local state police office had received no notice of his coming or of some continuing drug investigation.

A typical holier-than-thou attitude of federal agencies, keeping the local police in the dark while they did their own investigation, Al thought contemptuously. *Well, if he had let us know, he still might be alive.*

The forensics report did not reveal that there had been anything else in the automobile. There were a few fingerprints in addition to those of the deceased, but they might be from any passengers who had been in the car in the recent past. Well, he'd do his best to try to match them with Andrews' known friends and acquaintances. There were a couple of other prints on the steering wheel that would also have to be checked out. He'd also better check to make sure there had not been a second passenger in the car that night, and probably the best person to ask was that Kendrick guy. There had been no blood in the car and no evidence of a struggle.

The preliminary DNA report on the blood that Dick

Hines had found on the ferry's vehicle deck would not be ready for several days, but the blood type was a definite match with the deceased. Its location, right under the large porthole and on the edge of the porthole itself, was a pretty good indication that something violent might have occurred there, and its location was consistent with someone being pushed out of the porthole. They had taken some fingerprints from around the porthole, but the crew used that area so frequently it was doubtful there would be anything significant there. Hines had not found any other evidence on the boat, including around the area where Andrews' car had been parked.

Al had been given a list of the passengers on the Friday night trip, which included the owners of all of the vehicles, cars, and trucks. There were no reservations necessary and thus no lists kept for walk-on passengers. Also, the names of other passengers who might have been in the vehicles were not known; in fact, in some cases, the reservation had been made by a business and there was not even the driver's name but only the name of the company. In addition, he had a list of those walk-on passengers who had paid with a check or by credit card at the ferry office in Hyannis, but this did not include those people who had purchased their tickets prior to traveling. What a goddamn mess! Well, he'd have to have Hines do the follow-up on each name. Maybe he should ask Campbell for some additional help.

He would need forensics to check the various fingerprints from the different locations to see if there were any matches, and then check with the FBI fingerprint data bank for any matches. This was going to take some time, and Al was apprehensive that everyone would be getting more impatient. He suspected that the state police lab put a small community like Nantucket at the bottom of its priority list, although you'd think they'd speed things up since this case involved a federal officer. He knew it was important to keep busy so others would believe he was working hard on the case.

He also needed to get hold of Jack Kendrick and arrange to interview him in more detail. At this point Kendrick was the only one close to being a witness to some of the events of that evening.

24

On Monday afternoon, Jack Kendrick went with the news team to cover a press conference called by the Drug Enforcement Administration. The Boston media had been clamoring for more information on the death of the DEA official and had not been successful in getting details from the state police or the Nantucket police. Local TV stations had set up their news trucks outside the Boston DEA headquarters and tried to interview whoever came out of their building to try to learn more. After talking with his superiors in Washington, the Boston DEA director, Jim Cassetti, concluded it would be better to give the "newshounds" something to chew on, rather than let their imaginations and desire for headlines dream up a scenario that created more problems for the agency.

The room was filled with perhaps twenty-five news people—TV, radio, and print, along with their crews. Cassetti approached the microphone:

"I will read a statement concerning the death of Bill Andrews, the deputy director of this office, and then will take a few questions. I should emphasize at the outset that this investigation is ongoing and therefore I hope you'll understand that I won't be able to answer many of your questions.

'William G. Andrews, the deputy director of this office, was found dead Saturday morning on a beach on Nantucket Island. He was a passenger on the Steamship Authority's ferry that left Hyannis the previous evening for

Nantucket, but he did not disembark from the boat when it arrived. It is assumed at this point that his body entered the water sometime during the steamship voyage from Hyannis, which normally takes a little more than two hours, and was washed up on the beach sometime Friday night or Saturday morning.

'There is no conclusion at this point as to the cause of death; however, a full and complete investigation is being conducted. The Nantucket Police Department is leading the investigation, and the Massachusetts State Police and this office are assisting.

'Bill Andrews was a valued employee of this agency and a close personal friend of mine for several years. He had planned to retire at the end of this year and was looking forward to relaxing and traveling with his wife, Barbara. Those of us who worked with him on a daily basis will miss him, and I know you all join me in extending our sincere condolences to Bill's entire family.'

"I'll now take some questions." Cassetti recognized a reporter from the *Boston Herald*. "Yes?"

"Mr. Cassetti, we understand that Mr. Andrews' death may not have been accidental. Can you confirm that?"

"The investigation is still in its early stages, and the exact cause has not yet been determined. We have not ruled out anything at this point."

"A follow-up question. What did the autopsy show?"

"I understand that the autopsy is complete and that the medical cause of death was drowning," Cassetti replied. "However, other parts of the investigation are ongoing and the entire case has to be looked at before all of the circumstances surrounding his death can be determined."

"Mr. Director," came a question from radio station WBZ,

"was Mr. Andrews on agency business, and can you tell us the nature of that business?"

"Bill Andrews was conducting an ongoing investigation, but I am not at liberty to give you any more details at this time. At this point we have no reason to believe that his death is related to that investigation."

And from the *Cape Cod Times*: "Was there any evidence of a physical struggle or violence discovered in the autopsy?"

Cassetti hesitated and said, "The body had been in the water and exposed to the elements for some time before being discovered. The only thing I'm able to tell you at this time is that the actual cause of death was drowning."

"Do you believe he may have been pushed overboard?"

"All possible reasons and explanations as to why Bill Andrews went overboard from that ferry are being considered."

"Was he in good health? Could he have fainted or had some kind of an attack and become disoriented?

Again, Cassetti replied, "We are considering all possibilities."

Ed Boise, the reporter on Jack Kendrick's team from TV channel BOS, asked, "Why are the Nantucket police heading this investigation? If he was on DEA business, shouldn't the FBI be involved, and isn't this case beyond the capabilities of a small police department like Nantucket?"

Cassetti, a little irritated at the question, said sharply, "At this point we have no reason to believe that the death was anything but accidental. As I said in my earlier remarks, the Nantucket police are working closely with the Massachusetts State Police as well as this office. One final question!"

"Was Agent Andrews alone on this trip to Nantucket, and

did he bring a vehicle on the ferry? And if so, did the vehicle reveal any evidence?"

"He did take his own car on the ferry, and obviously that vehicle is a part of the forensics investigation. To our knowledge, he was alone on this trip."

"Mr. Director, we are aware that your agency has been concerned about the increased flow of drugs into the Boston area. Was Andrews' assignment a part of this investigation, and can we assume that your department believes there might be a Nantucket connection with the drug trafficking?"

"I'm sorry, but as I said earlier, I cannot give you any more information at this time as far as the nature of Bill Andrews' current assignment. Thank you, and we will keep you informed of further developments as they occur."

And then one passing question from somewhere in the crowd as the director was leaving: "Isn't it unusual for the deputy director to be assigned to field work?"

Cassetti left without stopping to reply.

25

The town of Quincy is only a few miles southeast of Boston on the coast. Today it is principally a bedroom community for the city, helping to make the major Southeast Expressway one of the busiest commuter highways into the city during the weekday rush hours. There are frequent traffic back-ups during even the slightest automobile breakdowns, and a ride that in normal traffic might take fifteen minutes could easily stretch to a half-hour and often longer. It was perhaps the most difficult commute into the city, and the continuing growth of new homes in most South Shore communities continued to exacerbate this already difficult problem.

Quincy was the hometown of the second president of the United States, John Adams, although in the eighteenth century it had been a part of the town of Braintree. Subsequently, that area of Braintree closest to the ocean was split off and the town of Quincy was formed. The ancestral home of John and Abigail Adams is now a national museum. It enjoyed many thousands of visitors in the early twenty-first century, although in the past it had not been a particularly popular historic attraction. In recent years there had been a sort of rejuvenation and a greater appreciation of Adams' role in the Revolutionary War, as well as his impact on the development of our Constitution. He was not an attractive man, especially in comparison to Thomas Jefferson, and his personality and demeanor were such that he was not a particularly popular figure. His frankness often brought on criticism, in spite of the fact that his innovative legal mind shaped the design of the Constitution probably more than any other individual. In recent years his image had been somewhat rehabilitated, the result of several books detailing his contribution to the founding of our country, as well as a greater appreciation for the critical role his wife Abigail had played in influencing his decisions.

Jack and Amy had bought their first home in Quincy for its proximity to Boston and the fact that the price was more attractive than in some of the more expensive suburbs. Jack picked up the morning paper from his driveway at around 6 a.m. on Tuesday morning, well before he normally would have been up, because he had not slept well. Since the DEA director's news conference the previous afternoon, he hadn't been able to get out of his mind the implications of some of the answers to the questions that had been posed. It was pretty evident that the authorities had not concluded that Bill Andrews' death was a suicide. As a matter of fact, it was clear that the director was being deliberately evasive, and not very convincing, in answering specific questions about the cause of death and the autopsy findings. The question about a drug investigation had added a new dimension to the investigation, as well as the fact that two DEA agents were now either dead or missing—one of them since last May.

He sat down at the kitchen table with a cup of coffee and opened the paper. On the bottom half of the front page was a story:

DEA AGENT'S DEATH MAY BE MURDER

The *Boston Globe* has learned from sources close to the investigation that it is likely that the death of Drug Enforcement Administration (DEA) Deputy Director William G.

Andrews, whose body was found on a Nantucket beach Saturday morning, was likely a murder. Although the autopsy report has not yet been released and the cause of death as cited by investigators was drowning, there was a deep wound to the head that was likely the result of a severe intentional blow with a blunt object. Sources close to the investigation said during a press conference that the nature of the wound is such that it is unlikely that it was caused by the victim striking his head while either accidentally falling or intentionally jumping from the ship. Investigators assume he was unconscious from the blow when he entered the water of Nantucket Sound.

DEA Director Jim Cassetti would not say whether Andrews was on official business to Nantucket; however, other sources close to the investigation, who wish to remain anonymous, indicated that he was involved in an investigation of possible drug trafficking between the Island of Nantucket and the mainland. Recently suspicions have been raised that one of the major sources of drugs in the Boston area may be the Cape Cod area. As reported in the *Boston Globe* Sunday edition, another DEA agent, Edwin Proctor, has been missing since May and had been involved in this investigation.

Apparently Deputy Director Andrews was a close friend of Agent Proctor's and had allegedly been very disturbed over his disappearance. An investigation of Proctor's disappearance was conducted internally over the past several months by the DEA but with no results. Andrews was reportedly frustrated and angered over the failure of this investigation, and may have taken it upon himself to try and determine what had happened. Sources allege that one opinion developing within the department is that Andrews was getting too close to uncovering the reason for Proctor's disappearance or too close to discovering the source of the drugs and consequently was murdered on the steamship trip from Hyannis to Nantucket.

Responding to concerns about the Nantucket Police Department handling the investigation of a deceased federal official who was allegedly involved in an ongoing DEA investigation, Cassetti expressed confidence in the way the investigation was proceeding. He stated that both the Massachusetts State Police and his own office were actively involved and that there were no plans to move the investigation from the local police force to state or federal authorities. He emphasized that the resources of the Massachusetts State Police, the FBI, and the Drug Enforcement Administration would be made available to the Nantucket police.

The last murder investigation on Nantucket was sixteen years ago.

The impact of the murder and the drug investigation on the tourist trade on this popular vacation island is unknown at this time, but unsolved violent crimes may cause vacationers to reflect on their own personal safety.

Jack sat back and thought about the fact that if this report was true, he was likely to be further involved. This had all the makings of a good mystery novel—with a high-profile federal employee murdered, drug trafficking, the killer still at large, and a popular exclusive vacation island at the center of the investigation. The press was already on this in a big way, and he knew from his own experience at the TV station that this would make headlines for some time, and that the press would be digging for their own information. It would probably mean his name would eventually surface with the news media, and he'd better alert his boss at the station.

As he was getting his second cup of coffee, Amy came into the kitchen. Before they exchanged their good morning kisses, Jack showed her the headline and told her what the article said.

She sat down and read the article herself. "Well, they seem pretty certain that it wasn't a suicide and that he was murdered," she said.

"Yeah, and it looks like the feds are going to be taking a more active role, and that's probably a good idea. I think now it's more likely that someone will want to talk with me further."

"And they'll undoubtedly have a lot more questions. I just hope you don't have to make another trip to Nantucket."

"I hadn't thought about that, and I really can't afford any time right now with all that's going on at work. Maybe if they want to see me, the interview could be arranged in Boston, since the DEA office is right there."

Amy was silent for a minute and then asked, "Have you thought about the fact that if Andrews was murdered, then the killer was on the boat with you and may have seen you talking with him?"

"Yeah, and that sure doesn't make me very comfortable."

"Do you recall anyone else talking with Andrews at any time on the boat?"

"No, I don't think so. You know, I didn't pay much attention to him until he sat down with me, and I didn't notice anything special after he left. He certainly didn't say anything about meeting or knowing anyone else on board the ferry. He didn't seem upset or anxious—just a regular guy."

"Well, it probably would be a good idea if you went over in your mind the conversation you had with him, just in case you do get another call."

They turned on the television to see if there were any more details on the morning news.

26

Joe Hinkle sat in front of the TV, having just heard the local news and the fact that Agent Andrews' death was now thought to be a homicide. He stared blankly at the TV for a moment and then turned to another local channel to see if there were any more details. The morning news anchor was showing a picture of the steamship wharf in Hyannis and then the beach on Nantucket where the body had been found. They had conducted an interview with the police chief in Nantucket, who hadn't come right out and said it was murder, but the newsman said his source had told him the investigation was leaning in that direction.

Hinkle got up to nervously pace the room. Should he call Bennie Haas, or wait for him to call? He decided it might go better if he called first, so he dialed Haas' number.

"Hello, Bennie, this is Hinkle. Have you been watching TV?"

"You mean the story about the DEA agent who was found dead?" Haas asked.

"Yeah, that's what I'm calling about."

"I've been reading the paper, and they seem pretty sure it's murder. Tell me you're not involved in this, Joe!"

Joe hesitated before his reply and then said, "No, it was an accident. Nobody intentionally pushed him overboard."

"What the hell are you talking about?" Haas yelled. "What do you mean 'pushed overboard?' Joe, for Christ's sake, quit lying to me—you are involved, aren't you? What the hell happened?"

"Well, we got into a little scuffle and he tripped and fell overboard. It wasn't intentional. It was just an accident."

"Jesus Christ, you dumb jackass. Don't you know this could blow the whole business? I've worked for years to get this setup going, and now it's in jeopardy because of your dumb-ass temper. Did anyone see you with this guy?"

"No, I'm pretty sure no one did. Most everyone was upstairs in the passenger lounge. I was really careful."

"Not careful enough! How did you get involved with this guy in the first place?"

"Well, I saw him snooping around my truck and then noticed that he was from the DEA." Joe then began to improvise. "I asked him what he wanted and he got kind of nasty—belligerent. We shoved each other, and then he lost his balance and went overboard. We were near a large porthole."

"As simple as that, huh? Come on, Joe, that just doesn't hold any water. If anyone suspects you, you'd better have a better story than that. You've already got a record of getting into trouble because of your fuckin' temper."

Joe didn't reply, and Haas went on. "So what are you going to do?"

"I don't know," Joe said after a pause. "Wait and hope it blows over."

"Fat chance, if they believe it's murder. Also, what's this about another agent disappearing a few months ago? Did you know about that?"

"No, that was the first I'd heard about it," Joe quickly lied.

"I hope you're telling me the truth, Joe, because I've got a lot at stake here. Jesus Christ, I can't believe this! Look, you keep me posted, and I think we'd better lay off any more deliveries for a while. I think I'd better begin to think about another way of handling my business."

"I still have my weekly NEEx trips scheduled for Nantucket, you know, and we've got that special pickup in a couple of weeks," Joe reminded him.

"Yeah, but I don't want to take any risks right now. Goddamn it! You've really screwed things up!"

Joe, concerned about losing his extra income, said optimistically, "I really think this'll blow over in a few days."

"I don't know about that. I'll give you a call later this week."

27

Ahmed had been in Halifax for three days and was getting nervous. The Silver Wave, the fishing boat that was to be his next means of transportation on his mission to the United States, was supposed to have been in port within two days of his arrival. Everything had gone according to plan to this point, but he worried now that someone had dropped the ball on this next step. Did he have the wrong date or even the wrong port? Or perhaps something had happened to the fishing boat, like engine failure or a storm delay.

During the last few days he had become a little familiar with this small port city, especially the area around the waterfront, and was pleased to have a chance to use his English frequently prior to reaching the U.S. He wasn't getting any unusual or difficult personal questions from people he encountered, and he found that his English was well understood. He noticed that some words were pronounced differently here than in the English he had learned, but assumed this was due to Canadian pronunciation. The first time he heard a Canadian say the word "about," which had sounded like "aboot," he had been taken aback and wondered if he had been pronouncing it wrong. He was really sensitive about anything in his speech that might raise questions when he got to the United States.

Yesterday he had worked up the courage to ask at the harbormaster's office if they knew when the Silver Wave would be in port. He had explained that his brother was on board and he hadn't seen him for some time. The clerk at the harbormaster's office had said the fishing boat schedules were not very dependable, and usually they didn't know until the day before arrival—sometimes not until the boat actually arrived. He had suggested that Ahmed go to the fish processing plant where they might have a better idea, but Ahmed had decided to wait before he aroused any more suspicions.

Early on the morning of the fourth day, the Silver Wave finally arrived in Halifax. It was a U.S. registered fishing trawler that regularly stopped at this Canadian port for fuel before returning to its homeport in Nantucket. There was a constant tension between Canadian and United States fishermen because they disagreed about each other's laws regarding restricted fishing areas. Most American boats stayed away from Canadian ports, except for emergencies, but the Silver Wave had frequented the Halifax port for years and the captain was well known.

Like many commercial fishing boats, the Silver Wave didn't look very substantial or well kept at first glance. However, on closer observation one could see that all of the essential tools and equipment for deep-sea fishing were state-of-the-art. The engine itself was more than adequate to power the vessel through the North Atlantic weather, and a skilled mechanic could tell from its sound that it was well cared for. The conditions that existed on all commercial fishing boats were such that it was difficult to keep the surface areas of the vessel and equipment looking clean. Salt air, wind, oil from fish, and the various kinds of ocean vegetation that were dragged up on the deck all worked to make it almost impossible to keep ahead of the slimy appearance until the trip was over and the crew had a chance to wash and scrub down the boat in port.

Ahmed found his way to the boat and was told by the captain, Ed Gatious, that they would be leaving that afternoon, and that the trip back to Nantucket would take about two days, depending upon the weather. Gatious was a gruff sort of man with a scraggly beard that was beginning to turn gray around the edges. His weather-beaten clothes smelled of the fish catch of the past ten days. He had apparently had a pretty good trip and the hold was about full. He explained to Ahmed that the weather the past two days had been really rough and that they might expect the same as they moved toward the southwest and home. The fall saw many storms make their way up the North American coast, some of them ferocious with hurricane-force winds.

Gatious seemed to take a great deal of pleasure in painting a hazardous picture for Ahmed of the voyage ahead of him, while at the same time stressing that he must stay out of the crew's way since they had work to do. Ahmed wondered if part of his demeanor might be due to the apprehension he felt about taking a passenger illegally into the U.S., but he was surely getting paid well for the risk. Ahmed's bunk was in a small cabin with two of the crew. He hoped the next two days would go quickly, especially since he had never been at sea before and was concerned about becoming seasick.

When Ahmed had first arrived in Halifax he had called the telephone number he had been given before leaving Israel, and made arrangements to pick up a suitcase of materials that he'd need for his work in the U.S. It was very heavy, but he didn't have much in the way of other personal belongings, so the crew of the boat would not be suspicious as to why he was carrying so much baggage. He had decided not to open the suitcase until he got to his destination in the U.S., although he was very anxious to make certain that all the materials he would need were there.

28

David Mier woke from his deep sleep with a start. At first he wasn't sure just where he was, and then the sound and the smells quickly reminded him that he was on an airplane, some-where over the Atlantic Ocean. He looked at his watch and real-ized that the eleven-hour flight was almost over and he would be landing at Washington, D.C., within the next hour. The flight attendant offered him a warm, damp towel, a truly refreshing benefit of flying first class, and David thought at that moment that it alone might have been worth the extra expense. He wasn't sure what made that particular service seem so special, but mused that it must be a combination of getting rid of the dryness and stuffiness of the cabin environment, the long trip without any exercise, and the fact that he had just woken up. There were indeed certain times and places when a simple act, like washing one's face, brought special pleasure.

As he sat there he recalled the dream he had just had, and wondered why after so many years Ahmed Kahlil had come to his mind. The dream had not been an unrealistic one but had simply taken David back to his youth, when he and Ahmed had been close friends; indeed, Ahmed had been David's closest friend. In the dream they were playing soccer with a group of local boys in a vacant schoolyard—sort of a pickup game of the kind they had played frequently in their neighborhood. On this particular day, Ahmed and David were on the same team, and their abilities and skills were quite similar. The other players varied in age and ability, but they tried to pick the teams so there was an equal balance of skill. Usually it worked out pretty well, but some days it did not. This was one of those days, and the opposing team had more than its fair share of older and larger boys. One boy in particular was physically larger and stronger than anyone else on either team, and although he didn't have the best soccer skills, he seemed to take pleasure in hitting and knocking other players around, especially if they were smaller. David was on the small side and was frequently the target of this particular bully, and David wondered at times if he deliberately went after him because he was a Jew. In the dream, David was dribbling the ball down the field toward the goal, and just as he made a pass to Ahmed, this older boy tripped him and pushed him hard. He went down hard, but in the dream he jumped up quickly, ran around the boy toward the goal, took a pass back from Ahmed, and kicked the ball through the goal. His teammates all ran to give him a high five; and Ahmed, with a big smile, gave him a big hug. It was one of those dreams that never had happened in real life.

He and Ahmed had truly been close, and David regretted the fact that their lives had moved along different paths since he had gone to private school away from Nazareth, but he knew that was not so unusual. They had shared so many experiences as young boys and had such similar interests. He wondered what Ahmed was doing at the present time and tried to remember when he had last seen him. David didn't get back to Nazareth very often, but he recalled that his mother had told him that Ahmed was working for an electronics or computer service company. He thought to himself that it was too bad Ahmed had not gone to a four-year school, since he had been such a good student, but few Arab students went to even a two-year program, usually because of financial limitations.

David recalled that his mother had showed some concern about Ahmed getting involved with the "wrong kind of crowd," but he had never followed up on what she had meant. He had assumed it had something to do with one of the more militant Arab groups, since many Arab youths seemed to gravitate in this direction, especially during the past few years of the intifada. He remembered that Ahmed's brother Hassim had been killed in Nablus during a serious altercation with the Israeli security force. This must have had an effect on Ahmed and his family and undoubtedly driven him in a more militant direction. He tried to imagine himself in a similar situation, but in spite of the fact that he knew the deep animosity and hatred that existed between Jews and Palestinians, he could not picture himself with the deep hatred of many Palestinians.

David thought about the proposed peace treaty and the establishment of a Palestinian state and the effect this would have on Arabs such as Ahmed. He saw it as a chance, perhaps a final chance, to begin to heal deep wounds that over many decades—in many cases centuries—had bred this hatred. How long would it take for each side to begin to trust each other? Growing up in Nazareth, he had not experienced the hatred that he knew existed in the occupied areas of Gaza, the West Bank, and the Golan Heights. He had come to realize through his Foreign Service job that there were groups on both the Israeli and Arab side that did not want peace and would do anything to prevent the proposed treaty from being signed. The violence and the suicide bombings were the visible signs of this hatred, but he had also seen in many instances how the more moderate factions on both sides feared taking positive steps that would offend the extremists. It was this reluctance, often over very minor issues, which had slowed down the negotiation process and still threatened to delay the final agreement. Similar to many national and international political situations throughout history, the polarized positions of extremists too often influenced the outcome of events, while the silent majority lacked the leadership to affect an outcome that truly represented their desires. David felt that this proposed peace treaty was one example of where the silent majority was speaking.

He would truly like to get together with Ahmed again, not only to try to renew their friendship, but also to learn from an Arab he had grown up with just how he felt at the present time. He made a promise to himself that when he was in Nazareth the next time, he would make an attempt to get in touch with him.

The flight attendant's announcement interrupted David's thinking.

"We will be landing at Dulles International Airport in approximately twenty minutes. The in-flight entertainment system will now be turned off, and at this time you should place your seats in their upright position and store your tray tables. Please turn off any electrical equipment, such as personal computers, and place all of your carry-on luggage in the overhead bin or under the seat in front of you."

29

Jack Kendrick was sitting in the lobby of the Drug Enforcement Administration waiting to meet with the director. He had received a call the previous evening asking if he would be available the following afternoon to talk further about having seen Bill Andrews on the steamship trip.

In many ways it was a typical government building—plain and nondescript, a lot of gray metallic furniture, pictures of the president in the lobby and, of course, entirely lacking in finely polished walnut woodwork that you'd find in a private office building in downtown Boston. The DEA office was in the federal office building, which was located in a section of the city with other government buildings, including Boston City Hall.

The receptionist displayed the temperament of too many government employees that he'd met over the years: coolly efficient, but with little in the manner of the good "customer relations" common in the private sector. Jack thought to himself that it was probably the result of the almost guaranteed job security, the seniority system, and the lack of competition in the public sector that subconsciously resulted in people treating others in a more casual manner. She had taken his name, told him to take a seat, and she'd tell Director Cassetti that he was here. No smile, no offer of coffee, only one newspaper that was being read by someone else, and only out-of-date magazines to read while one waited. The meeting had been set for 2 p.m., and he had taken time off from work for the rest of the day since the person who called him couldn't schedule it later in the day when he would have been available. Again, not the kind of customer relations he'd expect to find in the private sector. It was almost twenty minutes after two, and he'd been waiting more than thirty minutes with no further explanation from the receptionist. He was about to get up and question her as to how much longer it would be when the door opened up and a middle-aged woman came toward him and asked, "Are you Jack Kendrick?"

As Jack nodded, she said, "Come with me"; and before he could reply, she took off down the corridor.

The meeting room was just what he'd expected: a grey metal table and six chairs that were well worn, with one of the chairs in the corner having an arm hanging loose. There was a tape recording machine on the table, but otherwise it was entirely bare. After waiting for a few more minutes, a man wearing a shirt with an open collar and a tie hanging—as if it was rarely firmly in place—came into the room, followed by Detective Al Collins from Nantucket and another person.

The man with the open collar took a seat at the head of the table and introduced himself as Director Cassetti. He introduced the third person as his assistant, who was assigned the case. Jack said hello to Al Collins and they briefly shook hands.

Without any preliminary casual conversation the director said, "My agency is working with the Nantucket police and we're anxious to find out just what happened to my close friend and deputy director. We have reason to believe this was not an accident, and I'm going to see that no stone is left unturned in getting to the bottom of his death. Now, Detective Collins here tells me you saw Bill Andrews on the boat last Friday, and even though I know you already gave Al some information in Nantucket, I'd like to hear directly from you what happened that evening. We're trying to put all the pieces together. Oh, incidentally, we'd like to tape this interview for our records. OK?"

"Sure, that's fine," Jack said. "I'd like to do anything I can to help in your investigation."

"OK, then let's get started. Why don't you tell me when you first met Bill Andrews, and try to remember as much detail as you can. Every piece of information you give us may prove to be an important clue." His assistant turned on the tape recorder and they looked at Jack expectantly.

Jack took a moment to gather his thoughts and then began to recite his initial contact with Andrews in as much detail as he could remember from that evening, beginning with when he had first met Andrews when they had parked their cars on the steamship deck. He recounted their sitting together in the passenger lounge and that they had both been reading books by the same author. It took him no more than a few minutes to describe what had happened, and he ended by saying, "Well, that's about all I can remember. The next thing that happened was the call from Detective Collins on Saturday morning asking me to come down to the police station."

Cassetti and Collins looked at each other, and then Cassetti said, "OK, let's go back over this a bit. I have a few questions. You say you first saw Bill Andrews after you had parked your car behind him inside the ferry, but weren't you parked behind him on the dock before you were loaded on the ferry?"

"I don't think so; at least I don't recall seeing him."

"How long were you in line waiting to board the boat?"

"Oh, I guess I arrived about thirty minutes ahead of time. I had time to take my dog for a short walk before we boarded."

"So the first time you remember seeing Andrews was when you got out of your car inside the boat."

"Yeah, that's right," said Jack.

"Did you notice whether or not he locked his car when he went up to the passenger area?"

"No; I wasn't really observing that closely."

"Did you notice if he was carrying anything with him from the car?"

"No, I don't recall that he was carrying anything, although he must have had the book with him that he was reading later."

"And, Mr. Kendrick, you don't recall seeing Andrews before you arrived at the steamship? For example, at a restaurant along the way from Boston, or at a gas station, or anywhere, or at any other time?"

"No, I don't recall ever meeting or seeing him before."

"After you invited him to sit with you in the passenger area, you say you had very little conversation. Did he tell you why he was going to Nantucket? That would seem a logical discussion."

"As I said before, he did say he worked for the government and that he had some kind of business on Nantucket. He didn't say any more than that, and I didn't ask him."

"Did he ask you what you were doing?"

"Well, I don't remember who asked whom, but I do recall telling him we had a place on the island and I was going down to close it up for the winter. He really wasn't very talkative and we both put our heads into our books."

"Did he have anything else with him besides the book, like an envelope or a folder?"

"Like I said a few minutes ago, I don't recall that he had anything else with him. I think I would have noticed if he had put anything on the table."

"Did you see Andrews talking with anyone else at any time?"

"Well, I really wasn't looking that carefully, but I sure don't remember his talking with anyone—certainly not while he was sitting at the table with me."

All during the conversation Detective Collins sat staring at Jack, almost in a challenging or belligerent manner. Jack couldn't figure out what his role was and why he didn't participate more in the conversation if he was really heading up the investigation.

"What time did you say Andrews got up and left?" Cassetti asked. "It's really very important that we try to reconstruct his movements as carefully as possible."

"As I told Detective Collins earlier, I think it was about halfway into the trip, but it might have been closer to Nantucket now that I think about it. He had finished his book and left it on the table for me to read. I told him I'd probably finish mine before we arrived and he could take it with him. Both books were by the same author, David Baldacci, and we had talked a bit earlier about how much we liked his mysteries. I think I was pretty close to finishing my book when he left, because I had time later before the boat docked to get a Coke from the snack bar. I thought he was coming back, because he had said something about needing to stretch his legs."

"And where did he go when he left the table?"

"I really didn't pay any attention. I don't know."

"So, he could have gone down to the vehicle deck right then?"

"I suppose so."

"Where is the book that he left on the table?"

"I left it in Nantucket, figuring it would be a good read next summer."

"Was there anything in the book? Any papers or markers?

"No, nothing that I recall, but I really didn't look through it."

"So, you didn't see him again after he left you at the table? Down on the passenger deck or at the snack bar?"

"No, I never saw him again."

Cassetti leaned back in his chair, frowning. "I've been in this business of investigating my whole life, and one of the things I don't like is coincidences. I've learned over the years that coincidences just don't happen that often, and when I see one it's a red light to me."

Finally Collins came to life and said, "Yeah, I feel the same way."

"You were also on the ferry back in May," Cassetti continued, referring to a paper in front of him, "on May twenty-third." It was a statement of fact, not a question. "What were you going to Nantucket for at that time?"

"My wife and I came down in late May to open up the house. I guess it was sometime around then, although I don't recall the exact date. We came down for the weekend, and we do it about the same time each year."

"Why did you bring your car over on each trip? Isn't that pretty expensive just for the weekend?" The tone of Cassetti's voice had become challenging, almost accusatory.

Jack paused for a moment, trying to figure out what was going on, and then said, "Well, we had a car full of things to bring over in May. It's the trip when we usually bring over everything we're going to need for the summer. We have two young children, and all of their paraphernalia almost fills up the car by itself. There's no way we could carry it on board by hand. On the last trip, we had some clothing and other things to bring back. Also, it's easier for the dog to travel in the car."

Cassetti was visibly agitated. "I said I don't like coincidences, and I don't. You've heard that we had another DEA agent disappear last May while investigating possible illegal drug trafficking in the Cape area. The coincidence is that he disappeared on May twenty-third, and we have reason to believe he may have been on a steamship headed for Nantucket. And now my deputy has been murdered, also on the steamship, and also one where you again were a passenger. That's two coincidences, and then there's the further coincidence that you happened to be parked behind Andrews on the boat and that he just happened to sit with you. I don't like even one coincidence, and here we have multiple ones. And also, you just happened to have left your fingerprints all over Andrews' car when you left the book there. What do you think—a few too many coincidences?"

Jack was obviously flustered and confused, and looked toward Cassetti's assistant and Detective Collins for their reactions to Cassetti's statement. They were each stone-faced, but Jack sensed a little smirk on Collins' face that he read as a sign that he was enjoying Jack's discomfort.

"I don't know where you're leading with this," Jack replied coolly, "but I've told you exactly what happened. I don't know much about coincidences, but I guess that's what has occurred in this situation."

Collins broke into the conversation. "We're still working on tying together a lot of loose ends. We'd like to see the book that Andrews gave you. You said it's at your cottage. Do you have a key to the cottage with you, or is there one hidden somewhere that we could use to get in and retrieve the book?"

"I don't have one with me, but there's one hung in the outside shower stall in back of the house. You're free to use it, and I'm pretty sure I left the book in the living room on the coffee table. If it's not there, I guess I'd look in the bookcase against the wall."

"Well," said Cassetti abruptly, "I guess that's all we have for now, but I'm sure we'll be getting in touch with you again. This case is my top priority. Andrews was a close personal friend and I aim to get to the bottom of it and find his killer, and when we do I think we'll have the killer of the other agent as well. You're free to leave, but if you think of anything else give either Detective Collins or myself a call. We need to bring together any information that may help us find this bastard."

As he got up to leave the room he muttered, "I don't believe in goddamn coincidences."

Jack looked again at all three individuals, thought about saying something but couldn't find the words to overcome his confusion and growing anger over the way he was being treated and the way this meeting had ended. He sat there for a minute and then got up and left without anything further being said.

30

Jack took the rest of the day off. He needed some time to clear his head and figure out what was really going on. It was almost like he had been interrogated in that meeting and that they really thought he might have been involved in the agent's murder. He couldn't believe this was a serious possibility, but he couldn't ignore it either. Were they just trying to bait him, or were they taking their frustrations out on him at not being able to solve the case? He assumed that the officials were under some pressure from the press and their higher-ups to solve the murder quickly.

Amy listened quietly to him describe what had happened at the DEA office and then said, "Are you sure you understood what they were saying and that you're not overreacting? It just doesn't make any sense."

"No, it makes no goddamn sense at all. It's crazy! But that's what they said and that's what I heard. Maybe that's a common technique early in investigations to question and try to intimidate everyone." He paused for a moment. "I just don't like the feel of this. I think they may really feel I had something to do with this. You wouldn't believe the belligerent tone of their questions toward the end of the meeting."

They both sat quietly for a while. "Do you think maybe you ought to speak with Scott and get his opinion?" Amy asked at last.

Scott Abrams was a lawyer and a friend who had gone to school with Amy and was now with a Boston law firm, building a career in criminal law. He was the godfather of one of their children and someone they included in their small circle of close friends. He had tried a few small cases, but nothing of this magnitude.

Jack hesitated before saying, "I can't believe we're even talking this way. Here we are minding our own business, raising our family, struggling to make ends meet, and now we're talking about spending money on a lawyer." He walked to the picture window and looked out across the street to the row of houses in their middle-class neighborhood. It was a development that had been built in the mid-1960s; many of the houses were of a similar Cape Cod design. He noticed that his lawn needed to be mowed at least one more time and that shortly the leaves would have to be raked. This season had been a good one for fall foliage in northern New England. Even in neighborhoods close to the city the beauty of the reds, yellows, and oranges of the maple trees made it easy to forget that winter was rapidly approaching.

Discouraged, he turned back to Amy. "I guess it would be a good idea to get someone else's advice, and Scott may be able to get some input from other lawyers in the firm. You know, Amy, I was almost at a point in that meeting where I wasn't going to answer any more questions without talking to a lawyer. I'll give Scott a call."

3I

Joe Hinkle drove his truck up Route 3 toward Boston, and was glad to see that the traffic was light as he approached the city. During the week this highway could easily become bogged down with commuters and really upset the delivery schedule of a truck driver. During the summer months the traffic on this highway to the Cape was especially congested on Friday and Sunday evenings as people traveled to and from their vacation homes.

Joe picked up his passenger along with two suitcases at the usual pickup spot on the waterfront. Ed Gatious, the boat captain, had been there but didn't bother to introduce the passenger and was anxious to leave as soon as Joe arrived. After they left Gatious, Joe tried to engage his passenger in conversation, but this guy just didn't want to talk about anything. He answered Joe's questions with as few words as possible. He was really a rude bastard, and except for the fact that Joe was being paid good money—five times as much as a regular trip to the island—he would have thrown him out by the side of the road. He wondered who this guy was, and why he had arrived in Nantucket on the fishing trawler. He was sure he wasn't one of the regular crew, since he wasn't dressed like one and his hands looked a little too soft for a fisherman. Deep-sea fishing was hard and dangerous work, and he had heard somewhere that it was probably the most dangerous of all occupations. This guy just didn't look the type.

He said his name was Cahill and he spoke pretty good English, but there was some kind of an accent that made Joe think he hadn't been born in this country. *This guy, Cahill, sure isn't from around here,* he thought. *I don't know what he's into, but it's sure not legal. Someone wants to get him into the country without having to go through customs. Well, I'll drop him off in Boston and that'll be the end of it.*

This had been pretty easy money, and there was no problem on the steamship this time. Bennie Haas had come close to saying he would have someone else handle this pickup, but since two weeks had gone by since the guy went overboard and nothing further had developed, he had let Joe make the trip. Bennie had threatened Joe again and told him he wasn't satisfied yet with his explanation of what had happened to the DEA official. To demonstrate his continued concern and uneasiness, he had said there wouldn't be a drug pickup this time—just to be cautious in case Joe was stopped or questioned with the passenger on board.

Joe hadn't slept very well the first several nights after the incident, but now he had almost forgotten about it. It sure looked to him like it was going to blow over the same way the first one had. He'd still better be careful, and he needed to get back to the point where Bennie had confidence in him. He needed that extra money, and the regular pickups were usually so easy—so much a part of his normal routine. He wondered if he had overreacted to the two DEA agents, and that perhaps they really hadn't suspected him of anything. As each day went by, he had become more and more confident that he'd gotten away with two murders. Still, he planned to talk with Bennie Haas and tell him he wanted him to find someone else to do the Nantucket pickups. The fear of a lifetime prison sentence was too real for him to ignore.

32

Ahmed slouched down in the truck, closed his eyes, and tried to make the driver believe he was asleep. This seemed to be the only way of keeping him from persistently asking questions. Ahmed preferred to say as little as possible so that the driver would know nothing about him. But it was really difficult with this character who just continued to press him into conversation. He would be relieved when he got to the bus station in Boston. The driver had said it would take about ninety minutes, and they had already been on the road for about half an hour.

The boat ride had not been as bad as he'd feared. The sea had been rough at first, but the Silver Wave seemed to take the seas in stride. The first day his stomach had felt a little queasy, but by the second day he had gotten his sea legs. He thought the crew was a little disappointed that their landlubber passenger didn't get sick. It had really been pretty boring—just open seas for scenery, and because they were going straight to Nantucket there had been no fishing. Ahmed had remained in the small cabin except for meals, in order to avoid conversation and questions from any of the crew. The constant strong smell from the fish in the hold had been a permanent reminder of what this boat was really all about, and Ahmed would have liked to have seen how all the strange equipment on the boat worked and to learn the meaning of the words that the crew used, apparently nautical terms that were also not a part of his English vocabulary. Fortunately he hadn't gotten any questions from the crew as to who he was and where he was going. The captain ran a tight ship and must have laid down the law to the crew. The only information they had been given was his alias passport name. Art Cahill had sounded really odd to him at first, but the surname did sound somewhat similar to his real surname, Khalil. By now he was sort of getting used to the name and found he was beginning to respond quickly when someone called him Art, without having to think twice.

He was getting close to his final destination, and so far so good. He was more than a little apprehensive about the next step. Boston was a big city with more sophisticated people than he had run into so far. He'd have to be especially alert to using and responding to this new name. He continued to be somewhat apprehensive about his English, even though it seemed to have gone without a hitch so far. He had been warned that slang words and expressions and other colloquialisms were things to be especially on the guard for.

Arrangements had been made for him to stay in a section of Boston called Alston, but other than that he would be on his own. The suitcase he had picked up in Halifax was in the back of the truck, and just about all the special materials he needed were there. He would pick up a few other items at a hardware store once he got settled.

He hoped that everything connected with his temporary employment was all arranged. Even though he had been assured that all those details had been worked out, he knew that piece of the puzzle was critical to the success of the mission. He would feel a lot better when he had found his room and made contact with the sound and acoustics firm he was to work for. He felt the excitement of getting close to the end of a long journey, but he also felt he was realistic about the dangers that lay ahead. He would be almost entirely on his own for the next couple of weeks, and although he had been given a number to call in the Boston area, he had been warned to use it only in a dire emergency. The fewer people who saw him and could tie him to this mission, the better off he was. If everything went the way it had been planned he would not have to meet anyone face-to-face who knew who he was or what he was all about.

He looked out the window and noticed a sign for Plimouth Plantation and recalled that the town of Plymouth was where the Pilgrims had landed almost four hundred years ago. They had been escaping from religious persecution in their homeland of England and were seeking freedom on a new continent. Ahmed thought there were some similarities with the plight of the Palestinians and their fight for freedom. They were also being persecuted in their homeland, and indeed their land had been taken away from them by the U.N. resolution in 1947, but they would not run off to another country as these Pilgrims had. He had become convinced since his brother's death that the only solution for Palestinians was to regain their rightful land and property—by force and terrorism if necessary. Their freedom wouldn't be achieved until the injustice done to the Palestinian people almost sixty years ago was reversed. His mission was an important part of that goal, and in spite of the personal risks he felt enormous pride in being the one called upon to carry it out. He almost spoke out loud, *May Allah give me the strength to go through with it. The peace treaty must not happen!*

Well, at least the driver was now quiet, and Ahmed made up his mind to keep his eyes closed for the remainder of the trip to Boston.

33

David Mier looked out of the window as his plane descended toward Dulles Airport in Virginia, where most of the international flights to the Washington area were routed. To the northeast he could make out some of the larger structures of the city—the Capitol and the Washington Monument. He'd stay here only a few days before he flew on to Boston, where the peace treaty would be signed. Faneuil Hall had been selected as the sight for the signing, and the Palestinians were particularly pleased with the significance of a historic building whose history was tied to national freedom and independence.

His job was to make certain the Israeli foreign secretary had all of the materials he needed for each of the several meetings that would occur over the next few days as they tried to iron out the last details of the agreement. Sometimes he felt like a gofer, but at the same time he knew that this was an exceptional experience and that everyone went through this kind of a phase as they began their careers. There were occasions when the foreign secretary would ask him what he thought about a particular problem, usually not one of great importance, but one that was annoying the secretary and needed to be resolved. He wished these instances were more frequent because they made him feel he was contributing something of significance. However, more irritating issues had arisen as this sensitive project and the negotiations drew closer to this historic meeting. Which countries would be invited to sit in the auditorium at Faneuil Hall and observe the signing was a particularly sensitive question for each side. Both the Palestinians and Israelis wanted to make certain their "friends" were equally represented. And then there was the question of press attendance—both television and newspapers. There would have to be a pool representative, since there simply was not enough room in the hall for all of the foreign press; but each side wanted to have its own pool representative. Finally, after much discussion, the question had been resolved. Yet agreement on the final seating arrangements for the dignitaries had taken days of discussion and still had not been entirely resolved. It appeared to David that each side was reluctant to give in on any issue, even one involving the minutest of detail, since it might be taken as a sign of weakness and send a message that would negatively affect other negotiations. Furthermore, once a position was taken publicly there was even less likelihood of compromise.

The security arrangements were a particular concern for everyone involved because of the deep divisions that still existed and the threat of violence by extremists. Security would be extremely tight, both in and outside of Faneuil Hall. This was being left principally to the Americans, but the Israelis and Palestinians were insistent on making certain that their own interests would be protected. In addition, other countries from the region that were to have representatives at the signing were anxious about the security for their own officials. The extremists' statements continued to be threatening over the resolution of the "Jerusalem question." It was the most unique city in the Middle East, and indeed possibly in the world, where several religions had special and emotional historic ties. The Jews and Muslims both claimed important religious shrines, and this had been an almost impossible hurdle from the beginning of the peace talks, with each side claiming that the city should be a part of its territory. In addition, the Israelis had moved their capital from

Tel Aviv to Jerusalem, and this had added more complications. Indeed, several previous peace attempts had broken up over an impasse on the Jerusalem issue.

Those in the Christian minority in both Israel and Palestine also laid claim to the city's significant role in their history, especially the trial, crucifixion, and resurrection of their Christ. Perhaps because of the bloody encounters on both sides in the early twenty-first century, the majority of Israelis and Palestinians had finally been willing to accept a compromise that would place Jerusalem under a United Nations protectorate—a city that would be governed by the U.N. but with access provided to all religions. Since it was a solution that benefited neither side in the dispute, it was ultimately, although reluctantly, accepted. Without this agreement there would be no peace treaty whatsoever. The question of what countries would be responsible under the U.N. banner for security in the city still needed to be resolved. Each side wished to see a predominance of those countries that were especially friendly to their cause.

During the next several days, the communication of the Israeli position to the necessary parties involved in the arrangements was part of David's job, and was the reason he would be traveling on to Boston before the rest of the Israeli delegation. He knew that as the date for signing drew closer that the pace of his work would increase dramatically.

34

Jack Kendrick sat in the law office waiting room reading over the news wire printout he had picked up at the station that morning. It was not a long article but simply one more in the growing list of press reports on the death of Bill Andrews.

The Drug Enforcement Administration (DEA) does not appear to have made any significant progress in the investigation into the death of its deputy director, William G. Andrews, whose body washed up on a Nantucket beach some ten days ago. Under questioning, a spokesperson for the DEA continued to insist that the investigation is proceeding well and being managed by the Nantucket Police Department, but that his office is staying very close to any developments. When questioned further as to whether they had determined conclusively that Andrews' death was an accident, suicide, or murder, the spokesperson said it looked less and less like an accident and that murder had not been ruled out.

When asked if there were any leads or suspects, the spokesperson said that reporters should speak with the Nantucket police, but that he understood several leads were being pursued. Passengers who were on the ferry the evening of Andrews' death, who may have any information, or who may have observed anything unusual, were urged to contact either the Nantucket police or his department. He said as near as they could estimate there were about seventy passengers on that particular ferry trip, and some of those passengers must have come in contact with Deputy

Director Andrews. Even if that contact appeared to be very brief or minimal, he urged passengers to come forward, since any piece of information might significantly help to further the investigation.

He then pointed out that if Andrews had been deliberately pushed overboard, then the person who pushed him had obviously been one of the passengers on the ferry. He said the investigative team was examining the passenger list in detail to determine if there were any links to Andrews or the DEA in the past. He further said that in his own experience, careful investigation would eventually give them the clear answer to Andrews' death and to the murder, if it was indeed a homicide.

Another source close to the investigation said that the investigative team was now working on the assumption that Andrews had been deliberately murdered and pushed overboard, but that they were not quite ready to announce this publicly and conclusively—perhaps because it would increase the public's anxiety and pressure for an immediate arrest.

Jack read the article several times and didn't know whether to feel better or worse than he had after his meeting with the DEA director and Detective Al Collins. They hadn't indicated that they had a suspect under investigation, but at the same time the DEA spokesman had obviously not revealed all he knew. Jack began to wonder if he should have made this appointment with Scott Abrams, or if maybe he was overreacting. When he thought about it logically he kept telling himself that it was ridiculous to think that the DEA might consider him a suspect, but then he kept running over in his mind the specific questions they had asked him yesterday and he was less sure. And then he remembered the belligerent tone of the meeting and the almost accusatory position taken by the DEA director, and real fear began to well up in his belly. He had lost track of how many times he had gone over in his mind the conversations since yesterday's meeting, and indeed much of that time had been when he had lain awake last night.

Scott Abrams came down the corridor, greeted him warmly, and invited him into a small conference room. After settling into the room, Jack said, "Scott, I'm really a little embarrassed to be bothering you with something that may amount to nothing, but Amy and I thought you or someone in your firm might be able to give us some advice."

"Well, we're friends and you shouldn't feel that way. Why don't you tell me what's going on? If it's something that's bothering you and Amy, then it's important enough to talk about."

Jack spent the next fifteen minutes describing in some detail exactly what had happened over the past two weeks, and especially the meeting he had had yesterday with the investigators. Scott interrupted him only a few times to clarify something Jack had said, or to ask for more details.

At the conclusion of Jack's lengthy description of the events, Scott said, "I really don't know what to tell you, Jack, and we're quite frankly into an area where I don't feel comfortable without getting someone else's advice."

One of the things Jack had always liked about Scott was that he didn't have a big ego. He wasn't afraid to say when he was wrong or when something was beyond his expertise—a quality that many professionals lacked.

"Let me see if one of the partners with more experience in criminal law is available right now," Scott added. "I'd rather have someone listen to your story directly rather than second-hand from me and then have to have you come back." He got up and left the room to find one of the partners.

Jack concluded from the concern he saw on Scott's face as he had described yesterday's meeting that there was at least no more doubt about whether he was overreacting. Amy had been right in pushing him to see their attorney friend.

35

Al Collins was truly enjoying the celebrity status that the investigation had given him, even though the chief continually reminded him that he'd better do things "by the book" and that he "didn't want any screw-ups." He wasn't sure what to make of the questioning of Kendrick at the DEA office, but at this point he was the only person they had been able to establish as having had any contact with the dead man. Although the DEA was being careful to publicly state that he was heading up the investigation, Al knew that one misstep would result in the case being turned over to the feds and the Nantucket jurisdiction would cease. He had sensed during his meetings with Cassetti that he was not entirely comfortable with Al heading up the investigation.

As he drove out toward the Kendrick cottage, he felt as though this was just one more piece of the investigation that was not likely to produce any worthwhile additional information. He had brought along his assistant, Dick Hines, just as a pre-caution—to have another set of eyes present and also to cover him and verify any evidence he might find. The cottage was of modest size and had been built some thirty or forty years ago, but was neat and clean—obviously a place that had been kept in decent repair.

Jack Kendrick had given them permission to enter the house and find the paperback novel that supposedly Andrews had given to Kendrick on the boat. Having the owner's permission avoided the cumbersome procedure of having to get a search warrant that might not even have been granted. Al found the key where it was supposed to be and entered the house with Hines. It took only a few minutes to locate the paperback on the coffee table in the living room, and Al took the precaution of picking it up with rubber gloves and placing it in an evidence bag. He would hand it over to the state police forensics team to examine for fingerprints and any other evidence that might be of help in the investigation.

Since they had permission to be in the cottage, Al decided to look around and see if there was anything else of interest. Kendrick had said he had come to the island to close up the cottage for the winter. If so, there should be some evidence that he had done so. Al and his assistant checked to see that the water had been turned off and the system had been drained. They checked to see if the screens had been removed and that all of the outdoor furniture had been put away as Kendrick had said.

As they were about to leave, Hines called Al over to look at a cap he had found on the floor in a corner of the sitting room. "Hey, Al, come over here for a minute!" he said. "Do you remember that one of the reports from the DEA mentioned the college Andrews went to?"

"Hell no, and why would I want to know that?"

"Well, I seem to remember that it was a school called Drexel. It sort of stuck in my mind because it was an unusual name and I'd never heard it before. Take a look at this cap," he said as he pointed toward the article with his foot. "Do you see the large 'D' on the front? Over on the back side in smaller letters is the word 'Drexel.'"

Al came over and turned the hat over with his foot and was quiet for some time.

Hines said, "I wonder if this could be Andrews' hat, and if so how it got here."

"I don't remember any mention of a college, but I guess I could have missed it in one of those reports. Are you sure it said Drexel? It's also possible that it could belong to Kendrick and that he went to Drexel."

"Yeah, I'm pretty sure," said Hines.

"Jesus, Dick, another goddamn coincidence! It's beginning to look like this guy Kendrick may be the murderer. Every place we turn he seems to show up with some kind of link to Andrews."

He told Hines to go to the car and get another evidence bag. When Hines returned, Al marked on the outside of the bag where and when he found the hat, and then picked it up with plastic gloves and put it inside the bag. He reminded Hines that since Kendrick had given them permission to enter the house that they had some freedom to look around and pick up anything else that might have a bearing on the case. He was only a little concerned that the district attorney might have wanted him to get a search warrant before he picked up anything other than the book. But his anxiety to move on with the case and solve it overrode any realistic concerns he should have had.

"If this hat did belong to Andrews, then how and why did it come to be in Kendrick's possession?" he wondered aloud to Hines. "Forensics is going to have a field day with this one. We'll make sure they examine it for any evidence of blood or hair from a DNA analysis, and also whether there are any fibers that match the ones found in Andrews' car. Maybe it's nothing, but maybe it's the one mistake that a murderer often makes in a crime and ends up leading to an arrest. Let's take some more time and look around for anything else that may be of interest."

"Al, do you think we should get a warrant before we pick up anything else?" Hines asked, somewhat hesitantly.

Al brushed him aside. "Look, let's just look around a little more and see if we can find anything."

After another twenty minutes of looking thoroughly throughout the house and in the cellar, the two detectives were not able to find anything else that might be related to Andrews' death.

"OK, Dick," Al said at last, "let's take the hat and book back and give them to the forensics guys and see what more we can learn about Kendrick's involvement."

36

"Well, what did Scott say?" Amy asked.

"He brought in one of the senior partners, a fellow named Ted Andriolli, and after I briefly described what was going on, the senior partner said we were right to seek legal advice. I then went over the whole story in detail again and Andriolli said it's probably nothing, but it's better to take some necessary precautions to avoid any problems that may come up later. He was particularly interested in the tone of the meeting I had at the DEA office. He also said he would do some checking around to see if he could learn anything from some sources he has at the state police, and he wants me to call him immediately if we have any more contact with the DEA, FBI, or the Nantucket police. He said at this point he would advise me to have counsel present if there are any more meetings or interviews. He also said to be careful of anything I might say on the telephone if any of the police officials should call. I told them I would call them if I heard anything more."

Amy was quiet for minute and then said reassuringly, "That's probably routine legal advice, but something you should certainly listen to. Let's just hope there aren't any more calls."

"I asked him what this was going to cost us, since I was worried about the fees such a large and well-known firm might charge. He said not to worry about it right now, that unless something more definitive develops that there wouldn't be any fee for the meeting today. I guess we have our friendship with Scott to thank for that, but I'm still worried about the cost."

"Let's not think about that right now, Jack. The important thing is that we've got some good advice and need to listen to it."

"Yeah, I know you're right, but it really pisses me off to think that we may have to eat some legal expenses for something we're not responsible for. You know these guys charge big bucks by the hour. We haven't got any extra money to throw away, and whatever savings we have are for the plans to open up my photography business. You know I haven't even been able to think about that for the past two weeks. Here's something that I've always dreamed about doing and I was getting so close to being able to quit the job at the station and finally go into business myself. Now I just feel as though I'm walking around with this big storm cloud over my head that I can't get away from. Jesus, it just isn't fair!"

"I know, Jack, and it really isn't fair, but we have to try to get along with our normal lives and have patience while this thing plays itself out."

Jack knew Amy's advice, as usual, made sense; but how could he possibly be making plans for the future with all that was going on?

"You know, Amy, I've been thinking about this whole crazy situation. I couldn't get to sleep last night going over the meeting with the DEA and the Nantucket police, and it struck me that we don't know what other investigations or suspects must be in the picture. If Andrews was murdered, and it looks as though he was, his murderer was one of the passengers on that same steamship. Don't you think they must be going over the whole passenger list?"

"Yeah, I'd think so, but remember that walk-on passengers just buy a ticket and don't have to give their names."

Jack paused. "Yeah, I forgot."

37

It had been two days since Ahmed had arrived in Boston and found his way to the apartment in Alston. The rental had been arranged for him by someone whose name he didn't know, but who obviously had sympathy for the Palestinian cause. He had been told that there were thousands of people scattered throughout the United States who were either Palestinian or Arab and who believed as he did. Some provided financing for the terrorist cause and others were willing to provide help as needed. The room was simply furnished. It had its own bath and was situated on the third floor of an old apartment building, a building similar to many in the neighborhood that had been tenement houses built for working-class people some seventy-five to one hundred years ago. It was close to the Boston public transit system that Bostonians called the "T," and he would be able to commute to his "job" in the city easily. He had already taken a practice ride into Boston and felt pretty comfortable in finding his way around.

The rent had been paid for two months, and the land-lord was told that Ahmed was doing some research for several months at Boston University. BU was a school with a very large percentage of foreign students, some from the Middle East, and he had been assured that his slight accent would not raise any suspicions. Still, he had been apprehensive about accepting all of these arrangements and assumptions on the faith and trust that whoever had done the planning knew what he was doing. Ahmed was by nature a careful planner and was the kind of person who liked things in his life very orderly and with no loose ends. To depend on someone else—and indeed someone whom he had never met—for arrangements that might well affect his personal safety made him very uncomfortable. He was overly conscious of people who looked at him for longer than a few moments, suspicious that they might have learned something about who he was and what his plans were.

The job with the sound and acoustics firm had also been arranged by someone unknown to Ahmed, perhaps even the same person who had found him the apartment. He was even more apprehensive about this situation since he would be working closely with these people on a daily basis and they had to accept who he was under his alias of Art Cahill, as well as be comfortable with his technical skills to do the job. It seemed unusual to have been given a job without being interviewed, but the acoustics firm had had an immediate need for someone who could wire the listening system for the meeting where different languages would be spoken and the need for simultaneous translation existed.

Ahmed had been with a sound and acoustics company in Nazareth and had been involved on a few occasions in setting up fairly complex speaker systems for conferences and meetings that required translations into several different languages. It not only required skilled translators to simultaneously translate into the various languages involved, but also required the electronic speaking and listening systems so that some participants could hear through earphones what was being spoken in their own language while other participants were listening in still another language. On occasion Ahmed had worked on systems where there were even five different languages involved—not unusual in the Middle East. The wiring necessary to make certain that the right person received the right translation could become quite complicated, but it was an area where Ahmed felt very comfortable.

The Boston sound and acoustics firm that had obtained the contract for the meeting had contacted a New York company in the same business that did some of the sound work for the United Nations and for other international meetings in the New York area. The Boston firm requested the temporary services of a technician, and one of the senior managers of this firm who apparently was sympathetic toward the Palestinian cause had made the arrangements for Ahmed to fill the job. The firm in Boston had been led to believe that Ahmed was employed by the New York firm and had been loaned to them for the duration of the job.

Ahmed was a little concerned about the type of equipment and materials that were necessary for him to do the job. How different would the materials be from what he was used to in Israel? He had been told that there might be some minor differences, but here again he was uncomfortable putting his trust in someone else—especially in a foreign country where he felt uneasy anyway. On the other hand, he was confident of his technical training and felt he could probably work his way through any problem. So far all of the connections and arrangements had worked out exactly as planned, and he tried to take some comfort in that fact.

The most dangerous part of the work would come toward the end of the assignment, when he had to find a way to set up the explosive device without being detected. In the meantime he had to go ahead and wire up the meeting room for the simultaneous translation as if the signing of the treaty was to proceed without any difficulty. When he stopped to consider the magnitude of his assignment, not to mention the risks involved, his apprehension returned. He found that the only way he could overcome this fear and apprehension was to concentrate on the fact that he would be avenging his brother's death while at the same time striking a major blow for the Palestinian cause.

38

Bennie Haas called Joe in the evening after he had returned with his passenger from Nantucket. "Well, tell me you didn't do anything stupid on this trip!"

Joe held his temper but replied with some irritation. "There were no problems at all. I picked up the guy like I was supposed to and dropped him off at South Station. No problems!"

"You better be telling me the truth, Joe! That incident a couple of weeks ago was really dumb, and I have to tell you, I was only an inch away from pulling you off this thing altogether. I've got too much at stake to have someone like you who can't control himself screw up the entire deal."

"I know what you're saying, you know, and I've got a lot at stake too." Joe was concerned when Bennie hinted that he might pull the plug on this extra income deal. Thinking it would be best if he sounded a little more cooperative with Bennie, he said, "I'll really be careful in the future."

"Well, make goddamn sure you are. There are plenty of other people who would love to have some easy money and whom I can trust not to do something foolish." He paused and then said, "This guy who you picked up may need a ride back in the other direction in a couple of weeks, so keep your nose clean. I'll give you a call."

"OK, Bennie, I'll wait to hear from you."

Joe hung up with a big sigh of relief that he had convinced Bennie to let him stay.

39

Al Collins picked up the phone and called Jim Cassetti at the DEA. "Jim, this is Al Collins in Nantucket."

"Oh, hi, Al. What's going on out there where all the rich people live?"

Al paused and almost gave a smart-ass reply; he always got irritated when people off island assumed that everyone on the island was loaded. "Well, it's really only the summer people with the money. The rest of us have to work for a living and deal with all the high prices over here that the rich people can afford. Look, I'm calling to bring you up to date on what I think are some interesting developments on our case. I'm not sure where it'll lead us, but thought you'd want to know."

Cassetti sat up a little more alertly at his desk, "Well, what have you got?"

"You remember when we interviewed Kendrick that he agreed to have me go to his house and pick up the book that he said Andrews had given him on the boat?"

"Yeah, I remember."

"Well, we went to the house yesterday and found the book, and I've given it to forensics to go over with a fine-tooth comb. While we were there we found a cap on the floor that we think may have belonged to Andrews. I decided it was OK to pick it up since we had Kendrick's permission to enter the cottage. We picked up the cap and have turned that over to the state unit also."

"What makes you think the hat belonged to Andrews?"

"Well, I remembered that in one of the newspaper reports it said that he had gone to Drexel University, and the cap has the word 'Drexel' on it." Al didn't even consider mentioning that his assistant was the one who had found the hat and remembered the article about Andrews and Drexel.

"Well, that is interesting, and you're right—Andrews did get his degree from Drexel," Cassetti said. "He remained pretty interested in the school and even did some recruiting for them. As I think about it, I'm pretty sure I remember him wearing a cap on occasion. That's good work, Al. What do you think it means?"

"I don't know yet, but if it is Andrews' cap, then Kendrick has some real explaining to do. Where did Kendrick get it? Did Andrews leave it on the table they were sitting at along with the book, and Kendrick picked it up and brought it along with him? If so, why didn't he leave it in Andrews' car along with the book he says he left there? Why didn't Kendrick mention it? There's no way that cap could have gotten into his cottage without there being more contact with Andrews than he's been telling us. I've told the forensics people that we need a real rush on this, and they said they'd try to get back to me by tomorrow."

"Was there any blood on the cap that you could see?"

"Not that I could see, but I was very careful in handling it so I wouldn't contaminate the forensics work."

"Did you find anything else in the house?"

"No, and after we found the cap we really went over the place with a fine-tooth comb. We didn't leave anything un-turned."

"Have you got the forensics report back on Andrews' car and clothing?"

"No, they've been pretty slow. But they said today they'll

try to have it all ready tomorrow. I wish I could have used the FBI rather than the state police."

"It sounds like we're going to need another visit with Mr. Kendrick, and this time we'll put some real pressure on him. Have you looked further into Kendrick's associations when he's been on the island?"

"I really haven't had time to look into that with everything else that's been going on."

"Al, I'd really like you to have someone do a thorough check on that from your end. We've been looking at things from here, especially Kendrick's associations in the Boston area, and haven't been able to turn up anything other than that small drug incident when he was in college. If he's involved in trafficking and was the reason that Andrews and Proctor were on their way to Nantucket, then there's got to be some evidence on the island. Do you want me to send someone down to give you a hand?

Al hesitated for only a moment. "No, let me get on it myself and I'll get back to you if I find I need some more help."

"Okay, well, give me a call when you get the forensics report, and thanks for keeping me up to date. I think this hat may really be significant, and now we need a breakthrough on Kendrick's drug involvement."

Collins hung up the phone and looked out the window toward the waterfront. What a stroke of luck it would be if they could tie the cap to Andrews through DNA. As Cassetti had said in Boston, there were just too many coincidences that were beginning to link Kendrick to this crime. *What a big boost it would be to my career if I solved this quickly,* he couldn't help but think. *If I handle this right, it may be the stepping stone I need to a future chief's job.*

He picked up the phone to call forensics and check again on their progress.

40

Jack got up in the middle of the night, something he very rarely did, but he continued to have this horrible thought in his mind that the investigation was focusing too much on him. Frequently in the middle of the night things came clearly into his mind when he was relaxing that didn't surface during the day when he often was trying to focus too hard on a particular subject. Usually he could easily get back to sleep after such revelations, but tonight that wasn't possible. As he thought more and more about who could have been responsible for the deaths of the DEA agents, he came back to the fact that whoever it was had to have been on the boat with him—not only on the last trip, but probably on the previous trip that the investigators had questioned him about. *Maybe Collins was right to question me about so many coincidences.*

The total number of people on the steamship at this time of year was not terribly large, and he wondered if there was a way of getting a list of the drivers of vehicles and then checking to see what names came up on each of the trips that he had been asked about.

Would the steamship company provide that information just for the asking? Jack thought. *Probably not, but there must be a way to get hold of it. One of the investigative reporters at the station might be able to help me out.*

He remembered that both of his trips had been on a Friday, and he wondered if there was some pattern involving other persons on those trips. He had read that Bill Andrews had been investigating drug trafficking into the Boston area from Cape

Cod, and Andrews had told him he was going to Nantucket on business.

His mind began to consider possibilities:

There are only two ways that drugs can get from Nantucket to the mainland, and that is either by air or boat. But the real question is how would drugs initially get to Nantucket? They have to come from out of the country, and Nantucket isn't an international terminal of any sort. Is the airport security so lax that a private flight from Canada or even the Caribbean could smuggle illegal drugs and regularly land at the Nantucket airport without fear of being caught? The airport is large enough to handle twin-engine jets, and at least in the summer there are a lot of them coming to the island. But that just doesn't make sense, since there are hardly any private jets after the summer vacation period ends.

The only logical way is by boat. From the way the press is covering the story, there is a regular influx of illegal drugs, not just an occasional thing. What kind of boat would be making regular trips to the island from outside of the country? There is a constant flow of pleasure boats, large yachts, and sailboats to the island during the height of the summer vacation season. As a matter of fact, there are several sailboat races throughout the summer that draw sailboats from up and down the eastern seaboard and from the Caribbean, Bermuda, Canada, and occasionally Europe. But these boats, even though they may come from outside of the United States, do not make regular year-round trips to the island. It doesn't make any sense that there is a year-round drug ring bringing drugs on private yachts to the island through the winter months.

Jack was puzzled and frustrated with the problem. He was tired and he was angry that this crazy set of circumstances had put him and his family in a situation where he feared he might even face some legal action for something where he was truly an innocent bystander.

He went back to thinking through the problem. *The only way it makes sense for Nantucket to be the source of illegal drugs is for them to arrive somehow on the island by water from some international location and then later be transported to the mainland. Then it would make sense for Andrews to come to the island to try to locate the source.*

Jack mused further: *One hundred and fifty years ago, when Nantucket was the whaling capital of the world, there were many opportunities for illegal things of all kinds to be brought to the island and that probably happened with some frequency, especially since the laws were much more relaxed at that time.*

Jack finished his second cup of coffee, poured a third, and grabbed a few oatmeal cookies—by far his favorite cookie snack. He sat down and continued to think through his puzzle. *Most of the illegal drugs in the past have come into the United States over its southern border; however, Canada has also been a favorite route because it has more of an open border with relaxed customs procedures. With the extra border security since 9-11, however, it has become more and more difficult to move things by land across the Canadian border. On the other hand, American commercial fishing boats that go out to the Grand Banks come close enough to Canada that they could pick up the illegal drugs there and transport them to the States. Large commercial fishing ports like Boston, New Bedford, and Gloucester have probably had their security tightened up since the World Trade Center disaster. Nantucket used to have a small fishing fleet, but today there are only a handful of commercial boats that regularly go out from the island. The problem is that any catch brought onto the island has to then be shipped to the mainland market. Because of its size, is it possible that Nantucket is a loophole in the region's security?*

There just was no simple answer, but the more he thought about the possibilities the more it seemed that if there was a drug trafficking problem at all out of Nantucket, then the sea had to play a role. It was now 5:30 a.m. The three cups of coffee had woken him up and it was too late to go back to bed anyway. In any event he would try to get some help at work and see how he might get hold of the passenger lists from the Steamship Authority.

41

Detective Al Collins had quickly glanced at the detailed forensics report in front of him. He had seen enough to excite him about the possibility that the findings might lead to a solution to the case and that his growing suspicions about Kendrick appeared to be right on track. He closed the door to his office and told his assistant not to disturb him.

He sat back and began to read the report in detail. The first section was the autopsy report on Agent Andrews, and it confirmed that he had suffered a severe blow to the back of the head and even a slight fracture of the skull. The examiner concluded that the blow was severe enough to render Andrews unconscious for several minutes, but that the actual cause of death had been drowning. It was probable that he had drowned while still unconscious from the blow to the head, since the condition of the lungs and tissue showed no evidence of a struggle to save himself from drowning. There was a deep cut on his right arm that had perhaps occurred when he went overboard, since the small number of paint particles in the wound were consistent with tests he had run on the steamship's paint. An examination of residue under the fingernails was inconclusive, since the ocean water had washed away most incidental residue, but the remaining amount did not show any tissue or material that might have been lodged from scraping against someone else's skin or clothing.

There was evidence of beach sand under the finger and toenails, as well as scrapes on the arms and face that were consistent with the body having rolled and washed up onto the beach.

There was no evidence of alcohol in his blood, and after checking his medical history with the DEA there was no past history of seizures or fainting. He did not believe Andrews had gone into the water from a great height, since the body was otherwise free of contusions or broken bones. The observations were consistent with the victim having gone into the water from the vehicle deck, which was only some seven or eight feet from the water line. The forensics on the major organs were completely negative, and there was no evidence that Andrews might have had a stroke or heart attack. The report went on to say, "He was a man in his early sixties who might have expected many more healthy years in his retirement." The DNA and blood analysis confirmed that the body was indeed that of Bill Andrews.

The forensics report discussed the analysis of the deceased's clothing. "A detailed examination of the clothing doesn't reveal any unusual or extraordinary information," it read. There was no evidence of tears and no unusual fibers that could not be explained. Here again, the report emphasized that the "ocean water would have in all probability washed away most evidence."

Al hesitated at this point. Was this a CYA (cover your ass) comment by the forensics people? He'd much rather have a clear and definite statement that didn't offer any loopholes for a smart-assed defense attorney to latch onto. But he couldn't argue with the conclusion because several hours in the water, in salt and surf and sand, would logically have destroyed the types of residue and fibers that you might expect to find on a corpse discovered on dry land. The rest of the report on the clothing talked about the presence of salt from the salt water and large amounts of sand and beach residue consistent with a body having been in the water for several hours and washed up onto the beach. There was even evidence of small seashells caught in the clothing and in the pockets of the pants.

The next section of the report dealt with the forensic analysis of the materials gathered from Andrews' car. Al skipped through the routine parts of this section quickly until he came to the fingerprint section. Most of the prints on the interior and exterior of the automobile were identified as belonging to Andrews—just what you'd expect from his own car—however, there were other prints that clearly did not belong to the deceased. Three prints on the paperback book found in the car, on the steering wheel, and on a manila folder found on the front seat belonged to another person. The report had a footnote that said, "See Section F analysis of fingerprints found in the Nantucket cottage on evidence that was picked up in the Nantucket police investigation." Al jumped ahead quickly to this section and found the statement he was looking for:

> The fingerprints from the evidence taken from the cottage can be identified as belonging to three separate individuals. One group belongs to a small child; a second group probably belongs to a medium-sized female, based upon the size and contour of the prints, as well as the fact that most of these prints were found in the kitchen area and on female toiletries that were found in the bathroom and the bedroom. The third group undoubtedly is that of a medium-sized male and was also found in multiple places in the cottage, and was the only one found on the various male toiletries. This set of prints is also consistent with those mentioned in Section C that were found in the decedent's automobile—not those of the deceased, but specifically those unidentified prints found on the steering wheel, the manila folder, and the paperback book.

Al stopped reading, banged his fist on the desk, and said out loud, "We've got the hook set into you, Kendrick; now all we need is a little more to reel you in!" He knew this wasn't enough to arrest Kendrick, but it was consistent with his growing belief that he was the murderer.

He went back to Section C of the forensics report and began to read further.

A note found in the book shows fingerprints of both the deceased and the same individual whose prints were found on the book itself. The note also had the following handwriting:

Jack Kendrick
392 Plymouth Road
Quincy, MA 02170

Why did Kendrick give Andrews his address? Al wondered. *Did he expect the book to be returned to him?*

The last sentence of this section recorded various fibers found in the car, most of them consistent with the fibers found on the clothing of Andrews. It then listed several fibers that could not be identified as consistent with the clothing that the deceased was wearing; however, Al concluded that they most likely were from some of Andrews' other clothing. He did make a note, however, to try to get hold of some of the clothing that Kendrick had been wearing the evening of the ferry trip to Nantucket.

Section D dealt solely with the DNA analysis of the residue that was collected from around the steamship porthole, where Andrews was believed to have gone overboard. This part of the report was somewhat inconclusive.

An analysis of the residue indicates that it is human blood and consistent with the blood type of the deceased. The scarcity of the sample was not ideal for a conclusive DNA analysis; however, the limited analysis indicates that the DNA may also be consistent with that of the deceased.

CYA again, Al thought. *The words "limited" and "may" don't help this case one bit. Why can't I hedge my bets in my job? Well, at least this doesn't rule out the assumption that the porthole is where Andrews went overboard. As a matter of fact, it really strengthens this assumption.*

Section E read:

CAP FOUND IN COTTAGE WHERE NANTUCKET POLICE INVESTIGATION CONDUCTED
This well-worn blue and gold cap carries the lettering "Drexel" in gold letters. On analysis it was found to be saturated with calcium chloride (consistent with immersion in salt ocean water) and has many particles of sea sand embedded in the fabric. There are also multiple fibers that on examination are those of hair from the canine species. (See Section F for a match of these fibers.) The most significant findings were from the sweatband on the inside of the cap. Although the hat had been immersed in salt water for some period of time, the sweatband on this well-worn hat contained sufficient material for us to perform a DNA analysis. Our conclusion is that this sweat residue is that of the deceased, and human hair found underneath the sweatband is also that of the deceased. In addition, there was residue found on the hat that on DNA examination is consistent with canine saliva. The fact that this was present and not washed away by the salt water causes us to conclude that this saliva was deposited after the hat was removed from the water.

Again, Al banged his fist on the desk and said out loud, "Strike two, Kendrick." How could he explain away the presence of a cap belonging to Andrews in his cottage? The only thing that puzzled Al was the concentration of salt water and sand. It meant that Kendrick had not gained possession of the hat on the boat but after it had gone into the water. *Did Kendrick find the body on the beach first and not report it?*

Al had already read the part of Section F that had to do with the fingerprints found in the cottage, but now he read this entire section that dealt with the materials collected from the cottage. It stated that the dog fibers found on the hat were the same as those found in numerous places throughout the house. *Well, that's no surprise,* Al thought. *Kendrick has a dog that was probably shedding most of the year. The dog was probably playing with the hat and that explains why it was found on the floor with canine saliva.*

Al picked up the phone and dialed Cassetti's number at the DEA.

42

Ahmed rose early on this first morning of "work" after a somewhat restless night. He wondered whether the difficulty in sleeping was a result of tension over what he was to do over the next several days, or if the noise from the traffic on the street in front of his room had kept him awake. He continued to be amazed at the number of cars he observed everywhere in the United States, and the fact that they were much larger than in Israel. In the Palestinian sections and towns in Israel, most people could not afford their own automobiles, and the most common means of transportation was by bicycle, moped or public bus.

Why is it that Americans needed so many and such large automobiles? he wondered silently. *It is just more evidence of the decadence of the United States and the way in which material things are so important.* He had learned from his Palestinian friends that materialism, sexual permissiveness, nudity, and other examples of loose morals were all symptoms of Western decadence and that these cultural practices were being exported to Arab youth through television, movies, magazines, and videos. The way in which Western women were exploited through their dress was perhaps the most tangible example of this decadence. He had been convinced that if this continued then it would gradually deteriorate traditional Islamic culture. God had spoken to Muhammad, and the respect for women was a fundamental teaching of the Koran.

He walked the short distance to the T stop and waited a few minutes for the next trolley car. He was surprised with the age of the trolleys he had seen—they were old, not very comfortable, and very slow. With all the money in America, he thought they would have one of the most modern transit systems in the world. The trolley was busy during this heavy commuting hour, and Ahmed was forced to stand and hold onto a strap from the ceiling as the car rocked and rolled over the noisy tracks. On both sides of the trolley there were hundreds of cars involved in their own commute into the city. The trolley ride from Alston to the Park Street subway station in Boston took only about fifteen minutes, and he left the car and went down a level to get the underground subway to Government Center, the closest stop to Faneuil Hall.

He was supposed to report to work at 8 a.m., and since it was now only twenty minutes after 7 a.m. he decided to walk around the area. The subway stairwell exited onto a large open area that led to Boston City Hall and beyond that the Federal Office Building. Faneuil Hall was only a block from the Government Center T stop and was on the edge of a shopping district called Quincy Market. As he walked around the three large old warehouses that made up the principal market area, he observed hundreds of people rushing to work—obviously not tourists by the speed of their walk and the serious looks on their faces. He had heard that Americans were consumed with their work, although he admitted to himself that most Palestinians and Israelis probably looked the same as they went to their appointed jobs each day, even though the typical Palestinian workday began much later in the morning.

He had read that the buildings in Quincy Market were more than two hundred years old and had been warehouses on the waterfront before the area had been filled in and the actual piers moved farther out into the harbor. They had been rehabilitated a few decades ago, and now the market area was one of the busiest places in the city. At this time of the morning, none of the shops were open and the only place he noticed doing any business was a coffee shop, where the bustling workers would stop and pick up their coffee to take to work.

At 7:45 a.m. he was back at the entrance to Faneuil Hall. The building was surrounded by pedestrian walkways, and the small shops on the first floor of the building made it a part of the entire market atmosphere. Its history went back more than two hundred years to the American Revolution, and the hall itself had been the site of many important meetings and speakers throughout its history. It was one of those many historic sites in Boston that had played an important part in the city's history and was revered by many as a symbol of democracy and freedom. Ahmed had read a lot about Boston's history and the Freedom Trail, which was a walking route that led tourists on a tour of many of the city's famous historic sites. The trail was actually found by following a path of bricks laid in the middle of the concrete sidewalk that wound its way through the city and included Faneuil Hall.

The auditorium of the hall was on the second floor, above the retail shops, and could be reached by climbing a long staircase in the front of the building. The public was normally allowed to walk through the auditorium during the day, but it was now shut off while work crews began to prepare it for the major historic event that would take place in a few days.

There was a security guard at the entrance to the hall, and Ahmed presented his forged New York driver's license and his letter from the sound and acoustics firm that confirmed his temporary assignment to the project. The guard asked him to wait a minute and called someone on his security phone to get instructions. He repeated over the phone what Ahmed had told him, read a couple of sentences from the letter, and after a minute told Ahmed that someone would be down shortly to see him.

Ahmed naturally become a little apprehensive at this point and wondered if something had gone wrong with all the arrangements that were supposed to have been made for him.

In about five minutes—though to Ahmed the period of time seemed much longer—a middle-aged man dressed neatly in work clothes came down the stairs and introduced himself as Charlie Edgerly, the foreman in charge of all the lighting, acoustics, and sound for the project. As the guard handed him the letter and driver's license, Edgerly said to Ahmed, "You must be Art Cahill, the guy who's to solve all our electronic problems. We're really glad to have you here because this is really something new for us."

As Edgerly looked at the license and letter, Ahmed shook his hand and relaxed somewhat, but as he began to reply he quickly thought of his accent and whether he would pass this most important test.

"Hi, Mr. Edgerly, I'm glad to be here and I'm pleased to help out in any way that I can."

"Please call me Charlie, Art, and let's get going right away. The rest of my crew will be here in the next few minutes and then we'll have a quick get-together and you'll get to meet the people you'll be working with. There are a lot of other workmen here handling the seating arrangements and logistics for the meeting. My boss, who owns the business, is here today and he'll have a few words to say. He shows up every day for a few minutes in the morning to check and make certain everything is on schedule. We're under a lot of pressure to do this thing just right because of all the international media attention. You probably saw some of the TV trucks when you came in."

As they walked up the stairs, Edgerly gave Ahmed back his license and the letter.

43

Amy and Jack had spent the morning walking around the Quincy Market area of Boston. It had been Amy's idea to try to find a way to take Jack's mind off the events of the past several days, and to convince him to take the morning off from work to pursue something she knew had been a dream of his. Perhaps by concentrating on his photography hobby for a few hours, he would forget the events on Nantucket.

In addition to Jack's working at home on his photography book, using the collection of human interest pictures he had collected over the years, he and Amy had discussed the possibility of opening his own photography studio. He had done well at WBOS as the TV video camera specialist, but there was really no opportunity for advancement, and the hours were not on a dependable schedule. That was becoming more of a problem with his growing family and his desire to spend more time with them. In addition, Jack had always dreamed of having his own business where he would be his own boss and not subject to either the schedule or the constraints of a large corporation.

The thought of converting his photography avocation into a full-time career was something he and Amy had recently talked about with more and more enthusiasm. It had passed the point of being only a dream and was beginning to take on the excitement of something that could really happen. He was not interested in a photo shop where he would process film and sell camera supplies, but rather his plan was to operate a studio that would sell framed and unframed prints of high quality for people to display in their homes or offices. He thought that many of the human-interest photographs that he had accumulated over the years would be a good foundation for building the business. He would, of course, display other photographers' works, but he would be very selective.

Many of his photographs were not only studies in human nature, they also had a Boston-area connection or theme. Some were connected with various Boston sports teams, such as candid photos of individuals he had caught at the Red Sox's Fenway Park—especially during the 2004 World Series celebration. He had found the most interesting subjects were either very young or very old people reacting to the enormous excitement and celebration that had surrounded the first Red Sox world championship in eighty-six years. He had pictures of people celebrating in the streets, as well as the parade that had lasted for hours through the streets, and even along the Charles River. The shots that he liked the best were not those of the mass celebrations, but rather the individual, close-up photos that truly caught the emotion of the individual experiencing the "impossible dream."

He had photographs of Celtics, Bruins, and Patriots events—some showing the elation of victory and others the agony of defeat. He had caught some of the players in unscripted situations that he felt truly showed the honest excitement and anguish of the professional athlete at a time when many of the fans felt that highly-paid professional players were only in it for the money and had little interest in the outcome of the sporting event. Jack felt that he had caught the athlete's honest inner feelings at the instant of the event. One of his best shots was of Tedy Bruschi, the Patriots linebacker and captain, playing with his two young sons on the field just before a Super Bowl game. It had showed a gentle side to a football player who was one of the most aggressive linebackers in the game.

He had a large number of still pictures, which he had taken with his personal camera while on various assignments with the video team for WBOS. Most of these had been taken while covering various news events around the Boston area. Like most professional photographers, he was very critical of his own work and he selected as his "best" examples those photos that not only exhibited excellent photography but also had a captivating human-interest theme. The picture of a mother holding her eighteen-month-old child out of the third-story window of a burning tenement house just before she had dropped it into the waiting arms of a fireman had showed the anguish and fear in the mother's face, while the child had appeared surprisingly calm in the protective arms of the mother. He recalled that the mother had been rescued and the child uninjured from the fall, but had suffered severe burns.

Jack had been in Copley Square the night of the 2004 presidential election and had caught John Kerry and his family at the edge of the podium before Kerry had gone up to give his concession speech. You could see the strength of conviction in Kerry's eyes and face over what he was about to do, but at the same time the photograph had clearly shown the tiredness and disappointment in the countenances of his family as they realized the long campaign was ending without a victory. Their concern for their father and husband had caught the human side of an otherwise bitter campaign.

Boston was a city proud of its heritage and proud of its many educational institutions. Indeed, education was one of Boston's largest industries, and one of Jack's favorite photos was of a Hispanic-appearing man looking into the eyes of his son who had just received his degree from Northeastern University. To Jack the picture said so much about America, the city of Boston, and the history of the immigrants' pride in seeing their children excel in their new country.

Another photo that showed the rich history of Boston's immigrant community had been taken right outside of Faneuil Hall. Once a year the swearing-in of newly naturalized United States citizens took place inside the hall, and Jack's photo showed the gathering of a family on the steps of the hall after the ceremony. It appeared to be a group of more than a dozen relatives and probably friends who had come to celebrate the occasion, and they were taking a picture of a new citizen with his wife and two small children, holding his official document proudly in front of him. Jack had always thought that it would make a perfect subject for a Norman Rockwell-type painting.

Quincy Market had dozens of stores and shops selling all kinds of goods that catered to both residents and tourists. It was one of the busiest retail areas of the city and attracted large crowds the year round. Jack had thought that this would be an ideal location for a photo studio, and Amy had convinced him that they should take this day and look around and push his dream a bit closer to reality. She had seen an ad for open space in the market and now steered Jack toward the location. It was in one of the warehouses with a heavy volume of pedestrian traffic throughout the day, and which she thought an ideal location for the studio.

After pointing out the space, Amy suggested to Jack that they go to the property manager's office and get some details on when the property would be available and what the lease cost would be. Jack was hesitant about even inquiring about the property. "Look, Amy," he said, "this has been a great day just getting away from things and dreaming about my own photography business, but it's unrealistic to pursue this right now. First of all, we don't have the money to invest in a start-up business. It will take months to generate enough business to really make a go of it, not to mention the initial costs of furnishing a store and providing a stock of photographs to sell. Second, my mind is so occupied with this Nantucket thing right now that I can't really focus on anything else."

"I know now doesn't seem to be a good time," Amy agreed, "but what's wrong with talking to the property manager and getting some information? We're not going to make a decision today. As far as the money is concerned, we talked before about the possibility of my father making an investment in the business. He has money he invests in many different ventures, and if we convince him this would be a business deal that would make money for him, what's wrong with that? I know this murder investigation is something we can't ignore right now, but that's only a temporary problem, and this dream of your own business is something that affects our happiness for the rest of our lives."

Jack stopped and gave her a hug and a kiss. "OK, you win. Let's go find out how crazy our dream of my own studio really is."

44

At the end of the day, Ahmed walked to the T station and retraced his route back to Alston. The day had gone pretty well and he was sure that no one suspected that his identity was a fake or that his accent had caused any undue suspicion. There were so many people in the Boston area with various ethnic backgrounds and accents that his did not seem to stand out.

He had gotten to meet a lot of the crew that would be working on the technical arrangements for the signing of the peace agreement. There were electricians, lighting specialists, and sound people, but no one who apparently had any experience in wiring multiple locations for simultaneous translations. The auditorium was a beehive of activity. Charlie, the foreman, had showed him the proposed layout for the meeting, the location of the electrical panels, and the supplies and equipment he'd be working with. Ahmed had felt a great sense of relief that nothing seemed really unfamiliar to him. The brand names of the supplies were somewhat different, but the electrical connections and materials looked pretty standard.

He figured the actual setup of the equipment for the simultaneous translation wouldn't take more than a couple of days, but there was much work that needed to be done by others before he could start. They needed to decide where the translators would be housed. They really needed to be in a soundproof room or booth. Where would the central control booth be that housed the person who made necessary changes in the equipment settings as the meeting was taking place? There was always the need in this kind of conference to turn microphones on and off, depending on who was speaking at any given moment. The conference table where the participants would be sitting needed to be laid out so that Ahmed could see where each participant would be sitting. He needed to know what language translation needed to go to each position, but more importantly he needed to know where the Israeli and the Palestinian representatives would be sitting in order to complete the task that had been given him by Hamas. At first the coordination of all of the tasks had seemed overwhelming, but as the day moved on he began to formulate in his mind exactly how everything would be laid out.

In the short time since he'd arrived in Boston he had begun to understand the history that surrounded this city and especially the key role it had played in the American Revolution. The many historical sights, from the Old North Church where the patriot Paul Revere hung lanterns to alert the people that "the British were coming," to the gold-domed State House, to the Old South Meeting House where the Boston Tea Party was organized, to the Old State House where the Declaration of Independence was first read in Boston, to Faneuil Hall where he would be working, were all important parts of America's history. It wasn't possible to stand in the large auditorium and not be impressed with the history surrounding you. The paintings of Revolutionary War heroes around the walls of the auditorium, the Early American design of the room itself, and its furnishings, all had the effect of taking one back in time more than two hundred years. From Ahmed's professional electronics point of view, however, the wiring in this old building made his technical task a little more difficult. He might be able to use this to his advantage as he planned the details of how to lay out the simultaneous translation equipment, and it also might help his need for freedom of movement throughout the building.

Ahmed brought his thoughts quickly back to the present. He couldn't afford to be sympathetic with either the people in this country or its independence history. Still, he couldn't help wishing that this country, its history, and its economic strength could be transplanted to the Palestinian people and a truly independent Palestine—a new country that encompassed all of the Palestinian people's land, a country without Israelis, a country whose boundaries were those before 1947. It was not fair that a country like America could have so much wealth and success while the Palestinian people were suffering in poverty, their land having been taken from them, and actually under the control of Israeli military terror for almost sixty years. His short-lived musing toward sympathy and admiration for America quickly disappeared as he recalled that it was America that was supporting the state of Israel and had propped it up over those six decades. *It is indeed true that America is as much an enemy of the Palestinian cause as Israel itself,* he thought.

Now that he had a good feel for the layout of the hall where he'd be working, it was time to begin to plan exactly where he would install the explosives and also begin to assemble the devices. He had most of the materials he needed, and any other items he felt certain he could obtain at a local hardware store not far from his apartment in Alston. The first step was to lay out on paper the wiring schematic and the various locations for each of the key players at the conference.

The T ride was somewhat hectic and crowded during this late afternoon commuting hour, but Ahmed felt the rush of confidence that everything was going better than he had hoped for after only a few days in Boston. He was even getting used to being called Art Cahill.

45

Jack and his attorney had been in the DEA interview room for more than an hour, and his worst fears were being realized.

Phil Blaisdell, the FBI inspector, had called him yesterday afternoon and asked if he could come down to DEA headquarters today, since they had some more questions. It was interesting that the FBI had called rather than the Nantucket police; but after all, Andrews had been a federal employee, and Jack reasoned that the FBI probably handled all of these kinds of investigations. He had called his friend and attorney, Scott Abrams, and they had agreed that Scott should go along with him to the meeting. Jack wasn't certain this was such a good idea, and asked if it wouldn't appear as though he had something to hide. Scott had said that at this point he felt it was the smart thing to do and that investigators were used to having attorneys present—even if they didn't necessarily like it.

"I'll make a brief statement up front and then I'll only interrupt if I feel their questioning is not appropriate," Scott had added. "So, my advice to you is don't rush to answer any question, but first give me time to speak if I think you shouldn't answer. One other piece of advice, Jack: don't embellish your answers, but respond only to the specific question asked. We don't know where they're coming from, and sometimes people only confuse things if they try to expand an answer beyond what's asked."

Jack continued to be uncomfortable about this meeting becoming too legalistic and that he might appear to be uncooperative, which was the last thing he wanted. On the other hand, this whole affair was something entirely foreign to him, and he'd have to rely on Scott's training and experience.

The meeting included Al Collins from Nantucket, DEA Director Cassetti, and the FBI investigator. It was obvious from the start that the investigation had taken a definite turn from the time he had first been interviewed. It appeared that the FBI was now assuming the lead role in the meeting, even though Blaisdell stressed that the Nantucket police were still leading the investigation.

At the outset, Blaisdell stated unequivocally that Andrews' death had been determined to be a murder, and that their investigation had turned up significant evidence. Blaisdell said he had listened to the tape from Jack's previous meeting with Cassetti and Collins, so he had the benefit of that background. "I'll try not to go over the same ground with you again, but there are some new questions that have come up," he said.

Scott Abrams held up his hand. "I'm here to advise my client if he should respond to your questions. Is he being interviewed as a suspect in this investigation, or only as a witness to his contact on the steamship with Agent Andrews?"

Blaisdell paused, looked at his two colleagues, and said, "Well, at this point I guess I'd say no one is a suspect and everyone is. We're still gathering information, and your client has already given us information and may have more that will be of significance to this investigation."

"We understand that you need to develop information, and I know you'll appreciate the need for me to protect the rights of Mr. Kendrick," Scott said.

"Can we proceed then?"

The attorney nodded, and Al Collins reached over and turned on a voice recorder.

Blaisdell began, "Mr. Kendrick did you ever attend Drexel University?"

Jack, looking somewhat confused, said, "No, sir, I attended the University of Massachusetts."

"Where was that U Mass campus located?"

"The main campus in Amherst."

"Did you attend Drexel University for any graduate work, or do you have any other connection with that university?"

"No."

"Have you ever visited the Drexel campus in New York?"

"No, I've never had occasion to."

Blaisdell paused, apparently for emphasis, and said, "You'll recall that when you were here last you gave permission to Detective Collins to enter your cottage on Nantucket and pick up a book that you said Agent Andrews had given you?"

"Yes. I told him where the key was and that he could enter the house."

"Well, we found the book, but also found some other things of interest. One of those things was a blue and gold cap with the letters 'Drexel' on it. Can you tell us where you got that hat?"

Jack looked at his attorney and shrugged. "I don't ever recall seeing a hat like that."

"Well, it was in your house on the floor."

Jack was mystified, looked at Scott, and shook his head in confusion.

Blaisdell went on, "One of the interesting things about the hat was that it had been soaked with salt water and had dog hairs all over it."

Jack thought for a minute. "Wait a minute!" he exclaimed. "I do recall Jessie, my dog, picking up a cap while I was out jogging on the Saturday morning when I was on the island. She's a Lab, you know, and always has to have something in her mouth.

She brought the cap home to the cottage, and I'd forgotten all about it. She must have left it on the floor."

"Where did the dog pick it up, Mr. Kendrick?"

"It was down on Step Beach, and she picked it up shortly after we went down the stairs onto the beach."

"Well, one of the further coincidences in this case is that Agent Andrews was a graduate of Drexel, so we had the hat analyzed to see if we could find anything. Our lab turned up the dog hairs as well as human hairs that under DNA analysis turned out to be those of Agent Andrews." All three of the officers were watching Jack intently to see his reaction.

There was a long pause until Scott Abrams said, "I'm beginning to get uncomfortable with this line of questioning, and at some point may advise my client not to answer any more questions. It appears to me that your tone is no longer one of gathering information but is somewhat accusatory."

"So, are we to believe that this is just another in the long line of coincidences?" Blaisdell asked.

"Mr. Kendrick is here to cooperate in your investigation and can't help what you may or may not feel are coincidences."

"Well, I hope you can see why we're interested in the circumstances surrounding this cap, since it did belong to the victim," Blaisdell said. "We did find the book you mentioned and it had Andrews' fingerprints on it as well as yours, which is what we'd expect. There was also a note inside with your name and address. Can you tell me why that was there?"

"I gave it to Mr. Andrews, since he said he'd return the book once he'd read it."

"So you say this note is your handwriting," Blaisdell said as he showed Jack a copy of the note.

"Yes, that's my handwriting."

"Well, we haven't compared it yet to either the victim's or

your handwriting, and would appreciate your giving us a sample of your handwriting before you leave today."

"Mr. Kendrick will be glad to do that," Scott answered for Jack.

Blaisdell again searched Jack's face for a reaction as he said, "We found your fingerprints in other locations in Agent Andrews' car. They were on the steering wheel and on a folder that was found on the seat."

Jack started to answer, but his attorney interrupted and said, "I think at this point I'm going to advise my client not to answer that question."

"OK. Still, it's a mystery to us why Mr. Kendrick's fingerprints are on the folder if all he was doing was leaving a book in the car. Incidentally, the folder was entirely empty. Curious, don't you think? Did you take anything from the folder, Mr. Kendrick?"

Jack quickly replied before Scott had a chance to interrupt, "No, sir, I took nothing from the car."

"I'd like the record to show that I object to the question and ask that Mr. Kendrick's reply be stricken from the record," Scott said quickly.

Blaisdell replied, "Your objection is noted."

Blaisdell looked at Collins and Cassetti and asked if either of them had any further questions. Cassetti said that he continued to be disturbed by the mounting number of coincidences that had occurred in this case.

Collins, finally trying to exert at least some control over the investigation, said, "We may have some more questions for you later, Mr. Kendrick, and I do have a couple of questions for you now. Do you remember the clothing you were wearing on the boat that evening?"

Jack thought for a minute and said, "Well, I don't recall which slacks I was wearing, but I do remember the sweater."

"We are trying to identify all of the fibers in Andrews' car, and since you were in it we'd like to be able to isolate yours."

Jack looked to Scott, who nodded his head and said, "If Mr. Kendrick remembers what clothing he was wearing, then we have no objection to letting you have it."

"Do you remember how many trips you took to Nantucket from, say, May 1st to the date of your last trip?" Al asked.

"Well, no, I don't right off hand, but since my family stayed on the island from late June to Labor Day I did make several trips, at least every other weekend."

"Would you have a record of the dates of those trips?"

"I think I could figure most of them out with my wife's help."

"Wouldn't the Steamship Authority have a record of your car reservations?"

"Yes, I suppose so, but I didn't take the car over every time I went."

"How many times did you go with the car?"

"As near as I can remember I took the car over in May, when we opened up the cottage, and then didn't bring it over again until I brought the family back in early September. And then, of course, that last trip in October when I met Agent Andrews."

"Will you put together a list of all of your trips and send it to Detective Collins?" Blaisdell asked.

Jack looked at Scott and then said, "Sure, I can do that."

Blaisdell stood. "Thank you for coming and, as Detective Collins said, we may have some further questions for you as this investigation moves ahead."

As Jack and Scott were leaving the building Jack said, "I don't recall either seeing or touching any folder in the car, but I guess it's possible that I touched something as I was leaving the book. I certainly didn't take anything out of any folder."

46

David Mier felt a rush of excitement as he rode in the shuttle bus from the air terminal to the Hertz rental car agency at Logan Airport. To be back in Boston and visit his old haunts had been something he had been dreaming of since his graduation from Brandeis. His hotel room was at the Boston Marriott Copley Place, about a mile or so from Faneuil Hall, but close to many other things that David hoped to take advantage of during his visit. The area had dozens of shops in both the Copley and Prudential malls and was close to the upscale shops on Newbury Street. A few blocks away were the Charles River and the esplanade, where he planned to take advantage of the picturesque jogging paths. There were paths on both sides of the river and there were always numerous joggers, rain or shine. The joggers always seemed to be a mix of Boston culture: students from Boston University, MIT, and Harvard; medical students and health workers from Mass General Hospital; and early in the morning dozens of upwardly mobile members of the business community trying to calm down their personal tensions before they began their daily routines.

There was much he had to do at the Israeli consulate before he could finally go to Faneuil Hall and check out the arrangements for the signing ceremony. The signing would not take place until Sunday and there were a lot of details to check on and arrange in the next four days. He was pleased and yet considerably anxious about the responsibility that had been given to him, even though he knew there were many others working behind the scenes. The Boston consulate had office space for him to coordinate the arrangements for all of the events that would take place—the arrival of the entire Israeli delegation on Saturday, the arrangements for a working dinner on Saturday evening, the confirmation that all of the electronic communications between the consulate office, Faneuil Hall, and Jerusalem were running smoothly, the details and timing of the press release following the signing on Sunday, and the preparation for the inevitable press conference that would follow the signing. The Israeli delegation included several technical specialists who were already at work with their assigned tasks, but David knew the foreign secretary would personally ask him if all of the arrangements were in place.

On Saturday he had to build in time in the afternoon to actually go down to Faneuil Hall and ascertain that everything was in order and consistent with the agreements made between the parties involved. Protocol demanded careful attention to the detail of seating, lighting, space for staff, and all of those seemingly insignificant things that might be perceived by the public or press as putting one delegation at an advantage or disadvantage. He knew that security was a major concern for everyone, and was thankful that Israeli security was in the hands of the Israeli security force, of course, working with the United States Secret Service. He was to contact them when he arrived at the hall on Saturday to ascertain that they had taken care of all of the foreign secretary's concerns.

Fortunately he was by nature a very organized person—some would call him obsessive, but over the years he had found it was the one way he could keep several things going at once without losing his focus. He had put together a time chart listing all of the functions he was responsible for with an estimated time for completion, giving proper weight to those that were the most important and would take the most time. He had been following this schedule since he had first arrived in Washington, and except for the fact that there had been a few more tasks added, he had remained pretty much on schedule.

He checked into the hotel and was given a room on the nineteenth floor that overlooked much of the Boston skyline. He asked to be shown the suite that had been reserved for the foreign secretary, as well as the rooms for the rest of the Israeli delegation, and confirmed that the entire nineteenth floor would be closed off to any other guests. He was told that it had already been arranged by Israeli security.

After unpacking his belongings he made a call to the consulate and said he'd like to see the office he would be using and get started right away. When he arrived at the consulate he could sense the great anticipation for the event that was to happen in a few days. He was shown his office and began to scan the list of tasks one more time to ascertain that no further changes or adjustments were necessary. He paused at the entry that listed his scheduled time to be at Faneuil Hall at 2 p.m. on Saturday and wished that it could be sooner, since this was where the culmination of all of the planning and negotiations over the past weeks, months, and even years would take place. This was where the dozens of reporters and all the TV cameras of the world would be watching on Sunday. This was the place where any potential disruption or act of terrorism at the signing would likely take place. However, this was primarily under the control of American and Israeli security, and his only responsibility was to make certain the communication and protocol issues were handled properly within the hall.

He found the person in charge of the security arrangements, a person he had worked with in the past back in Israel, and confirmed that everything from his end was on schedule. He could sense that all the people he talked to were taking their assignments very seriously; no one wanted to slip up on his or her specific task. As was always the situation when large groups of Israeli officials were involved, the security issues took on an importance that was unique, because historically the nation of Israel was always subject to great terrorist risks.

After spending two hours at the consulate and after satisfying himself that everything was on track, he returned to the hotel. The day was clear, with a crispness in the fall air. He changed into a T-shirt, shorts, and his running shoes and headed out toward the Charles River for a forty-five-minute jog.

47

As soon as the steamship left the dock, Jack went down to the vehicle deck. He had left his own car in Hyannis and bought a ticket as a foot passenger. Now, as he walked around the several rows of cars and trucks, he noticed that there were only a few drivers who had stayed with their vehicles, most having gone up to the more comfortable passenger deck to either relax, eat, or watch television. It was quite common to find passengers stretched out across several seats in the passenger lounge trying to catch a nap during the crossing.

He had decided on sort of the spur of the moment to make an overnight trip to Nantucket to see if anything seemed to tie together with his thoughts about how drugs could get to and from the island. After the meeting with Blaisdell he had had another sleepless night but had gone into work the next day and prevailed on one of the script writers to call the Steamship Authority and try to get some information on passenger lists. He had suggested that the writer say the station was going to do a story on steamship travel to the islands and wanted to get a list of frequent users.

He was surprised to have been successful in getting lists for the two trips he had made during the summer as well as the last trip when the DEA agent had disappeared. There was no list of walk-on passengers but the Steamship Authority had provided a complete listing of all the vehicles on each trip, most of them automobiles. The list included the license number of each vehicle and the name of the owner; however, most of the trucks listed a company as owner and didn't indicate whether the truck was an eighteen-wheeler or a pickup. There was no indication of who the actual driver of each vehicle had been.

Well, it's a start, Jack had thought, *and at least I'm not sitting around building up anxiety.* In studying the lists he had quickly seen that there were some matches showing the same vehicles on both trips—three automobiles and six trucks, including his own car and name. In some instances the truck license number didn't match, but the name of the company that owned it did.

He knew it was a little foolhardy to take off on a moment's notice and try to investigate something that should be left to professionals, but he just couldn't sit around waiting for something further to develop, especially since it had been strongly hinted by the police that he might be involved in some way. He had to check out some of his own assumptions, even though they might prove to be worthless. Amy had been very upset, told him he should let the police do their work, and angrily reminded him that he had a family to think of. It was one of the few times in their marriage that they had had a serious disagreement. He had tried to reason with her as to why it was important to him to follow up on some of his thinking, but she had been adamant that he should not be taking risks in an area he knew nothing about.

Finally they had both realized they were at an impasse and Amy had said, "OK, we're not getting anywhere, so go! I can see doing nothing is consuming you, but don't do anything foolish, and bring your cell phone and call me from the boat."

This was the same Friday night ferry that he had taken a few weeks earlier when the murder took place. Using the list of the cars and trucks that had been on all of the trips that the police had questioned him about, Jack began to methodically check the license plates of all of the vehicles. There were many more cars than trucks—only fourteen trucks in total, from large semi-trailer trucks all the way down to pickups. Most of the trucks were carrying loads of various kinds of construction materials, not at all surprising given the big building boom on the island. Over the years Jack had been coming to the island the amount of new building had continually grown, to the point where traffic congestion was a real nuisance during the summer months. Recent reports had shown that the new home construction growth rate was the highest in the entire state, although the town showed little inclination to limit the growth boom. There had been various attempts to restrict new growth through placing caps on new construction, but they had been largely ineffective. Although more than fifty percent of the island was either conservation land or owned by the town and therefore not available for new construction, there were still plenty of lots—many of them quite small—that were attractive to developers and buyers in this booming real estate market.

The Steamship Authority had listed the cars and trucks separately, and Jack made the following notations of vehicles that appeared on both trips:

CARS: Charles Adams, MA license #459-746; William O'Neil, MA license #296-BHV; John Kendrick, MA license #909-316.

TRUCKS: Marine Home Center, MA license #J73491; Stop and Shop, MA license #J24398; NEEx, MA license #K84297; Marine Home Center, MA license #J73488; Sid Warner, Inc., MA license #K99275; Sun Island Express, MA license #B35124.

Three of the truck license numbers were different than on the Steamship Authority lists, but since the name of the company was the same, he kept them on his list. The number plates on one of the Stop and Shop trucks, the NEEx truck and the Sun Island Express truck were identical to the numbers on both of the steamship lists.

Jack decided that most likely the vehicle he was looking for would be a truck, since many trucks made the trip regularly and would not be as apt to draw suspicion with frequent trips as would a personal car. He began to go down the aisles of vehicles looking for the same company names as were on the list. Only nine large trucks were on the vehicle deck, the rest being pickups. Two semi-trailer trucks had the Stop and Shop logo printed on them, and one had Marine Home Center, the large local store that carried everything from building materials to furniture to flowers. The only other truck with a name that was on the list was a medium-sized truck with the name NEEx that he recognized as a company that delivered packages throughout the New England region.

Next he began to check the license numbers against the list. He found this was not as easy as it would seem because the vehicles were parked almost bumper-to-bumper to conserve space. Also, he wasn't sure whether the number on the list was for the license plate on the trailer or the one on the cab. He didn't want to be seen examining the trucks too carefully for fear that he'd raise suspicions, since some truck drivers were still in their vehicles. Although he didn't want to be seen, he sure would like to get a look at the drivers' faces. He decided to check both the cab and trailer numbers against the list and moved around the vehicle deck cautiously.

There were two matches for trucks with both name and number; one was a Marine Home Center trailer and the other was the NEEx delivery truck. The second Marine Home Center truck had a number that was not on Jack's list. One truck had a driver in it, and in order to avoid drawing attention, Jack decided he'd come down to the vehicle deck later when the boat arrived at the dock and try to get a look at both drivers.

He then went back and checked all of the pickup trucks and the automobiles against the list but found no other matches. This took considerable time since there were more than two dozen cars on the ferry, and he frequently had to squeeze between the rows of cars and trucks because they were parked so close together. They were about halfway across Nantucket Sound by the time he finished, and he decided to go up to the passenger deck and get a snack and read the book he had brought along with him. However, he found he really couldn't concentrate on the book as his mind continually switched to the two trucks on the deck below him and who their drivers might be. He went over again his assumption that the drug traffic somehow got to the island by boat, probably a fishing boat; and then the drugs were shipped off the island by vehicle, probably a truck of some kind. He tried to find holes in his thinking, but the more he thought about it the more it made sense. Still it was only an assumption, and he couldn't take the idea to the police until he had more to go on.

48

Joe Hinkle returned to his truck on the vehicle deck after having a couple of hot dogs from the snack bar. They weren't particularly appetizing after rotating on an electric spit for God knows how long and for how many trips across Nantucket Sound. He preferred a hot dog that was grilled, preferably over charcoal, a little bit burned, and then served with a bun that had been smeared with butter and grilled on both sides. Plenty of mustard, relish, onions, and a generous helping of french fries, made a meal fit for any hungry truck driver. However, there wasn't much choice at this snack bar, and he had had to make do with a soft, non-grilled roll, packaged mustard and relish, and a small bag of chips. He had washed it all down with a large Coke and at least his stomach felt somewhat satisfied, even if his taste buds were not.

Another Friday night and another trip on the steamship to the island might be too long a week for some, but for Joe the ferry ride always meant he would be putting a few extra dollars in his pocket. Except for those two occasions when he had had that trouble with the DEA agents, the trip was always relaxing, as it allowed him the chance to get away from the normal hustle and bustle of the mainland. He'd follow his normal routine during the next twenty-four hours, a late night arrival at the inn, up early the next morning to pick up any additional items at the airport that had to be delivered, and then make those deliveries during the day. Just before he got back on the steamship late tomorrow afternoon, he'd make that last stop at the waterfront and pick up the regular package from Ed Gatious, the fishing boat captain. Joe had made a few trips since he had had the problem with the DEA agent in early October and everything seemed to be going OK—sort of back to normal.

Every once in a while he wondered what was happening with the police investigation of the missing agent, but there had been only a couple of small articles in the paper a few weeks ago, and nothing recently. He certainly didn't have any reason to believe he was a suspect, and he thought he'd know if anyone had been following him. He even picked up the latest edition of the *Cape Cod Times* on the boat, and there was no mention of the death of the DEA agent. No news was good news, and Joe, not always astute, felt even more at ease that he had gotten away with another murder.

He noticed there was a man walking sort of aimlessly around on the vehicle deck, looking as if he couldn't find his own car. Joe didn't pay much attention to him and settled back in the truck to take a snooze. After all, he had had a full day of deliveries on the mainland, and he wouldn't be at the inn until around eleven o'clock.

He woke up as he felt the jolt of the steamship hitting the pylons as it approached the dock in Nantucket. There were a few parked vehicles in front the NEEx truck, and after one of the rows of vehicles left the steamship the deckhand gave Joe the signal to drive off. The ramp from the ship moved up and down with the tide, and at high tide the ship was several feet above the level of the dock. That sometimes made it a little difficult to see the entire ramp from the high seating of a large truck. Joe was always prepared for that, but tonight the angle was not too severe and his exit from the ship was routine.

As he approached the ramp he noticed the same man he had seen earlier on the vehicle deck now standing by the exit looking at him and his truck as he drove by. It didn't make sense that a vehicle driver would be standing at the exit ramp while all the vehicles were being driven off. If he were a foot passenger, then he would exit on the upper level of the ship. The man seemed to look at him sort of purposefully and directly. When Joe looked back at him the man averted his eyes.

That's really odd, Joe thought to himself, *and I don't like people staring at me like that. If I hadn't been busy driving the truck off, I would have stopped and asked him what the hell he was staring at. He wasn't in any sort of police uniform, and there's no reason to think this has anything to do with the murder. The guy didn't look like the cop type anyway. I must be getting a little jumpy.*

49

The next evening, Jack took the twenty-minute flight on Cape Air from Nantucket to Hyannis, and then took a taxi to the lot where he'd left his maroon van. He sat in the van at the parking lot of the Steamship Authority waiting for the 7:45 p.m. boat from Nantucket to arrive. He knew he was taking a risk in continuing to try to solve the murder of Bill Andrews himself, but he had come this far and was determined to go the next step. Amy would be upset with him, his lawyer would be upset with him, but the police and the FBI seemed to be focusing their investigation entirely on him. He'd read enough mysteries and followed enough court cases to know that the police sometimes became fixated on a particular solution to a crime and didn't follow other leads. He felt that he was becoming the victim of one of these situations.

After the steamship had arrived in Nantucket the previous evening, he'd checked the three trucks that he was interested in as they drove off the boat. The two Marine Home Center trucks were driven off and then parked in the steamship parking lot by drivers dressed in the uniform of Steamship Authority employees. He had noticed in the past that some of the trucks were driven off and on by steamship personnel, a financial savings for the business involved, since they didn't have to pay for their own drivers to spend hours on the ferry. Marine Home Center would undoubtedly send their own drivers down to pick up the trucks in the morning. If this was the regular routine for these trucks, then Jack figured it was unlikely that either one was the one he was looking for.

The third truck, NEEx Express, seemed to be the more likely candidate, assuming that Jack's theory was correct, but the more he thought about it the more doubts he had. What made him think he had skills that the police and FBI didn't have? Well, he knew one thing for sure that the police didn't know, and that was that he had nothing to do with the murder or the drug trafficking.

He had stood close to the exit and watched the NEEx truck with red and gold lettering drive down the ramp onto the island and had looked at the driver, but had found it was really difficult to pick out detailed features through the windshield and looking into the headlights as the truck passed close to him. He was certain the driver had seen him staring at the truck, since just before the truck exited the boat they had made eye contact. The truck hadn't stopped in the steamship parking lot but had continued toward the center of town.

Jack had had no way of following the truck, since he had left his car in Hyannis. He hadn't been sure what to do next, but since he had to have transportation to get to the cottage and to get around the following day, he had taken a cab to the airport to rent a car. As the cab turned into the airport, he had noticed the NEEx truck in the parking lot of the Nantucket Inn.

Well, Jack thought, *it's too late for this guy to make deliveries, and he has to sleep somewhere.* He considered for a minute that he might take a room himself at the inn, but thought that might be a little too obvious and dangerous if this guy was the murderer. Instead he had rented the least expensive car available and driven to the cottage. It was cold and the water had been turned off, but he had turned on the electric heat and the house had warmed up quickly.

He had called Amy and told her that he had arrived at the cottage, but didn't fill her in with all of the details of the trip.

He told her that he was going to hang around the island the next day, and she had cautioned him again not to do anything foolish.

When he woke up in the middle of the night, he began to go over all of his suspicions again, and just what he might do the next day. He had to find out whether this driver was the one he was looking for, and had decided that the logical next step was to try to follow him around and see if anything unusual turned up. With the usual clarity of his brain working at 3 a.m. he recalled his previous thought that if the murder of the DEA agent was drug-related—and that really seemed to make the most sense—then it was possible that the driver might be making a drug pickup tomorrow.

When you think about it, it's an ideal cover for drug trafficking, Jack thought to himself. *Here's a guy working for a company whose business is picking up packages and delivering them all around New England. Everyone expects this sort of truck to make frequent stops and deliver and pick up packages.*

The problem for Jack was how he could follow the NEEx truck without being observed, and how he would know if and when the driver actually picked up a package that contained drugs, or indeed if any of them did. He had decided he'd get up early, have breakfast at the Downy Flake Restaurant, and then go out to the inn and follow the truck for a while. Maybe an idea would come to him once he got there. He assumed the deliveries wouldn't start until at least 8 or 8:30 a.m., when the stores had opened and people were up and around.

He had followed the truck at various times during the day, but purposely decided not to stay with it for the entire day for fear of being noticed. He was pretty sure the driver hadn't suspected he was being followed, especially since he was busy delivering and picking up packages. One advantage for Jack in following the truck was that its bright red and yellow markings made it easy to locate on a small island. And second, the uniform of the NEEx drivers was gold with red lettering. Even though this driver's uniform had probably faded, it had still been easy to recognize as he made his deliveries and pickups around the town.

Throughout the day there had been nothing suspicious about the driver's actions or whom he met, until the last stop at the end of the day when he had picked up two parcels from a man down on the waterfront near the town pier. All of the other deliveries and pickups had been at houses or businesses, but in this case the pickup was made on the dock and the man was waiting there for the truck. The man who gave him the parcels was dressed in fisherman's gear, yellow waterproof jacket and pants; and once he had given the two packages to the driver, he had headed back down the pier. There hadn't been much of a conversation between the two men—just the passing of the packages.

Jack had recalled his earlier thinking that drugs arriving on Nantucket would likely arrive by the sea, and he had to be careful not to overreact to his own assumptions. The NEEx truck then drove from the waterfront directly to the steamship pier. Jack had decided he would wait until the NEEx truck boarded the steamship, and then he would take the short flight back to Hyannis, pick up his car, and be ready to follow the truck when the ferry arrived. He knew the longer he pursued his suspicions, the greater the risks, but he couldn't just walk away at this point. One advantage was that it would be dark, and he felt he could follow the truck on the highway without being noticed.

The steamship arrived at the Hyannis dock pretty much on time, and Jack had parked his car facing out of the parking lot so he could follow the NEEx truck when it drove off. A few cars came down the ramp, and then the red and gold truck drove off and Jack followed it out of the Steamship Authority's lot, through the town of Hyannis, and out to Route 6 heading toward Boston.

50

Ahmed spread out the materials on the floor of his rented room. He had kept the suitcase with the explosives in the back of his closet since he'd arrived in Alston. At first he had been worried that someone might stumble upon them, but no one had needed to enter his room since he did all the cleaning himself.

The explosive material was made in the Czech Republic and the special wiring and fuses for the bombs were also in the suitcase. The explosive was called Semtex and was the same kind he had trained with in Israel. He had obtained some heavy tape, a nine-volt battery, and other necessary materials from the hardware store around the corner from his apartment. He had spent time over the past week looking in various stores for a compact clock that would be suitable for the timing device. Since he would be running wires for the simultaneous translation system from the conference table to a central location, he thought he could easily run a separate wire for the bombs to the same location without it being discovered. He could put the timer and battery in the same central control room with the audio equipment. That would mean that the bombs under the conference table would be less bulky and noticeable—something he was concerned about.

Before he left Israel he had been instructed as to how to build the explosive device, and it had been decided that he should use two small bombs rather than one large one. First of all, it would be more difficult to conceal a large device and, secondly, Hamas' objective was to kill only two of the people in the room. They had also felt that two small bombs, each specifically designed and placed to kill a single person, would have a better chance of success than one large one.

The targets were the Israeli prime minister and the chairman of the Palestinian Authority, both being the senior officials present from their respective governments. There would be many other Israeli and Palestinian officials in the room, but it was felt that if these two were killed then the signing would not take place. There would also be several representatives and observers from other countries—Arab states, the European Union, the United States, and the United Nations—but there would be no other heads of states present since it had been agreed that it would take away from the significance and symbolism of the Palestinian and Israeli leaders reaching the peace agreement without external influence. Everyone knew, however, that there had been tremendous pressure on the two parties to finalize this agreement. No one had played a more important role in brokering the treaty than the United States president; however, his presence at the table would have sent a very confusing and negative message, especially to the Arab world.

The Hamas leadership had felt that if these two leaders were killed, then not only would the treaty not be signed as planned, but without their leadership it would be difficult, if not impossible, for new leaders to step forward right away and continue the peace process. The Palestinian extremists felt that the Palestinian leader had betrayed the goals and aspirations of their people—goals that had been fought for with blood and hardship for more than fifty years. They felt that the death of this leader would leave a void similar to the one left when an Israeli extremist had assassinated Yitzhak Rabin in 1995 and the progress toward peace at that time had been halted. Hamas saw both the Palestinian and Israeli leaders as the ones responsible for the treaty, and without them the process would cease, similar to what had happened when Rabin was killed.

Hezbollah and the states of Syria and Iran had publicly expressed strong opposition to the treaty. They saw it as legitimizing the state of Israel and thereby undermining their stated goal of destroying that country.

There continued to be demonstrations, some of them violent, in both the Israeli and Palestinian sectors. They had increased in their ferocity and numbers as the date for the signing grew closer. Even though polls showed that the majority of the people on both sides supported the urgent need for peace, and consequently the treaty, the hardliners and extremists still held to their historical positions and saw the treaty as a surrender to the opposition. There had been dozens of arrests, both of Israelis and Palestinians, as well as several deaths as a result of the demonstrations leading up to the signing. The security personnel in Boston had been augmented by the federal Secret Service, as well as the security forces from each of the visiting countries to protect their own leaders.

Ahmed was well aware of all of the activities, both at home in Israel and in Boston, and the more he read and heard about the violence and demonstrations, the more he was convinced that he played the critical role in stopping the march toward an unjustified settlement. He focused his attention on his task. The making of the two bombs was not very complicated. The wiring to make certain that they would both explode, and simultaneously, was somewhat more difficult; but he felt confident that he could make the explosive devices work. His principal concerns were how and when he would transport the bombs to Faneuil Hall, where he would finally install them, and if he would be able to adequately conceal them. What steps would the security forces take to screen the conference room before the meeting, and how could he avoid detection?

The conference table was large, having space for about two dozen people; and because he was responsible for the wiring of the simultaneous translations, he knew exactly where each participant would be sitting. He was confident that the bombs would be large enough to kill the person at a specific place at the table, even though he was aware that the attempt to kill Adolf Hitler during World War II had failed because of the protection provided by a heavy conference table.

Explosives had improved since then, both in their destructive power and in their being more compact. The greatest concern he had was installing them before the meeting without being seen and without the bombs being discovered. Still, the thought of the critical role he was about to play excited him and gave him confidence. He was able to complete the assembly of the two bombs in one evening, and worked out in his own mind both how he would transport them to the hall and how he would attach them to the underside of the table.

He placed the small bombs in his canvas tool bag and put the rest of the materials back in the rear of his closet. Next Sunday was the day he had been waiting for, and he went to bed that evening running through in his mind the steps he would take to make certain that everything went off as he had planned.

51

Joe Hinkle locked the NEEx truck after backing it up to the loading dock at the terminal in Waltham. It was late on this Saturday evening and the truck wouldn't be unloaded until the next morning. As he walked over to his car, he noticed a maroon Dodge van, similar to the one he had seen earlier, drive by the entrance to the terminal and continue down the highway. He got into his own car and drove out of the lot, trying to catch up to the van; but when he reached the four-way intersection he had no idea which way to turn.

Maybe I'm going crazy, but that van sure looked like the same one I've seen a couple of times since I left Hyannis, he thought. He remembered the van because it was the same model and color as the one his sister owned, and when he had first seen it he had doubled checked to see if it was her. He had seen it first as he was driving off the steamship in Hyannis. The van had been parked near the exit to the parking lot at the dock, and when he took the second look at the van he even thought the male driver looked familiar to him. Later on, as he was leaving the interstate in Boston and driving toward the drop-off point for the two packages in South Boston, he thought he had noticed a maroon van in his rearview mirror, but had discounted it as his own jitters. Now he had seen it again and his anxiety increased even more. He drove down several side streets around the NEEx terminal, but could not find the van.

As he drove home he thought about his previous plan to "retire" from the drug pickup arrangement after the next couple of trips. He was getting gun-shy and couldn't get rid of the uneasy feeling that things just weren't right—despite the two instances of the DEA agents and his having to get rid of them, he had been lucky up to now. But he thought about the man on the ferry yesterday, whom he thought had been taking too close an interest in him as he drove off the steamship, and now the maroon van. It was time to stop the drug business, even though the extra money was something he could use.

He let his mind wander a little more and thought about his tickets to the Patriots game next Sunday. It had been a couple of years since he had gone to a game at Gillette Stadium, and this was billed to be a great divisional match-up with the Jets. The tickets had cost him a small bundle, but to see the three-time Super Bowl champions live was worth it, even though it was only every couple of years. It was something to look forward to and get his mind off his worries.

He looked in the rearview mirror and noticed lights following him. He quickly slowed down and pulled over to the side of the road. As the blue sedan passed he relaxed a bit, subconsciously relieved that it wasn't a maroon van.

Is it possible that the FBI or DEA is following me? Was the van at the terminal the same one I saw in South Boston, and did they see me drop off the two packages? If so, why hadn't they stopped me right there? He really was getting the jitters. With a start, he remembered that the man he had noticed as he was driving off the steamship yesterday in Nantucket could have been the same man he had seen in the maroon van when he drove off in Hyannis earlier this evening.

The next time he talked with Bennie Haas, he'd tell him he was done with the pickups, Joe decided. He remembered again that if he was arrested this would be his third time, and that "three strikes and you're out" meant a long prison sentence—maybe even a life term.

52

The October morning was crisp and there had been a frost overnight. Ahmed had turned on the television news first thing in the morning and learned that the temperature had gone down overnight to 28 degrees Fahrenheit, which he calculated was about minus 2 degrees Celsius. Plenty cold for someone from the eastern Mediterranean, where it rarely got even close to freezing. He noticed that most of the passengers on the T were wearing heavy clothing, but the heaviest thing he had brought with him was a sweater, and he hoped he wouldn't look too conspicuous. As he looked around, however, he noticed that most of the younger student passengers were wearing only sweaters or sweatshirts—typical of youth everywhere refusing to acknowledge the change in seasons.

His tool bag was heavier and bulkier today than usual because of the two explosives he had decided to bring to Faneuil Hall and hide until the day of the conference. Ahmed felt that the security on the day before the conference would be much more intense than this day, several days before the scheduled signing, and he had located a good spot to conceal them until that Sunday. He had been coming and going to the hall for the past ten days, and at no time had he been stopped or searched. His face was now familiar to the two security personnel, and they usually greeted him by either saying, "Hi, Art" or "Hi, Cahill." The informality of Americans was something he was getting a little used to, but he still wasn't comfortable in returning the same kind of greeting.

His wiring of the simultaneous translation system was coming along very well, and if anything he was a little ahead of schedule. The central room where the three translators would be located was on the same level as the conference room. There had to be separate rooms or booths for each individual translator in order to avoid the confusion of several different voices during the transmission to each individual attendee at the conference table. It had been decided that the only translations would be in Hebrew, Arabic, and English. There were other nationalities that would be represented at the conference, but it had been agreed that no other languages would be used. The only reason why English was to be used was because the U.N. secretary-general would preside over the meeting and preferred English, and it was by far the most common language for international meetings.

In addition to the Israeli, Palestinian, and U.N. delegations, there were individual representatives from Egypt, Jordan, Saudi Arabia, France, England, and the United States. Each location at the conference table had to be wired to receive all three translations, since some of the delegates spoke more than one language and no one wanted to presume that they would want to listen to only their native language. This had been the standard approach when Ahmed had wired other simultaneous translation systems, and the listener could control which translation to listen to by simply moving a switch at his or her position to one of three locations. Ahmed also had to provide wiring for translation to several additional locations for observers around the room, especially the press pool, including TV, radio, and print. The potential problem of a large horde of press people was solved by an agreement that there would be only nine press people in the room. Each individual represented a specific pool for the Israeli, Arab, or English speaking press, and this required three for television, three for radio, and three for print.

The wiring was fairly straightforward for Ahmed, but the time-consuming step was checking and double checking each separate location to make certain that each one had all of the technical functions necessary. He had spent the last two days verifying that each position worked and had found only a few where he had to make minor changes. His plan called for him to make one final check of each location on the Sunday before the meeting.

The Israeli prime minister and the Palestinian chairman would be located in the middle of the large oval table immediately across from each other. He had checked and double-checked the wiring at these two locations multiple times. These two places at the table had an extra wire running under the carpeting and intertwined with the translation wiring to the room where the translators would be located. There were so many wires from so many locations that Ahmed was confident that the two additional wires that led to the timing mechanism and the battery would not be noticed by even the most curious and diligent of security personnel.

More difficult was the problem of how to conceal the explosive devices under the table, where they would not be conspicuous but would be near enough to the targets to kill them both. Ahmed had constructed a plastic tube that would hold each bomb and could be taped under the table. He had installed the two tubes several days ago and filled them with extra wiring that was unnecessary and could be removed when he was ready to install the bombs. If anyone became curious about the two tubes, they would see they were filled with wires and assume it was a part of the translation wiring system. No one had asked him any questions, and he felt confident that this part of his plan was going well. Once he installed the bombs on the morning of the meeting, he could quickly attach the two wires under the table and then attach the other two ends of the wires to the timer that was hidden in one of the translation rooms.

Ahmed got off the subway at the Government Center T stop and made the five-minute walk to Faneuil Hall. He noticed that as the date for the signing came closer, there were more press people and paparazzi in evidence around the hall—apparently hoping to catch a photo or an interview with someone who could provide a story or a picture for the evening or next day's news. Also, he noticed that there were more people in plain clothes around the entrances to the hall, and he assumed that these were security personnel. There was no way of knowing whether they were American, Israeli, Palestinian, or U.N. people, but they all sort of looked alike, with the same kind of serious but bland expressions. Perhaps there was an international school for security personnel that resulted in their looking like they all had identical training by the same instructor.

As Ahmed reached the entrance to the hall, he felt a quick twitch in his abdomen that he knew was nerves. There had been several critical points during this assignment over the past few weeks, but today was one of the most dangerous. If he was stopped by one of the new security personnel and they inspected his tool kit, not only would he be arrested, but more importantly he would have failed in his task—failed to stop the signing, failed the Palestinian people, and failed Allah.

He walked without hesitation and with confidence toward the entrance where he knew the security people would be. As he approached the entrance, one of the guards said, "Hi, Cahill. You must be part polar bear to be out in this weather with just a sweater."

As the guard moved to let Ahmed through, he laughed and said, "Well, I didn't realize it was so cold until I was on my way and I spent most of the time on the subway." Within a few seconds he was up the staircase onto the conference room floor and into the translator's room, where he hid the explosives. It was only then that he realized he was perspiring and gave a great sigh of relief.

53

It was only two days before the scheduled signing of the Israeli-Palestinian peace agreement, and Jack was outside Faneuil Hall with some of the WBOS news team trying to decide where they would locate their equipment for their live broadcast on Sunday. They would not be allowed inside the hall, but there would be plenty of opportunity to get pictures of the dignitaries arriving, and certainly to get interviews with the large crowd that was expected to be present. The police were setting up barricades around the hall to keep the crowds from blocking the building. There were already a few demonstrators with signs and flags, some for and some against the treaty; some representing Palestinians and some Israelis.

Only a few yards away stood the store in Quincy Market that Jack and Amy had looked at a few days ago as a possible location for his photography studio. That seemed so long ago now, and he didn't dwell very long on his dream to start up his own business venture. In several ways he knew that this whole nightmare was beginning to affect his nerves. Neither he nor Amy slept well at night. He was having some difficulty during the day focusing on his TV filming in the way he normally did, doing those things with his camera that had always come so naturally. He even found that he was frequently looking around at people, especially those behind him, to see if he was being followed. There were occasions when he thought he noticed the same person several times during the day, and felt that it was likely FBI surveillance. On one occasion he had seen a man in laborer's clothes a few times one day and thought he might be the NEEx truck driver. He had not gotten a really close-up look at the driver at any time but thought he would probably recognize him if he saw him again.

So much had taken place during the past week that Jack was having difficulty separating it all in his mind—the unbelievable interview with the FBI, the unscheduled trip to Nantucket, then following the NEEx truck around the island, and finally following it into Boston.

The easiest part of that day had been following the red and gold delivery truck as it drove into Boston. There had been no stops, and Jack hadn't thought he needed to be overly concerned about being detected since it was dark and the truck driver wouldn't be able to pick out the make or color of his van because of the glare of the headlights in the rearview mirror. He had noticed the address on the side of the truck said "Waltham, MA," but there was no way of knowing whether the driver had been heading there or to some other location. Jack had decided he'd stop following him if the truck continued through Boston to some other location north of the city. He could be heading almost anywhere to another NEEx terminal.

When they had left the expressway in Boston, the truck drove into South Boston, only a couple of miles from the exit; and the driver had stopped and delivered to a small warehouse what looked like the same two packages he had picked up on the waterfront in Nantucket. Jack had tried to remain inconspicuous, but it had become more difficult as they had made frequent stops at intersections and the streetlights made his maroon van more visible. He had parked about a half-block away after the truck stopped to make its delivery. When the truck had turned around to leave, it had driven right by Jack, and his van had been clearly visible. Jack had ducked down in the front seat to give the impression that the "vacant" van was parked there for the night.

As Jack began to follow the truck again away from South Boston, he wasn't sure how much farther he should go, but the truck had left the expressway again, and after a few turns Jack had been quite sure it was heading for Waltham. He had looked at his watch and knew that Amy would begin to worry about him, so he had called her on his cell phone and told her he would be home shortly. She had been curious about what he'd found, but he had held her off by asking her to wait until he got home.

He had followed the truck to the Waltham NEEx terminal and drove by as the truck entered. He had considered for a minute waiting for the driver and following him when he left the terminal in his own car, but decided that he had pushed his luck far enough for one evening. He had turned the van around and drove back through Boston and then to his home in Quincy.

When he got home he spent a good hour explaining to Amy what he had done; she was obviously very upset. She had still been angry with Jack for having gone to Nantucket, and their frayed emotions quickly began to surface. Amy felt he had gone too far and taken too many risks.

"Jack, you're not the police," she had said at one point. "You're not some private investigator. You're taking risks following someone who is dealing in drugs and who may have killed two people. He's probably armed and wouldn't hesitate to kill again. What are you thinking of? You've got a family to think about. Why don't you leave it to the lawyers and professionals to sort this out?"

At this point Jack had lost his cool. "Should I just sit back and let the police and the FBI continue to believe that somehow I'm involved in the murders? There's no indication that they're looking at any other leads, and here I am, an amateur, following up on some logical conclusions and perhaps finding the person who's responsible for the murders and you want me to drop it. Amy, I've got too much at stake and I don't want to be rail-roaded!"

"I want you to go back to our lawyer and at least let him know what you've found out. Ask Scott what you should do and where you should go with your suspicions."

"I don't know what to do. I'm not sure anyone will listen to me at this point. I really don't have any proof at all that this man I followed is involved or that it might be some other NEEx driver, or even some other company and driver entirely. I've been following up on my assumptions about how the drug trafficking might have come to Nantucket, and from there to the mainland. So far, my assumptions are holding up pretty well, but I don't know whether that will make any sense to the police. They sure haven't shown any interest in believing me up to now, and on top of that I don't think they've shown any interest in pursuing other leads."

"Jack, will you please call our lawyer?"

"Let me think it over, Amy. After I sleep on it overnight, I may decide it'll be foolish to do anything further."

"Promise me you won't try to follow anyone again?"

Jack had moved to Amy and put his arms around her. "I've had enough excitement for one day, and I know I've taken some risks that weren't very bright. I won't go any further, other than to decide where and when I should go with my suspicions."

Later in the day, after the news team had left Faneuil Hall, Jack went back to WBOS headquarters and made a telephone call.

"Hello, is this New England Express?"

"Yes, this is the NEEx headquarters in Waltham."

"I wonder if you can help me. I was on the steamship last Friday to Nantucket and met one of your drivers, but I forgot to write down his name. Can you tell me who your driver was on that 5:30 p.m. boat to Nantucket?"

"Sure, that's not hard to do. The Friday/Saturday trip is usually made by Joe Hinkle, but sometimes we do make a change. Let me check." The clerk was gone from the phone for a minute or so and then returned. "Yes, it was Joe—Joe Hinkle. Is there any problem that we should know about?"

"Oh, no—no problem at all. We just had a nice conversation and I wanted to get in touch with him. And, yeah, that does sound like the name. Can you give me his address?"

"Well, we're not supposed to give out addresses, but I can give you his telephone number."

Jack decided it wouldn't be a good idea to press her further and said, "OK, I'll give him a call."

The clerk gave Jack the phone number. He hung up and thought, *Well, at least I've got a name, and she did indicate that he was the usual Friday driver. Maybe someone at the TV station has a way of finding out exactly where this telephone number is located.*

54

As he picked up the phone, Joe heard Bennie Haas say, "Hinkle, this is Bennie."

"Oh, hi, Bennie. How're things goin'?"

"Yeah, well, I should be asking you that question. Any more trouble on your trips to Nantucket?"

"No, everything's fine. It's really blown over." Joe wasn't about to tell him about his fears that someone was following him, especially since he wasn't sure it was anything but his own nerves.

"Well, I'm not so sure and I hope you're keeping your nose clean and not doing anything else stupid."

"I hear you, Bennie."

"Look, Joe, I need another 'special' pickup, but this time it's a pickup in Boston that needs to go to Nantucket."

Joe thought for a minute that this really didn't make much sense. Why would Bennie have a drug pickup in Boston going to the island? After a moment he said, "OK, what's the deal?"

"We need you to pick up the same guy you drove from Nantucket to Boston a couple of weeks ago. He's ready to go back and you'll drop him off at the same place with Ed Gatious at the pier."

"Yeah, OK, when and where do I pick him up?" Joe wondered to himself what this was all about. Why did this guy need a ride back all the way to the island? Why couldn't he get there on his own by plane or by bus to Hyannis and then take the boat over himself? He was reluctant to question Bennie about how strange this was since he knew he was still treading on thin ice with Haas and didn't want to press him too much.

"The pickup needs to take place next Sunday and get him to the island late that afternoon. I know that's not the usual time for your trip to the island, but you've changed it a few times before in order to meet Gatious' schedule in port."

Joe hesitated before he said, "Yeah, I guess I could arrange to switch with the other driver who usually makes the Sunday trip."

"You remember what the guy looked like and that his name is Art Cahill?"

"Yeah, I remember. He sure wasn't very talkative and had sort of a funny accent. He hardly said anything at all from Nantucket to Boston." Joe paused. "Oh, wait a minute, Bennie, I've got a conflict on Sunday. I've got tickets to the Patriots-Jets game in Foxboro."

Bennie came back quickly and belligerently. "Look, Joe, do you want the extra cash or not? I'm gonna double the amount we paid you the last time, since it's not your regular trip. That means 10,000 big ones in your pocket. If you don't want it, I can find someone else easy."

"No, Bennie, I'll do it," Joe hurriedly answered. "It's just that I've been looking forward to this game all year, and you know how hard tickets are to get." The extra bucks always came in handy, and he wasn't about to let someone else begin to make the Nantucket connection. He didn't really buy Haas' explanation that he was doubling the amount because it wasn't Joe's regular trip. He knew that this guy Cahill was probably in the country illegally and that's why all the secrecy. This meant there were risks involved and that's why Bennie was doubling the amount. Well, he'd picked up this guy the last time with no trouble and he'd do it again. Boy, how he hated to miss the

Pats' game! "So, when and where do I find this Cahill guy?" Joe asked.

"As I told you, it'll be on Sunday and you're to meet him outside the Union Oyster House restaurant near Quincy Market. You know where that is?"

"Yeah, sure, but that's a busy area to be hauling around a large delivery truck, especially on a weekend."

"Well, I thought you could use your own pickup truck and then go to the terminal and get the NEEx truck."

Joe paused. "Yeah, I guess I could do that. What time are we talking about? I need enough time to get to Hyannis before three o'clock in order to make the ferry."

"That won't be a problem, Joe. He needs to be picked up in the morning. He said somewhere between 10:30 and 11 a.m., but I think you should get there by 10 just to make sure. That's not a problem, is it?"

Joe thought to himself, *Boy, you're really screwing up my plans,* but he said, "Yeah, OK, I guess I can do it."

"No guessing, Joe, this is important. I need you there at 10 a.m."

"Yeah, I hear you. I'll be in front of the Union Oyster House at ten o'clock."

"One last thing, Joe—make sure you're wearing your NEEx uniform. That's the way Cahill will recognize you."

"Sure, the gold and red colors can't be missed by anyone unless they're color blind, but make sure he knows I'll be in my red Ford pickup. I may not be able to get out of the truck for him to see the uniform."

"OK, I'll make sure he knows. Joe, I'll call you again on Saturday evening just to make certain everything's all set."

"You don't have to do that, but if it makes you feel better, then OK."

Joe hung up the phone and sat there for a while trying to sort out why this had to be done on Sunday and why this guy couldn't get to the island by himself. *Well, the $10,000 will make it almost worthwhile. Shit, I'm going to miss the Pats' game. I've gotta find someone to buy the tickets. Maybe they're worth more than when I bought them since both teams are doing so well.*

55

Jack again found himself sitting in the law office waiting to see their friend and lawyer, Scott Abrams. He wasn't sure just how much he should tell Scott about his suspicions or about his "detective work," but Amy had been insistent that he needed to keep Scott fully informed. He knew she was right, but he also felt that up until now he really hadn't been able to depend on anyone else for help in this nightmare—not the police, not the FBI, not the lawyers. He felt some personal satisfaction at having followed up on his hunches and suspicions, and to this point they continued to make sense. At least he was doing something constructive and not just sitting around worrying and imagining things—like he would be charged with the murder. The more his suspicions seemed to tie together, the more he felt that his own explanation for the murders and the drug trafficking really made sense. The frustration that continually came to his mind was, *How can I get the attention of the authorities so that something will be done to stop all this ridiculous suspicion that points at me?*

Scott called him into his office and they spent a few moments passing the time of day before Jack got to the point. "Scott, I've been following up on a few things since we met with the FBI last week. As you know, I was really upset with that meeting and came away with the obvious feeling that they felt I was somehow involved in the murders and the drug trafficking. Even more disturbing to me was that there was no indication they have anyone else under investigation."

Scott nodded. "Well, I can certainly understand your frustration, but as I told you, when the police are conducting a criminal investigation like this they try not to leave any stone unturned. In doing that they sometimes take an aggressive and accusatory tone with anyone they think might be involved, and I think that's what we were experiencing the other day. Jack, we really don't know whether they're following other leads in their investigation or not, but we mustn't overreact and read things into the process that may not be there."

Jack listened, but really wasn't satisfied with Scott's attempt to explain and downplay their session with the FBI. He didn't respond directly to Scott's comments, but went on to explain what he been doing since that meeting. He described in some detail his thinking over the past several weeks about the events on the steamship that day when Andrews had disappeared. He explained to Scott how he had arrived at his conclusion that the person who killed Andrews and the first DEA agent had to have been on the same two steamship trips that Jack had been on. He explained why he thought the drug trafficking must be getting to the island by sea and then how it was probably getting from the island to the mainland. He went on to tell him how he had concluded that it was likely that the drugs were leaving the island by truck, and that it also had to be a trucking company or an individual who made frequent trips back and forth to the island.

"Jack, you've been doing a lot of thinking and making a lot of assumptions," Scott said, "but this kind of investigative work really isn't anything where you have any training whatsoever. I think you'd be better off leaving this to the professionals."

Jack hesitated before going any further, but then said, "I'm not finished yet, Scott, and remember that from where I sit the so-called professionals haven't done a damn thing for me yet."

He then went on to tell Scott about his latest trip to Nantucket, that he had called the Steamship Authority and gotten the list of vehicles that had been on both of the trips in question, his surveying the trucks on the boat, his following the NEEx truck around the island, and finally the fact that he had followed the truck into Boston and then to Waltham. He mentioned that he had seen the driver pick up two boxes at the waterfront in Nantucket and then drop them off in South Boston.

"You've been taking some big personal risks, Jack," Scott said sternly. "I wish you'd called me before you took off on your own investigation. I have to advise you as your attorney that I'm really not comfortable with this. You may end up complicating this whole problem."

Jack decided not to tell Scott that he had checked further with NEEx Express and had been given Joe Hinkle's name. "Well, Scott, I have to tell you that I'm not entirely comfortable with what I've done either, but I really had to do something." Jack paused for a minute and then said, "Is there something I should be doing with the information I've gathered? Should I pass it on to the police or the FBI? Or do you think they'll even be interested?"

"I really don't know. I do know they won't be happy to hear that you've been poking around like a private investigator, especially when they're probably investigating some of the same leads. Let me think about it and talk with some of my colleagues here. I would like you to take a few minutes right now and write down the series of events, your assumptions, your suspicions, exactly what you've been doing, and your conclusions so that I can refer to the specifics. If we do decide to pass the information on to the authorities I'll need those specifics anyway."

"Yeah, I can do that."

"And, Jack, please don't do anything more on your own; don't go acting like a detective, for God's sake, and don't try to do any more surveillance. If your assumptions are close to being right, you're dealing with someone who's already killed two people and won't hesitate to kill again."

"I hear what you're telling me and I'll try to remain calm, but I would feel much more at ease if I knew the police and FBI were following other leads. I'd like to think that some of the information I've dug up would be helpful to them and they wouldn't feel threatened."

"I'll get some input here from some of the other attorneys and let you know what we think," Scott said. "My major concern right now is not doing anything that's going to increase the suspicions in your direction. The best decision right now may well be to do nothing. These investigations tend to move at their own speed. But again, please don't do anything further without talking with me first."

"Thanks for your time, Scott. I really appreciate all you're trying to do for me."

Jack left, not entirely satisfied that he'd been able to convince Scott of his anxiety and sense of urgency, or that Scott would even talk with the FBI or the police.

56

The month of October is one of the most enjoyable times of the year for the year-round residents of Nantucket. The hectic tourist season is over, the merchants have an opportunity to catch their breath, the traffic jams have disappeared, one can find a place to park in the center of town, and the weather is superb. Because the island is thirty miles out at sea, the cold winter ocean tends to delay the start of spring, and some say there is no spring weather to enjoy at all. However, the opposite is true in the fall. After the ocean has warmed up with the summer sun, the temperature and the summer warmth continues into September and brings delightful weather through October and even into early November. The water is still warm enough for swimming and the harbor and coastline are less crowded with boats, so the locals can truly enjoy all that the island has to offer.

Al Collins was also enjoying the slowdown in activity at the police department, and it was the time when most of the police officers took some vacation. During this last week in October, he was eagerly anticipating the scallop season that had already begun and planned to take a week of vacation time himself to get his annual catch. His gear was ready to go and, like most local scallopers, he was optimistic that this would be a plentiful season.

Since the last meeting with Jack Kendrick in Boston, he had been frustrated that nothing else was developing in the investigation. They had received Kendrick's sweater that he had told them he wore on the day of the steamship trip when Andrews had been murdered, but the fibers did not match any of those found in the car. Still, he felt that they already had enough information to make an arrest and press charges against Kendrick. He had discussed this with the FBI and with the county district attorney, but they were hesitant to make an arrest until more information developed.

He felt he was at a dead end and had done as much as he could. They had proven Kendrick was on both steamship trips—the one when Andrews was murdered and the other trip when the first DEA agent had disappeared. They had found Kendrick's fingerprints all over the place in Andrews' car—on the steering wheel, on the manila folder, and on the door handle. There was no logical reason for his prints to be in so many places if all he did was toss in this paperback book. He had probably taken any information that was in the manila folder. There was no other explanation for it to be sitting there empty. They had found the note in the car with Kendrick's handwriting. They had searched his cottage and found the hat that had belonged to Andrews and Kendrick didn't have a good explanation as to how it got there. Al felt that this was the most important piece of evidence tying Kendrick to the crime. There was simply no logical reason why he should have the hat. Andrews wouldn't have given it to him. Kendrick had probably picked it up on the boat after he pushed Andrews overboard, and then for some reason took it with him. Most criminals usually make one stupid mistake.

And finally, they had found information that Kendrick had a drug history, even though it was back in college, and they knew that he made frequent rips to Nantucket—often enough so that he could be trafficking drugs. Sure, it was all circumstantial, but anyone who had any sense would have to conclude that there were just too many coincidences to ignore. Al felt sure this guy was trafficking in drugs and that he was the murderer, and he'd like to have an opportunity to put more pressure on him. He felt if he could do his kind of interrogation he could get Kendrick to admit to the crime.

He was really upset that the FBI was taking more and more of the lead in the investigation, even though in public they still said it was being handled by the Nantucket police. There was even some question as to whether a criminal trial, if it ever occurred, would be under the Nantucket County jurisdiction or whether it would be in a federal court. If it could be shown that Andrews' death was related to his job as a DEA official, then it was likely that it would be in federal court. On the other hand, if the death was not related to his job, then the jurisdiction might remain in the local court.

Al recognized that more evidence would greatly improve the chances of indicting Kendrick, but didn't know where else to turn. The FBI still had surveillance on him in Boston and nothing had turned up yet. He had suggested to the district attorney that perhaps they should convene a grand jury to review the evidence and let it determine if an indictment should be handed down. This approach would take some of the heat and responsibility off of the shoulders of the district attorney and place it with a jury, but here again the DA was not ready to move.

Well, the only thing Al could do at this point was wait and see if anything turned up from the surveillance. At least the pressure from the press, as well as the police chief, had died down. He guessed it was probably old news at this point, but he decided he would wait a week to see if anything further developed and then talk again with the DA. There had been some discussion over the phone last week with the FBI and DEA as to whether they should broaden the investigation and include others. This subject had come up before and they had gone over the possibility of other suspects, but Al had found no evidence that led in any direction other than Kendrick.

57

Saturday at Quincy Market is always bustling with shoppers and tourists, and this last Saturday in October was no exception. The weather was close to Indian Summer and many people were relaxing on the benches while others were casually moving around the market area. The middle building of the three principal buildings that formed the market area was one long food court, and no matter the time of day it always seemed to be busy. Between Faneuil Hall and the middle market building a small crowd with many children watched the outdoor performers—mimes, jugglers, and acrobats. At other sites around the hall, demonstrators for and against the peace treaty had been gathering all during the day. Mostly they were quiet, but occasionally the two opposing sides had shouted at each other. The police lines were set up to keep the two factions as separate as possible. One wondered whether this was truly a good location for the signing because of the large numbers of people in and around the market.

Ahmed had arrived at the hall around midmorning on this day before the planned signing of the peace treaty. The security on entering the building was the tightest he had experienced, and even though he was now recognized as a regular part of the crew preparing for the meeting, he not only had to pass through the metal detector, but he was also hand-frisked for any weapons. The security guard—someone he had not seen before—took more than the normal amount of time to examine his picture identification card that he had been given to wear around his neck. Even though everything had gone exceedingly well during the three weeks he had been in Boston, this level of screening made him uneasy.

Is it possible that they suspect something and are looking for me? he thought to himself. After he was cleared through the screening, he quickly concluded that there probably was nothing to be concerned about and the increased security was because the meeting was to be held the next day. He knew if he had waited to bring the bombs into the building today, he would have been in big trouble. As he thought about the magnitude of the risks he was taking and what was at stake he could feel some beads of sweat trickle down his back. As the signing date came closer and closer, his anxiety had naturally increased.

He spent the remainder of the morning checking the equipment and making certain that all of the headsets at each of the listening locations worked properly. The foreman, Charlie Edgerly, along with another member of the crew, stayed with him the entire time assisting him, making certain that there were no bugs in the system. They were on the international stage and obviously Edgerly was under substantial pressure. Toward the end of the morning a third person showed up who was introduced to Edgerly as part of the security team. After Edgerly gave him a tour of the meeting area, the man came back to the conference table and said he needed to examine the electronic installation and the equipment and might have some questions.

Ahmed watched as the agent meticulously went over the various locations in the room and finally looked under the table at each one of the twenty-four seats. When he came to the seats at the center of the table, where the prime minister and the chairman would sit, he asked Ahmed what the plastic tubes were for. Ahmed had been prepared for this question and told him they were filled with excess wiring that he didn't want to cut and splice. He pulled the wiring out of both tubes and that seemed to satisfy the agent. Ahmed silently let out a big sigh of relief. The security person also checked the translation booths and left, satisfied that everything was in order. The timing device for the bombs remained hidden and was not discovered. There were still a couple more hurdles that Ahmed had to clear before the explosive devices were armed and ready, but getting past the tubes under the table was a big one.

In early afternoon, as he was leaving Faneuil Hall, he heard a voice across the room that made him stop and look. His subconscious had picked up a familiar voice, but it wasn't until he turned and located the source that he became startled.

He caught himself almost saying out loud, "David, what are you doing here?" He was certain even before he took a second and third look that it was David Mier; not only the tone of the voice but the way the person stood, sort of leaning to one side, brought back memories of those easy-to-recognize, unique characteristics of a familiar person. He was about the same build as the last time Ahmed had seen him, but in his business suit he looked more mature and confident.

Ahmed left the large meeting room quickly and went to the secluded area where the translation booths were. He was certain he hadn't been seen and he began to try to logically put together an explanation in his mind for David's presence at the hall. He knew that David worked for the foreign secretary and so it was possible that he might be in the United States with the secretary for this important event. What a coincidence that the two of them, close boyhood friends so long ago, would be in the same place so many thousands of miles from Israel.

Ahmed then began to think ahead to the next day. There were still things he had to do in the morning before the meeting for the signing of the treaty at noon. He would be at the hall early, and the principal task was to place the bombs in the plastic tubes and make the final connection to the timer. He'd have to be in the meeting room for several minutes installing the bombs. How could he be sure David would not be there? He would have to be extremely careful and alert. There was no possible way he could explain his presence to David.

As he paused to think further, he realized that he was again perspiring and felt that flush of heat that accompanies great anxiety. *Would David be in the room at noon when the explosion took place?* All of a sudden he realized that up until this moment the mission he had been on for the past several weeks had been very impersonal. There had been no one who might be affected by the explosion that he knew personally. In fact, the two targets for the bombs were indeed enemies of Hamas and therefore the Palestinian people. Even though the chairman was a Palestinian, he did not represent the best interests of the people, and Hamas believed he was solely responsible for caving in to the horrendous terms of this treaty. But the thought that David might be in the room when the explosion took place genuinely frightened him.

After a few moments he began to think through the process more clearly. The two bombs were designed to kill only the Israeli prime minister and the Palestinian chairman. It was unlikely that anyone else would be killed, although there would be others injured. The people sitting at the table closest to the two targets would be the most vulnerable. He had worked with the assigned seating list of officials at the table as he set up the simultaneous translation equipment and he knew David's name was not there. As he thought about it more calmly, he realized that David was relatively new at the foreign secretary's office and would not reasonably be expected to have a place at the table. He might not even be in the room. His presence there today was probably as an aide to make sure everything was set up properly.

Nevertheless he would have to be very careful on Sunday morning.

Ahmed left the hall, still shaken, and walked over toward the Union Oyster House on Union Street. There were more crowds and more demonstrators than when he had arrived in the morning, but they were still peaceful. The Union Oyster House was a well-known Boston restaurant and had the distinction of being the oldest in the city. It was only a couple of blocks from Faneuil Hall and an easy walk. When he left the hall tomorrow, after completing the final electrical hookups for the bombs, he wanted to make certain as to where he was going to meet up with the NEEx truck driver.

58

The last several days in Boston had invigorated David and he had been able to not only accomplish what the foreign secretary had assigned him, but also had had time to relax and become reacquainted with the Boston area. He had gone out to Brandeis University, his alma mater, and had spent one afternoon just walking around the campus and being filled with the special nostalgia that came from remembering the four years he had spent there. As a student he hadn't fully appreciated how important that educational experience was. It had been his first time away from home for an extended period, several thousand miles away at that, and in a foreign country. He had come to understand the American people better the longer he was here and the more he was separated from the stereotypes that foreigners have of that country from seeing it only through television and the movies. America had its faults like all countries, and yet its strength came from being a melting pot of many nationalities and cultures over its more than two-hundred-year history. He had especially enjoyed the occasional jogs he had taken along the Charles River, and that morning he had run more than five miles—much farther than his usual distance. He felt invigorated and energized as he looked ahead to finishing the final tasks from his assignment over the next two days.

It was early afternoon and he had walked from his hotel in Copley Square to Faneuil Hall. As he approached the hall he noticed the plaques of the demonstrators. Most of them had sayings opposing the treaty, such as, "Our leader has betrayed us!"

and "Give us back ALL of our homeland!" There were others that called both the Israeli prime minister and the Palestinian chairman traitors. He thought most of the demonstrators were Palestinian, but there were also several who clearly were expressing the conservative Israeli viewpoint of "Don't give back any of our land!" and "Don't give up Jerusalem!"

There was a third group of demonstrators, not as large or as vocal, who supported the treaty. Their signs were fewer in number and the common statement was "Peace now!" David wondered if this group was made up of both the Israeli and Palestinian factions, demonstrating together and each supporting the signing of the treaty, but perhaps for different reasons.

The Israeli prime minister and the foreign secretary were both arriving in Boston late that afternoon. David's visit to the place where the signing would take place tomorrow was one of his last tasks before they arrived. The arrangements for the dinner this evening at the Four Seasons Hotel for the entire Israeli delegation had been checked and double-checked over the past few days. The nervousness he had felt over his responsibilities had subsided as the week went on, and he recognized that one of his personal assets was his self-confidence in high-pressure situations.

The foreign secretary had expressly asked that he make this trip to the hall on the day before the signing to make certain that everything was in order—especially that proper protocol was being observed. David had learned that often the minutest of details could be misinterpreted and send the wrong signals to the press and to the world audience. Where people sat, who sat next to them, the lighting in the room, the location of the television cameras, and the quality of the loudspeaker system were all somewhat minor incidentals to the observer, but in the diplomatic world the little things often made all the difference.

David had made a checklist of all of those things that might be sensitive issues and methodically went around the conference room checking each one. The Israeli security officer was already present, but he was not really concerned with protocol. David found that everything seemed to be in order and that the U.N., in charge of the arrangements for the meeting, had done an excellent job of being sensitive to the protocol issues on both sides. David spent considerable time examining the prime minister's place at the table and checked the earphone and microphone that were part of the simultaneous translation system. On each side of the prime minister would be other Israeli officials—one being David's boss, the foreign secretary. David made certain that all of the equipment at these locations was working properly.

He left the hall after about an hour and walked back to his hotel. He thought about his role on this historic occasion, even though it was a very minor one. But to be present at the signing of the peace treaty, which held the promise of a secure and permanent peace that had eluded Israel for more than fifty years, was something he was proud of. He felt that he had accomplished his assigned tasks well and hoped that would help his career advancement.

59

Late Saturday afternoon Joe Hinkle drove his pickup into Boston and down Congress Street to Union Street and the Union Oyster House. He knew the area pretty well, but he was anxious over the intensity of Bennie Haas' concern that everything go all right. He hadn't seen Bennie as nervous about any of the drug pickups as he was about making sure this guy Cahill got picked up on time and taken to Nantucket. Joe's major concern was where he was going to park the next day. Bennie had said to be there by 10 a.m. but that Cahill might not show up until 11 a.m. He had to find a place close by to park his car while he waited around in front of the restaurant.

Bennie had made a point of his wearing his NEEx uniform so that Cahill would be able to pick him out easily. It had been a few weeks since Joe had picked this guy up in Nantucket, but he was pretty sure he'd recognize him easily. There weren't any parking spots near the restaurant, which was open on this Saturday afternoon, but hopefully tomorrow morning it would be different. It suddenly occurred to him that the police might have some streets blocked off tomorrow and that he might have difficulty getting the truck close to where he was to meet Cahill. Well, he'd worry about that tomorrow, but he was sure he could find some way of getting to the Union Oyster House. He decided he'd better get there well before 10 a.m. so that he would have time to drive around until he found a spot. He was concerned about picking up Cahill, driving out to Waltham to pick up the NEEx truck, and then getting down to the Cape in time for the three o'clock steamship ferry.

Joe was still somewhat uneasy about being followed, although he hadn't noticed the maroon van or anything else that looked suspicious during the past several days. As he drove away from the Quincy Market area, he looked again in the rearview mirror to see if any vehicles following him gave him any concern. *I'm really getting the jitters,* he thought. *I've got to tell Haas that I'm all done after this trip.*

60

Jack woke up early on Sunday morning and turned on CNN to catch the morning news. Sundays were almost always a day off for him at WBOS, since he had some seniority over the younger cameramen, but today was the signing of the peace treaty and the WBOS senior crew would be on the scene for the events at Faneuil Hall. He had to be at the Quincy Market area by 9 a.m. to set up the equipment for the live broadcasts that were to start at 10:30 a.m. Even though the signing was not going to take place until noon, there was a great deal of background coverage that the station wanted to capture. They expected large crowds, including demonstrators; and there continued to be considerable apprehension about the possibility of violence. In addition, the tremendous anticipation of this event had generated interest around the world, and there would be international camera crews to record every minute leading up to the actual signing.

He was watching the 7 a.m. international news with a cup of coffee and toast, and neither Amy nor the children were up yet. All of the coverage for the first several minutes had to do with the signing of the treaty. It showed the arrival of the Israeli prime minister and his entourage at Boston's Logan Airport the previous evening, and then covered the Palestinian chairman and his staff as they arrived at their hotel. Both senior officials gave brief comments to the press—upbeat, positive, and anxiously anticipating the historic occasion on Sunday.

The news coverage went on to show scenes of the demonstrators who had been outside the hall on Saturday and the interviews with some of them. However, the most disturbing coverage was from Israel itself, where there had been violent demonstrations overnight in many locations around the country. The extremists were the most vocal and visible ones, and here again it was ironic that in this instance both the Israeli and Palestinian extremists shared the same goal of being unalterably opposed to the signing of the treaty. The TV commentator made a point of asking whether this was the only time in the past fifty years when the two extremes found themselves on the same side of an issue.

Security was especially tight in Jerusalem, where a suicide bomber had tried to explode his bomb close to the U.N. headquarters in that city. It had gone off prematurely, and though the bomber had been killed, only a few other people were injured. Jack recalled the demonstrators around Faneuil Hall yesterday and the security personnel trying to keep the crowd under control. He was certain the crowds would be larger today, and the larger the crowds the greater the chance that an incident might occur. The Boston police were used to large crowds and demonstrations, having recently hosted the Democratic National Convention, not to mention the enormous crowd control challenges with the Red Sox and Patriots championship celebrations, and the visit of the pope several years ago.

But this was different, especially with the threat of terrorist action of some kind. Jack hoped that the TV crew would not be restricted in their movements, and again this would depend on how volatile the situation became. One of the risks for the camera crew was getting drawn into the violence of a demonstration. On the one hand, you wanted to get close to the news event and capture the emotions of the people—and typically the demonstrators wanted to be on camera and would "put on a show" for the news team. On the other hand, there were clearly physical risks if the demonstration turned violent, and Jack was well aware of news reporters and cameramen being injured while covering events. As Jack thought about it, this particular historic event had more potentially volatile ingredients than any he had covered in his career with WBOS.

When he arrived at the hall, media personnel were every-where. All of the national networks were represented, of course, along with representatives from Israeli and Palestinian televi-sion. But in addition, there were crews from around the world, Middle East countries such as Jordan, Lebanon, Egypt, Saudi Arabia, and Iran, and many European TV networks as well as Russian, Japanese, and Chinese representation. Many coun-tries had multiple competing networks and therefore the total number of media personnel could be counted in the hundreds. Equipment and cables were strung out in all directions to the numerous satellite trucks that were parked some distance from the hall.

WBOS, along with most of the other crews, was interview-ing the demonstrators, as well as people in the general crowd of curious onlookers. After Jack's crew became organized they worked hard to alternate their coverage between Israeli and Pal-estinian demonstrators. Their coverage had to be coordinated with the newsroom at the TV station, some of it actually broad-cast live during a scheduled news program; but most was cap-tured and then transmitted back to the station to edit and air later.

When there was a lull in the interviews, Jack wandered over to the retail store buildings and took a look at the space he and Amy had talked about as a possible location for his photography studio. It still seemed to him that it was unlikely they could make it happen in the near future. He felt very reluctant about going to Amy's parents for a loan, and would rather find some way to finance it themselves. He absentmindedly took a photo of the location and then returned to where the TV crew had set up to interview still another demonstrator.

"The prime minister is a traitor to Israel," said one person. "He's forcing this treaty on the people of Israel, who have given their lives and their blood for our freedoms over the past fifty years. Some of us are being forced out of our homes. We are giving up our historic right to the city of Jerusalem. Palestinians still want to destroy our nation, and Hamas continues to breed hatred and bomb and kill our civilians. This treaty will not bring peace and it legitimates Hamas and other Palestinian terrorists."

And then there was an interview with a Palestinian student who was attending Boston University. "Our land was stolen from us by the Israelis. Our homes were taken from us. Our people have lived in poverty for more than fifty years. Now our leaders are accepting a treaty that only gives us back part of our rightful land, and we are forced to give up our legitimate right to the holy city of Jerusalem. We will be a weak nation, dominated by a more powerful neighbor. We are not even given the freedom to build an army to defend ourselves. Many of us will continue to fight until we receive all of the lands and the rights that belong to us."

It was more difficult to find demonstrators who favored the treaty since it was human nature to be more emotionally stirred by the negative than by the positive support for an issue. The supporters were also less vocal and visible; however, one person expressed the feeling of the quiet majority of both Israelis and Palestinians by saying, "We have had enough war, enough bloodshed, and enough hatred in our part of the world.

Both Arabs and Israelis have a historic right to live on this land, and this treaty is as fair an approach as we can find right now. Neither side gets everything that it wants, but it's a significant beginning. It gives us a structure to move toward a peaceful co-existence that will allow both countries to grow to be more economically sound and away from the destructive cost of violence and hatred."

There was substantial evidence of security all around the hall—hundreds of state and local police as well as some obvious plainclothes security personnel. The crowds were kept several yards away from the building with police barriers, and the area between the front of Faneuil Hall and the middle Quincy Market building was entirely closed off in order to give free access to the entrance for the arrival of the dignitaries. Jack found he had time between the interviews to take several human interest photos with his still camera. He felt he was getting some really excellent shots that not only would have some historic significance, but also captured the emotion of people on this truly historic day for so many around the world.

Maybe that dream of my own photo business will happen sometime in the future, he thought. *Amy certainly encouraged me and seems to be honestly excited. Some of these human interest shots will be really important additions to my collection.*

As the WBOS crew moved all around the exterior of Faneuil Hall, Jack was able to get dozens of shots of demonstrators, as well as the general public, who had come to observe the event.

61

Ahmed slept fitfully throughout the night, tossing and turning, partly from anticipation of finally completing his assignment and partly from anxiety over whether he would be able to finish the final assembly of the explosives without being discovered. His training by Hamas had stressed the personal commitment all Palestinians must have for justice and freedom, and that they should be prepared to give their own life for the cause and in the name of Allah. He felt a considerable degree of guilt when he realized that he was as concerned about his own safety as he was about completing the mission. Then he thought about his brother Hassim, and he tried to convince himself that he had to be prepared to give up his own life as retribution for his death.

What better way to honor Hassim than to prevent the signing of this unjust treaty? he thought. *My people will consider me a hero back home, and if I should die, Allah has promised a glorious life after death. I've been given the opportunity to do something for my people that no one else can do.* Still, he longed for his home, and was excited about the prospect of successfully finishing his task and then beginning the long, secretive journey back to his homeland.

There would be increased risks as he made his escape from Boston, traveled back through Canada, and then finally took the long flight home, because after the explosion there would be a worldwide manhunt to find the perpetrator. The plan was to escape quickly to Canada and then remain in Montreal for a few weeks before making the final flight to Israel. He longed to see his parents, and yet he was apprehensive because he knew they would not embrace the violent act that he was about to commit.

At other times during the sleepless night, he lay awake thinking about David Mier. One moment he would question himself as to whether it really was David he had seen, but then, as he went over the clear recollection of seeing him, he was convinced that it indeed had been David. *What an alarming and dangerous coincidence at this critical point in the mission to be in the same place, many thousands of miles from home, with my boyhood friend with whom I shared so much as a youth!* He thought about their years together back in Nazareth and the time they had spent playing games and sports, exploring the neighborhood where they lived, sharing things, and just fooling around as boys will do. *Will he be at the hall tomorrow morning? How will I explain myself if David should recognize me? Somehow I've got to make certain he doesn't see me.*

As he thought more about his presence he was certain that David would not be in the room when the treaty was signed. Ahmed had seen the list of the attendees, and they were all senior officials from various governments. He was sure David was not on that list. *He must have been at the hall only because his duties as an aide required that he check to make sure everything is in order for the Israeli delegation. The sooner I get to the hall and complete my work, the better the chance that I will not be seen.*

He arose early and finished packing his suitcase. He would pick it up later, after he returned from Faneuil Hall. He spent considerable time and was meticulous in gathering all of the unused bomb-making materials, and any other items that might be traced to him. He put them in another bag and planned to leave them in a dumpster that was in an alley a short distance from his apartment.

He arrived at Faneuil Hall around 9 a.m. and noticed that

the crowds and the media were already gathering. The security at the entrance to the hall was again very strict; he was hand-searched and his identification picture was scrutinized. He had gone over in his mind dozens of times just what had to be done on this Sunday morning. He felt pretty confident in the technical details, but knew that he had limited control over where the security personnel would be as he went about his work. He had worked out the details of when and where he would perform his final tasks so as to minimize the chance of the bombs being discovered.

The first thing on his list was to meet with Edgerly and once again go over the simultaneous translation equipment to make certain it was still in order. Edgerly had specifically asked that they do this first thing in the morning, and Ahmed suspected that the foreman was especially uneasy because he wasn't familiar with the translation equipment and its electronics. It took quite a while to check all of the locations, as well as the booths where the translators would be, and to double-check that the equipment was working at the seats for the prime minister and chairman.

Throughout their time in the meeting hall, Ahmed was continually on the lookout for David Mier. Everything went off perfectly. As Edgerly left he told Ahmed that there would be a final security check later. Ahmed had suspected this might happen but was concerned that it be done soon enough for him to make the final installation of the bombs. He knew it had to be done before 11 a.m. because all of the crew had been told that they had to leave the building by that time.

Ahmed made one final check of the timing device in the adjacent room and was satisfied that it was working properly. He had set the timer for the explosions to take place at noon—the exact time when the actual signing was to take place. He was confident that the two principals would be sitting in their chairs at that time, since the media networks around the world were to all broadcast live at that moment. Tens, and probably hundreds of millions of viewers, would see the explosions.

The three translators finally arrived. Ahmed explained the technical layout, made certain they were comfortable with their equipment, and assured them that everything was working properly. They were experienced translators from the U.N. headquarters in New York and appeared very nonchalant about their roles on this historic occasion. As he finished with them, the same security official who had checked under the table the day before showed up in the translation booths. After looking around that area to make certain that nothing had changed from the day before, he and Ahmed went into the large meeting hall and again went over the entire installation; although it was obvious that the official was somewhat less intense about his work than on Saturday. He had a mirror on a long pole and looked under the table in several locations. He paused at the seats of the prime minister and chairman, and Ahmed held his breath as he ran the mirror under the table where the plastic tubes were located. He looked at Ahmed and sort of nodded and went on about his work. Again, Ahmed kept a close watch as people entered the room, but saw no evidence of David.

As the security man left, Ahmed checked off in his mind that he had gotten by one more high risk in this assignment. He waited several minutes and then went to the area where he had hidden the bombs. He could again feel the perspiration running down his back, even more intensely at this moment, but forced himself to remain calm as he prepared to go through the final step in his mission. He had to take the bombs into the meeting room and install them, all without arousing suspicion. He decided that he had to wait several minutes to make certain the security official had left the meeting room and hope he didn't return while Ahmed was working under the table making the final electronic connections. The bombs themselves were quite compact and he was actually able to slide one in each of his pant pockets. They bulged somewhat, but were much smaller than a soda can and would not likely arouse concern unless someone was especially suspicious. He took a deep breath and opened the door, moving cautiously into the large meeting hall and looking carefully to make certain that neither the security man nor David Mier was present.

62

Jack was especially glad for the extra hour of sleep on this Sunday morning when so much was happening. It was the last weekend in October and the clocks had been turned back one hour last night from daylight savings to standard time. He often wondered why the government didn't just maintain daylight savings throughout the whole year, since it seemed to him that it was much better to have an extra hour of daylight at the end of the day than early in the morning. He guessed it was more important for school children to have daylight in the morning on their way to school. Still, the onset of evening darkness one hour earlier always seemed to him to be an abrupt warning of the shorter days and winter months to come.

During the morning his TV crew had done dozens of interviews, while back in the studio there had been continual coverage of the events leading up to the noontime signing of the treaty. Jack lost track of the number of human interest still shots he had taken, but he was on his fourth roll of film, taking almost anything that looked of interest, knowing that he would discard perhaps ninety percent of the shots. He had found over the years that as he had become more proficient, he had also become much more selective in the shots he saved that became part of his collection. His camera had a zoom lens, and he spent considerable time looking through the zoom to pick out subjects in the gathered crowd some distance from where he was standing.

During one of these moments he was panning the crowd away from the hall when he noticed a man in a faded gold uniform and focused on him more closely. As he magnified the image, he was quite certain that it was a NEEx uniform and that the man resembled Hinkle, the truck driver he had been following. He took several pictures through the zoom lens at its maximum magnification and then edged over closer to the subject. The man was not moving and didn't seem especially interested in the demonstrators around the hall, but was rather just standing in front of the restaurant and looking at people as they passed. Jack took several more pictures, and the more he looked the more he felt that it could be Hinkle. He would have to look over the pictures later.

For the next several minutes he continued to alternate between filming various WBOS interviews with the demonstrators and onlookers and taking some still pictures. His crew was moving around the area in front of the hall, and he wasn't always in a position to see the man in the NEEx uniform. At about 10 a.m. he was again in a position to see the Union Oyster House restaurant and saw the same man still there. He was closer to the subject at this time, and as he looked through the zoom lens one more time he was convinced that it was indeed Hinkle. As he was about take a shot, he saw Hinkle greet another man. Jack took several good shots of the two men before they moved off and out of his sight. He wondered what Hinkle was doing in his uniform on a Sunday—obviously not delivering parcels.

63

Ahmed looked at his watch and noticed that it was almost 10:30 a.m. He had to be out of the building by 11 a.m. when the dignitaries would begin to arrive. As he walked nervously toward the large conference table, he continued to look around at all of the people assembled. Many of them were ones he had seen previously, but there were several new faces. The TV crews that would be filming the event were setting up their equipment, and large electrical cords seemed to stretch to every corner of the room. He continued to be alert to the possible presence of David and was relieved that he had not yet appeared.

He moved quickly to the center of the table and sat down on the chair where the Israeli prime minister would be sitting. He put the headphones on his ears as if he was testing the equipment once again, and quickly slipped one bomb from his pocket and reached under the table, as if to make an adjustment to the equipment. He had practiced over and over attaching the final wires back in his apartment with his eyes closed, so that he hoped to be able to do it now without looking under the table. He pulled the wires from the tube and found the two with the clips and attached them to the bomb. He checked to make certain the connections were secure and then slid the bomb and the wires back into the tube. He slipped the headphones off and looked quickly around to see if anyone was observing him. No one seemed interested, and there was still no sign of either the security man or David.

He moved to the other side of the table to the Palestinian chairman's seat and again went through the same steps. For a moment he almost panicked when he could find only one of the clips; the other wire was missing its clip. He searched around inside the tube with his fingers, and after several anxious moments finally found it. *It must have slipped off the end of the wire,* he thought. *I'm lucky it didn't fall on the floor.* He attached the clip to the remaining wire and then to the connection on the bomb. He again looked around one more time and then stood up and placed the chair back against the table. Ahmed felt like running from the room, but fought to control his nervousness and walk from the room as calmly as possible.

One last check of the timing device and I'll be ready to leave. He went into the adjoining room, found the timer was still working properly, and checked again that it was set for the explosion to occur at noon. He had worked with similar timing devices when he was training with Hamas, and was confident that the microchip circuitry would work properly.

As he was leaving Faneuil Hall around 11 a.m., he saw David Mier and several other men approaching him from a short distance. He quickly reversed his direction and went around the corner of the building, hoping that David had not seen him. He waited nervously for several minutes, his body pressed tightly up against the building, and then regained his composure and cautiously moved away from the hall toward the Union Oyster House. *How many close calls am I going to be able to get away with?*

As he walked hurriedly in that direction, he said a short prayer to thank Allah for protecting him as he completed his mission. *The only thing remaining is for the explosive devices to go off and kill these two leaders.* He felt a tremendous relief at the completion of the assignment and began to focus on escape.

Ahmed picked out Hinkle in his gold uniform at about the same time that Hinkle recognized him. They briefly but coolly greeted each other, shook hands, and Hinkle led him away from the Faneuil Hall area.

Ahmed sat in the pickup truck and tried to reassure himself that David would not be in the meeting room at noon. Again, after thinking through the possibilities, he concluded that even if he was in the room the chances that the explosion would seriously injure anyone away from the conference table were minimal. He silently prayed to Allah, *Please keep David away from the hall and safe when the bombs explode.*

64

The day was brisk but bright as David ran along the Charles River. There were several other joggers out exercising, even though it was early on this Sunday morning, and he had thoroughly enjoyed this quiet time alone when he could energize himself for the day ahead. He ran by the Hatch Shell on the Esplanade, where the Boston Pops orchestra held its summer concerts, and over toward the public boating and sailing area. Most of the sailboats had been taken in for the winter, but the rowing shells were still available and there were several that David had seen out on the water. Close by the boathouse was a protected lagoon, where several geese and ducks were foraging in the weeds for their breakfast. The only hazard along his forty-minute run had been the bicyclists who shared the path in some places. He wished that his stay in Boston would last a few days longer so that he could reacquaint himself with some more of the city's surroundings and culture.

He got back to the hotel at about 8 a.m., with plenty of time to finish packing and get over to the hall with the folder that the foreign secretary had given him last evening. The extra hour—a result of the change back to standard time—had resulted in his waking up early, and he had been able to take the run that he had not planned on. He thought about the state dinner last night with the prime minister, and all of the Israeli dignitaries who had come to Boston to observe the signing of the treaty. The Four Seasons restaurant was one of the best in the city, and was frequently the venue for important gatherings.

Although David had been responsible for making the dinner arrangements for the thirty people in attendance, he had not expected to be present himself; but the foreign secretary had invited him at the last minute.

In addition to the delegation from Israel, there were the senior officials from the Israeli Washington embassy and from the Boston consulate, as well as some of the more influential and well-known American Jews from the Boston area. David had sat beside the president of Brandeis University and had had an enjoyable discussion about the changes in the school since David had attended. During the cocktail reception before the dinner, the foreign secretary had introduced him to the prime minister, who had personally thanked David for all he had done in making the arrangements for today's meeting. The men and women in the room were all important and powerful individuals in their government positions or professions, and David had been pleased and surprised to observe how relaxed they were in this social environment. He thought how very fortunate he was to have the opportunity to rub shoulders with these people on this historic weekend, and mused about the possibility of his being one of these officials later on in his career—perhaps even the ambassador to the United States.

He arrived at Faneuil Hall at about 10 a.m. with the sealed folder that he was to place on the table in front of the prime minister's designated place. The security around the hall was much more rigid than the day before, and he guessed that was to be expected. The thing that concerned him was that as a result it had taken him almost thirty minutes to get into the building and up to the second floor, where the large meeting hall was. They had scrutinized his identification papers for what seemed like an unnecessary length of time, and had called upstairs for one of the senior security officials to come down and examine them. Probably the concern was that he had mentioned he had some private papers for the prime minister and that had set off alarm bells.

When the senior official arrived, he fortunately had an Israeli security agent with him who recognized David, and he was then passed through quickly. He was concerned with the amount of time that had elapsed, since he wanted to be out of the building when the dignitaries began to arrive shortly after eleven o'clock. As he gradually calmed down, he chastised himself for his impatience with the security personnel. He of all people should understand the need for tight security at an event that was a logical terrorist target. Living with tight security was a daily way of life for him back in Israel.

He had watched CNN news before leaving the hotel, and had seen the live pictures of the demonstrators back in Israel. Security concerns and fears were especially high as the hour for the signing drew nearer. It would be evening in Jerusalem when the treaty was actually signed, and everyone at home—both Israelis and Palestinians, those supporting and those opposed to the treaty—would be watching their televisions. He knew that the careful security planning back in Israel for this day had involved the possibility of violent demonstrations and terrorist attacks right up to the moment of the signing and then in the aftermath. No one could predict how serious the demonstrations would become, but he was confident the security forces were as usual very well prepared. Here in the United States, they did not expect the same intensity of public demonstrations, but again they had to be prepared.

David finally reached the meeting room door and was again questioned before he was allowed to enter. The Israeli security agent was there to vouch for him a second time. He was asked to open the sealed folder for inspection, and reluctantly broke the seal and let them look inside. He hadn't been told what the papers in the folder were, but assumed they were the prime minister's remarks that were to be made at the completion of the signing.

It was almost II a.m. when he finally arrived at the conference table. While he was there he decided to make one final check of the translation equipment at the prime minister's place. He sat down, put on the earphones, and moved the switch back and forth between the English, Hebrew, and Arabic positions. He heard the translators testing their equipment, speaking in each of their languages, and for a minute lost himself in listening to all three of the languages in which he was fluent. Satisfied that everything was in order, he took off the earphones and straightened out the folder on the table that held the prime minister's papers.

65

It was an hour after the explosion, but the turmoil and utter confusion had not yet subsided. Ambulances and fire equipment still surrounded Faneuil Hall. Fire and police personnel were continually going in and out of the building. The black smoke that had poured from the broken windows on the second floor had now ceased, so one could assume that any fire that had occurred was now extinguished.

Jack and his crew had been interviewing people when the explosion occurred. They were located close to one side of the building at the exact time of the blast and were showered with glass fragments as the windows shattered. His crew immediately moved to the front of the building, and Jack began filming for WBOS to transmit the pictures live. It had been absolutely chaotic for several minutes, until the fire personnel arrived and the police began to gain control of the crowd. Immediately after the explosion, people in the crowd had panicked and hundreds of them, many screaming, ran away from the building. It was a natural reaction, since no one knew whether there would be more explosions, but the result was that several people had been needlessly injured as they tried to escape the immediate area. Jack was able to film the bedlam and transmit it back to the station immediately while the newsperson with his crew described what was going on.

Within a few minutes the fire and police pushed the crowd back at least a half-block away from Faneuil Hall. The numerous press people resisted the initial attempts to be moved away from the area, but the police quickly became forceful and pushed them back with the rest of the crowd. Some people who had been in the building were seen staggering out of the doors, some bleeding from injuries, some gasping for air, and many just terrified. Fire trucks and ambulances began to arrive in large numbers. Emergency personnel began to take charge of the injured, some of whom received treatment right on the street; they had left the hall while most of the emergency people ran into the building. Firefighters were dragging hoses through the doors, and ladder trucks were extending their ladders on each side of the building. By this time the initial bursts of black smoke had begun to diminish, almost before the fire personnel entered the building.

Most of the crowd that remained some distance from the building was stunned; however, very quickly those demonstrators opposed to the treaty began to cheer and celebrate. This resulted in clashes with some of the general observers. The police, who already had their hands full, were forced to break up several fights and make some arrests. The TV personnel—who lived for headline news—were in the middle of an extraordinary event that was being transmitted live around the world.

It was obvious to everyone present that there had been many injuries and probably some fatalities. At least a dozen ambulances had left with the injured, and the emergency personnel had treated at least that many people, who had not needed hospitalization. The news people were trying to interview some of the officials to find out who was injured. There was a great deal of speculation initially as to who was in the building, but Jack and his crew were quite certain none of the principals had arrived at the time of the blast. They had been on the lookout for the Israeli prime minister, the Palestinian chairman, and the U.N. secretary-general, but had not seen any of them arrive.

Still, some of the network broadcasts picked up rumors from the crowd that they had seen one or more of the principals go into the building. Sophisticated listeners knew that very often the early live news reports from big news events were either erroneous or exaggerated.

66

This son of a bitch, Cahill, is still as quiet and rude as he was the last time, Joe thought. *I'm not the most talkative person in the world, but this guy acts so high and mighty—like he shouldn't be in the same car with me. Well, the hell with him. I can give him a cold shoulder too. The money is the only thing that makes this all worthwhile. It's a damn good thing I got here earlier than Bennie Haas had suggested, because this guy showed up a lot earlier than I had been told.*

Joe Hinkle had arrived in the Quincy Market area a little after 9:30 a.m. and had had trouble finding a place to park his pickup truck. The extra police around the area were a nuisance, and Joe noticed that some streets had been cordoned off. After circling around Congress and Union streets two or three times, he finally parked in a no parking zone about a half-block from the Union Oyster House. He figured the police would be too busy today with all of the excitement over at Faneuil Hall to bother with parking tickets, and he could see the truck from where he was standing in front of the restaurant in case any cops showed up. He couldn't believe all of the crowds around the market area and the noisy demonstrators over in front of the hall. He knew there was to be some important event at the hall today that had something to do with Israel, but truly didn't know or care about any more details.

As Joe and Ahmed were pulling away from the curb, Ahmed said, "You know that you have to pick up my suitcase in Alston?"

"No, nobody said anything about that. Look, I've got to get to Waltham, make sure the delivery truck is loaded and ready, and then we've got to get to the steamship dock in Hyannis by around two o'clock. I also need to get some lunch. Where the hell do I have to go in Alston?"

Ahmed gave him the address and Joe muttered, "Christ, that's way out of the way, and on top of that I'm going to have to take all secondary roads. It'll probably take me twice as long. Look, I'll head toward Alston now, but if the traffic is bad and we begin to lose time I'm going to have to go straight to Waltham."

Ahmed gave no reply, and Joe made a turn to head toward the Charles River and Storrow Drive as they headed out of the city.

When they arrived at the apartment, Ahmed was gone only a few minutes before he returned with two bags. Joe threw them both in the back of the truck, and Ahmed then asked him if he could stop halfway down the block so he could get rid of one of the bags. Joe thought that was a little odd, since he had had both bags when he'd brought him from Nantucket a few weeks ago. When Joe stopped, Ahmed took one of the bags and threw it in a dumpster. He explained to Joe, "Those are some old things that I don't need anymore where I'm going."

Joe didn't say any more but drove away quickly as if he was really late for his schedule. He turned on the radio to a rock station and then adjusted the volume to a very high level—his way of expressing his disgust with his passenger. When they arrived at the NEEx terminal, Joe said, "Look, Cahill, I'm going to park my pickup over on the far side of the building and I want you to stay in the truck until I come by. We're not supposed to carry any passengers, but they kind of look the other way if it's a relative goin' along with us. So that's what I'm going to tell them if anyone asks. But it's better that you stay out of sight."

Ahmed slouched down in the truck and thought about the explosions that should happen any minute. He whispered the same prayer over and over again that the bombs would go off as planned and that David would not be injured. After what seemed like a long time, Joe drove up and called to Ahmed to get his bag and climb into the truck.

Joe wheeled the much larger vehicle out of the terminal and onto the highway. After a few blocks he stopped at a McDonald's and said he was going to get a hamburger and fries. He asked Ahmed if he wanted to buy anything, but Ahmed said no, that he wasn't hungry. Joe just sort of shook his head and went to get his food. He was quickly back in the truck, and after several minutes they arrived at Route 128 and headed south toward the Cape and Hyannis. "I wish we had more time, but I guess we'll make the ferry as long as we don't run into a lot of traffic," Joe said. "We've still got two hours to go and they'll start loading the ferry about 2:15 p.m."

Ahmed made no reply, and Joe turned on the radio to the rock station—again at a high volume. Ahmed looked at his watch and then slouched down in his seat and closed his eyes as if he was trying to go to sleep.

Joe was not really listening to the music but was rather thinking about the Patriots-Jets game that would start in about an hour. How he wished he were there. It was a perfect fall day, this was a division rival, and the Pats were only one game ahead in the standings. If they lost today, then the two teams would be tied for first place. It was only about halfway through the season, but every game against a division opponent was especially important.

Well, this is a home game, and that should give the Pats an advantage, Joe thought to himself. *I'll switch the radio over to the game in a while. At least I can listen to it. Goddamn it, I haven't been to a game in two years, and who knows when I'll be able to get tickets again!*

67

The explosion had occurred almost two hours ago, and Jack's news team was heading back to the WBOS station. Things had begun to quiet down around Faneuil Hall; only a couple of fire trucks were still present, and most of the crowds had left. The news teams were picking up their gear, since there was really nothing more to report at the scene. There had been an announcement by a United Nations official that no principals had been present at the time of the explosion, but no specific mention was made of either the prime minister or the chairman. The official was asked where they were and refused to answer. The security, police, and fire personnel were still on their highest alert around the city, in case there might be other explosions at other locations. It was clear from the official's comments that they were convinced this was a terrorist attack. When asked exactly where in Faneuil Hall the explosion occurred, he had replied only that it was in the room where the peace treaty signing was to take place. He didn't know what kind of explosives had been used, how the bombs had gotten into the building, or who might have been responsible.

Even those demonstrators who had been celebrating the explosions had begun to dwindle in number around the hall. Things were different in Israel, however, where both the Israeli and Palestinian groups opposed to the treaty continued to celebrate late into the evening. Some said the peace process had been permanently thwarted and that finally the two leaders had been made to understand that the treaty was wrong and would not be implemented.

Jack was anxious to get back to the station and print out some of the still pictures he had taken. There were definitely some that he believed were exceptional shots of the events of the day, which could be used by both the TV and the print media. Even though he was employed by WBOS, he had an agreement with them where he owned the rights to any still shots he took. On the other hand, dozens of photographers had been present at the hall, and so chances were good that his would not be unique. He didn't know what his news team would be doing for the rest of the day, but he had heard that there was supposed to be a United Nations news conference sometime in the next hour.

68

The traffic was light, and after they had been on the highway for a while Ahmed spoke to Hinkle. He had to speak loudly to be heard above the radio. "Would you mind turning to a news station for a few minutes?"

Joe looked at him and said, "Yeah, I suppose, but I'm really not interested in listening to news for the next two hours. There's a football game coming on shortly that I want to hear. I was supposed to be at the game, but this trip really screwed me up." He turned the dial and found the hourly news as it was first coming on.

"This is WBOS radio news on the hour, and we will continue to cover the events at Faneuil Hall as we have been for the past hour.

"There was an explosion at Faneuil Hall at about 11 this morning, and there have been multiple injuries. Emergency personnel from around the city are at the scene. This was to be the location of the historic signing of the Israeli-Palestinian peace treaty at noon today, and it is clear now that it will not take place. There is no official explanation at this time as to the source of the explosion, but emergency personnel confirm that it appears that at least one bomb was detonated in the great hall of the building where the treaty was to be signed.

"There is no official statement as to injuries or loss of life; however, there have been an estimated ten to fifteen people transported by ambulance to area hospitals. In addition, several people have been treated for minor injuries at the scene. At this time, it appears that the fire is under control since the black smoke that billowed from the broken windows on the second floor of the building has now stopped. Fire equipment and personnel, however, are still on the scene.

"There were hundreds of demonstrators and onlookers in this busy Faneuil Hall area at the time of the explosion; however, they were far enough away from the building so that they were not injured. There was some initial panic among the crowd, but the police quickly restored order."

As the news report continued, Ahmed sat up straight in his seat and leaned toward the radio. "What time did he say that explosion occurred?"

"I think he said eleven o'clock. Jesus, we were there less than an hour before that."

"I don't understand. My watch says it's a little after one o'clock now. He must have said twelve o'clock."

Joe shook his head and showed Ahmed his watch, "It's about ten minutes after noon right now, not one o'clock. Your watch is wrong."

Ahmed looked at his watch again and said, "No, it's ten after one."

"You must have forgotten to turn your watch back last night," Joe said with a laugh.

Ahmed looked at him, and his face paled with the realization of his error.

"We always turn the clocks back on the last weekend in October," Joe added.

The radio announcer went on to describe the scene around Quincy Market, and interviewed some onlookers live for the radio audience. Ahmed sat silently staring at his watch and figuring over and over in his mind what the error in setting the time device had meant. *Neither the prime minister nor the chairman would have been there at 11 a.m.,* he thought. *It was too early. The treaty signing didn't take place, and I've failed in my mission to kill the two key people.*

At 12:30 p.m. the announcer came on with updated information.

> "It has just been confirmed at a brief news conference by the fire and police chiefs that the explosions were caused by a bomb or bombs that were placed under the conference table that was to be used for signing the peace treaty. Furthermore, the bombs were placed at the seats of the Israeli prime minister and the Palestinian chairman. However, since neither individual was in the building at that time, it is speculated that the bombs must have malfunctioned and gone off prematurely.
>
> "There is a rumor that the prime minister and chairman may be meeting elsewhere in the city; however, for security reasons, no official will confirm or deny this. We also understand that a photograph of a man has been given to Boston television stations to broadcast. Apparently the photo is of someone the police and the FBI wish to find and interview in connection with the explosions."

69

Jack had spent the last several minutes back at the WBOS station looking at the still photos he had taken and waiting to see where the news team would be sent next. He had glanced up at the large television screen on the wall that continually broadcast the WBOS programs when he heard they were putting on a picture of a man wanted for questioning about the explosions. As he was about to return to reviewing his photos he took a second and more careful look at the picture on the screen. He concentrated for a few moments and exclaimed, "It couldn't be him!"

He had loaded his still photos on a CD and quickly flipped back through the dozens of shots until he located the ones he was looking for. He found four pictures he had taken of this man who had met Hinkle near the Union Oyster House that morning. He moved quickly over his computer keyboard and was able to isolate and then enlarge the face of the man. One of the pictures was a clear frontal view, and as he focused in on it he became more certain that it was the same man he had just seen on television. Both pictures showed a person in his late twenties or early thirties with dark, thick hair and a small mustache.

Jack sent one of his crew to the television studio to get a hard copy of the picture they had just shown on TV. They had said this man was wanted for questioning and had been part of the work crew involved in preparing Faneuil Hall for the meeting. There was no explanation given as to why they suspected that this particular individual had something to do with the explosion, but obviously they were very anxious to find him. They gave no other details.

His associate returned very quickly with the picture, and in the meantime Jack had printed out the blown-up image from the photo on his CD. He compared them side by side and asked his associate what he thought. They had both agreed that it looked like the same person. Jack got two others from his news team to look at the same picture and they all concurred. He told them how he had happened to take these particular shots and then thought, *What was this guy doing meeting up with Hinkle, and where were they going?*

He went into the office of his crew chief, showed him the pictures, and asked him what he thought they should do. As the crew chief carefully examined the pictures and considered what their options were, Jack had an idea. He picked up the phone and called the NEEx terminal in Waltham.

"Hello, I'm calling from the Steamship Authority and just want to verify that you're going to be using the reservation for a truck on this afternoon's ferry to Nantucket."

"Let me check," the NEEx employee said. After a moment she returned to the phone and said, "Yes, the truck is en route and should be there in plenty of time for the 3 p.m. ferry."

Jack hesitated a bit and then asked, "Can you tell me if the driver today is Joe Hinkle?"

"Yeah, I saw him here earlier. He switched with the driver who usually makes this run. Is there a problem?"

"Oh, no, I just happen to know him and wondered if he might be the driver. Thanks a lot."

Jack hung up the phone and then explained to the crew chief all of the background—who Joe Hinkle was, how Jack had happened to be taking the photos of the two men, and about the murdered DEA agents. "I think Hinkle is taking this guy to Nantucket," he concluded. "I don't know why for sure, but maybe it's somehow linked to this drug smuggling."

His boss looked doubtful. "We're really not one hundred percent sure this is the same person, and even if he is we don't know whether he's even in the truck with this guy Hinkle."

"No, I guess you're right, but there's a lot at stake here, and I still think I'm right. They do look like the same person to me."

"What time does that boat leave?" the crew chief asked.

"She said three o'clock."

"Well, it's almost 1:30 p.m. now, and we don't have time to drive to Hyannis, but I agree that this is potentially too big a story to miss. Let's get your crew together, and you take the helicopter down there and see if you can verify that this guy they're looking for is really in that truck and heading for Nantucket. In the meantime, I'm going to talk to the station chief and get his opinion about if and what government officials we need to notify at this point."

Jack quickly got his crew together, and they were ready and out on the helicopter pad within ten minutes. The Bell helicopter was just large enough for his four-man crew and their equipment and could make the trip to Hyannis in about forty-five minutes, but then the crew had to get to the steamship dock. As they were flying en route, Jack remembered his last conversation with his attorney, Scott, who had cautioned him to let him know of any further contact he had with the authorities. Jack decided he should call him right away.

He was able to reach Scott on his cell phone at his golf club and quickly filled him in on what had happened. It was difficult to hear over the noise of the helicopter engine, and Jack had to repeat himself several times. The lawyer had heard about the explosion but paused on the phone, trying to take in all that Jack explained and then relate it to Jack's problem with the murdered DEA agents. "Look, I need some time to think this through," Scott said. "What's your cell phone number? I do think we probably need to contact someone and let them know what you suspect, and it probably should be someone who's familiar with your situation. I'll call you back. But remember, don't take any risks or do anything foolish."

"OK, I'll wait for your call. And, Scott, thanks for handling this for me."

Jack sat back in his seat and tried to make sense of all of the events of the day. *Is the guy with Hinkle really the one the police are looking for? What is he doing with Hinkle anyway, and are they really on their way to Nantucket? If they're not, then I'll look really stupid. If it has something to do with the drug trafficking, how are they involved with the Faneuil Hall explosion?*

His thoughts were interrupted by the crew chief. "OK, we've got to decide what we do when we get to the steamship."

70

Scott Abrams left the golf club after talking with Jack and went to his office in the city. On the drive he went over in his mind what Jack had told him and realized he needed the advice of one of the senior attorneys. When he got to the office he called Ted Andriolli at home. Scott had discussed the case with Ted before, and they talked over the situation for a long time. They decided that a call should be made right away to the FBI to inform them of Jack's suspicions and where Jack was headed. They felt that they should present their suspicions about the passenger in Hinkle's truck as something they weren't sure of but felt the FBI should be informed. Andriolli didn't know Jack personally and wasn't as convinced as Scott that Jack wasn't overreacting, given the pressure he had been under. Scott knew that they would also have to inform the authorities of Jack's suspicions about Joe Hinkle and the fact that he had been doing some "investigating" on his own.

Scott had a great deal of difficulty getting the FBI to put him in contact with Agent Blaisdell. Obviously everyone was involved with the Faneuil Hall investigation and didn't want to be bothered with other matters. Scott had to emphasize to the person on the phone that he felt he might have information that was related to the explosion. When they finally got FBI Agent Blaisdell on the joint phone call, Scott went over the situation in detail from the time of the last meeting with them to the events of the morning. After several minutes and explaining Jack's suspicions about the passenger in the truck, there was a long pause on the phone. Finally Blaisdell spoke in a somewhat frustrated and angry voice.

"I'm not sure what to make of all of this, but I'm really upset that Kendrick has gone off on his own trying to solve this drug trafficking case and the agent's murder. It's not only foolish and dangerous, but it also might compromise our own investigations. You should know that our own investigations here have broadened and there are other vehicles we are checking out that were on all the same ferries where the crimes took place. One of those was a NEEx truck, and we are aware that Joe Hinkle was its driver on those occasions. We're also aware of Hinkle's violent past and criminal record."

Scott did not respond but was disturbed.

"Hinkle's past is one reason why it's foolhardy for your client to be sticking his nose in business that should be left to professionals. However, all of that aside, my main concern now is this passenger in Hinkle's truck and if it is indeed the same person we're trying to locate in connection with the bombings this morning. I've got to make some calls right away. What time did you say this ferry was to leave Hyannis?"

Scott was about to answer when his cell phone rang. He excused himself from the call for a minute and answered the call. Jack Kendrick was on the other end of the line.

"Scott, we arrived at the dock just before the boat was to leave. We decided that I should get on the ferry and see if I could locate the truck. The boat is just leaving the harbor now and I'm down on the vehicle deck where the trucks are. I've found the NEEx truck, and there is a passenger sitting in the truck that looks like the same man I saw in the photo. The driver, Hinkle, has gone up to the passenger lounge. I think you should go to the authorities and have them meet the boat in Nantucket."

"Ted Andriolli and I are on the phone with Agent Blaisdell right now," Scott answered. "We've just filled him in on what's happening. If you're right about this guy, you should get away from that truck and away from Hinkle. Wait for the authorities to handle it. Let me call you back and, again, don't do anything foolish. I should tell you that Blaisdell is pretty pissed off about your detective freelancing. I'll call you right back."

Scott got off the phone and told Blaisdell about his conversation. When the agent heard that the suspicious man was on the boat, he said, "Look, I've got to get on this right away. Tell Kendrick to stay out of the way. We're dealing with some killers."

71

Joe Hinkle sat in one of seats in the bow of the steamship and looked at the TV coverage that continued to carry information about the bombing. His face showed frustration and anger, and he thought to himself, *I'll sure be glad when this fuckin' trip is over. I couldn't stand another minute with that guy, Cahill. He's almost creepy the way he just sits in the cab, says nothing, and either stares straight ahead or out the window. He even seemed to get more nervous and fidgety as we got close to Hyannis.* He smiled to himself. *Maybe he's afraid of getting seasick on the ferry ride. Serve him right, but it better not be in my truck! I'll call Bennie as soon as I get back to Boston tomorrow and tell him I'm done.*

He looked around the room and began to focus on a man sitting on the other side. He thought the guy looked familiar to him. He glanced over a few more times, and at one point made eye contact with the person, who then quickly looked away. After a while it came to him that this guy might be the same one he had seen on his last trip to Nantucket—the same person who had watched his truck come off the boat in Nantucket and then was sitting in the maroon van in Hyannis on the return trip. *Are the police really following me, or am I just getting jumpy?* he wondered. *Christ, I should have quit this before.*

He was about to go over and confront the man when he noticed a picture come on the TV screen. He moved close to the television that was mounted on the wall so he could hear what the announcer was saying. The sound was turned down quite low and the background noise made it really difficult to hear. As he concentrated on the picture he actually whispered out loud, "Jesus Christ, that's Cahill!"

The picture remained on the screen while the announcer went on with his report.

> "The FBI has released this picture of the man they are looking for in connection with the bombings this morning at Faneuil Hall. His name is Arthur Cahill and he was employed by the firm that was doing the electrical work at the hall in preparation for the signing of the peace treaty. We are told he is in his late twenties, medium height, dark hair, and a mustache. He was at Faneuil Hall earlier this morning and apparently left shortly before the explosions. There is no more information as to where he may be at this time; however, if you have information about Cahill or think you may have seen him, please contact the FBI or the Boston police immediately. The FBI stresses that this man is dangerous and may be armed."

Joe stood there stunned for a minute and then stormed out of the passenger area toward the stairs that led down to the vehicle deck.

72

Ahmed did not dare leave the truck and had been trying to find a news station on the radio, although the steel hull of the steamship blocked reception. All he was getting was static; he had gone over the dial several times, but without success. It was important that he get an update on the explosions, and even though he knew it was unlikely that either the prime minister or the chairman had been there, at least the treaty had not been signed. He was frustrated, angry, and frightened. Optimistically he tried to convince himself that between the explosions and the demonstrations in Israel and in Boston, the political leaders would hold off any signing until things quieted down. That might give Hamas a chance to come up with another plan. *How can I explain what happened?* he thought. *What a stupid mistake after all the work I've gone through during the last few weeks!*

Finally it occurred to him that even though the AM stations wouldn't work, perhaps he could get the news on an FM station. He quickly switched the radio over to FM and began to search the dial again. He found a public broadcasting station that was providing news coverage.

"Here is what we know at the moment about the events at Faneuil Hall this morning. The explosion occurred at around 11 a.m. and there were multiple injuries and one fatality reported so far. Neither the Israeli prime minister nor the Palestinian chairman was at the hall at the time. The fire was quickly extinguished, although there has been substantial damage to the large auditorium in the hall.

"The FBI has released the picture of a man they are seeking as a suspect in the bombing. He is a Caucasian male in his late twenties, of medium height, with dark hair and a mustache. He was last seen in the vicinity of Faneuil Hall this morning before the explosions. His name is Arthur Cahill, and he was apparently employed by a company doing work at the hall in preparation for the signing of the peace treaty. There is an extensive manhunt now underway for Cahill. Anyone with information as to his whereabouts is urged to contact the FBI or the Boston police.

"The name of the man who was killed by the explosion has just been released. He was an aide to the Israeli foreign minister and was at the hall prior to the arrival of the rest of the Israeli delegation making final preparations. His name was David Mier, and he had been in this country only a few days as a member of the advance team for the signing of the treaty. We are told he was killed immediately by the explosion."

Ahmed began to shake uncontrollably and tears began to stream down his face. *What have I done?*

The announcer went on:

"I have just been handed a joint press release from the Israeli and Palestinian governments. It reads as follows:

'In spite of the unfortunate events of this morning at Faneuil Hall in Boston, we are pleased to announce that the historic peace treaty between our two governments was signed today at 1:30 p.m. The signing took place in the governor's office at the Massachusetts State House and was witnessed by the United Nations secretary-general and several officials from other nations who were here in Boston to observe the signing. We thank the governor of the commonwealth for offering his facilities to complete this historic occasion. We regret the violence and loss of life that occurred today, which represents the unsuccessful attempts by terrorists to destroy the prospects for a lasting peace in the Middle East. We rejoice today at the beginning of a new era for our two countries—one that will bring peace and economic prosperity to our two peoples.'

"That is the end of the official announcement, but it is clear that the violent actions of the extreme elements in the Middle East have been frustrated. We will continue to interrupt our regular programming as we receive more information concerning the events at Faneuil Hall this morning."

Ahmed was thunderstruck. He felt faint. So many things were rushing through his mind that he could not think rationally. Through his sobbing, he whispered rapid and disjointed thoughts. "David is dead! I've failed completely in stopping the treaty being signed! Will I even get out of the United States without being caught? Will I be able to get out of Canada? Will I ever be able to get back to my homeland? I've failed Hamas! I've failed the Palestinian people! What do I say to Hamas, even if I do get back? What do I say to my family? How can I even go back to Nazareth, where David's parents live? He was the one true friend I've had in my life."

Suicide is a mortal sin under Islamic law, but as Ahmed slumped in the truck, tears still streaming down his face, gripped with fear and depression, he saw no other way out of his personal hell.

At that moment the door beside him was yanked open and Hinkle reached in, grabbed him by his jacket, and pulled him out of the truck. He pushed him against the side of the truck and demanded, "Who the hell are you? Your picture is all over

TV and the FBI have a manhunt out for you because of the bombing at Faneuil Hall. Are you responsible for that?"

Ahmed, shaken, mumbled, "I don't know what you're talking about."

"Look, you sick son of a bitch, I think you're some kind of a fuckin' terrorist. All this secrecy about picking you up in Nantucket and now bringing you back. I think you're a goddamn Arab who sneaked into the country illegally. You've got me involved in this shit that I have nothing to do with. Do you realize the whole country is looking for you? Every cop has a copy of your picture!"

At this point, Ahmed pushed away from Hinkle and ran to the stern of the steamship near the large docking porthole. Hinkle pursued him and cornered him at the porthole, grabbed him, and threw a punch that glanced off of Ahmed's face. As they continued to struggle, Ahmed again pushed Hinkle away, turned, and swung one leg through the porthole. Joe grabbed hold of his jacket and threw another punch at him that struck him hard high on the temple. Without a second thought, Ahmed kicked back at Hinkle and dove through the porthole into the cold ocean.

Hinkle looked out the porthole and saw Ahmed slip beneath the waves, and then looked around to see two men running toward him.

73

Jack had observed Hinkle's reaction to the TV news report and followed him when he went down to the vehicle deck. The altercation at the truck happened quickly, but Jack's photographic instincts were such that he was able to get a picture with his camera.

He followed the altercation when Ahmed ran to the stern of the boat, was able to get another shot of their struggle at the porthole, and then was shocked to see Ahmed go overboard. At that moment he noticed one of the crew running toward the porthole, and he joined him.

The crewman grabbed the telephone by the vehicle exit door and Jack heard him say, "There's a man overboard! He just went out a porthole on the stern!"

Almost immediately he felt the steamship sharply lose power, and an alarm bell rang throughout the vessel. Hinkle was standing near the porthole, and as the two men approached he was repeatedly saying, "That guy jumped overboard! The crazy bastard jumped overboard!"

The crewman said, "We saw the two of you fighting, and it looked to me like he was pushed."

Jack looked at Hinkle's anguished face and said, "I saw you fighting with that man by your truck, and then you chased him back here and continued to fight."

"Listen to me! He's the terrorist the police are looking for. His picture's all over the TV! I didn't push him overboard! He jumped!"

The crewman picked up the phone again, explained what

had happened, and told the captain to hurry down to the vehicle deck. By the time the captain arrived, the steamship had reversed its direction and was going back to try to locate Ahmed. The captain had a revolver in his hand and said to Hinkle, "Look, I don't know who you are or what happened here, but I need for you to come to my cabin and remain there until we reach port. We will call ahead for the police to meet the boat."

The boat circled back and forth around the area where Ahmed went overboard, but was unable to find any sign of him. In the meantime, they had called the Coast Guard. After about forty-five minutes a Coast Guard cutter arrived to continue the search, and the steamship then continued on to Nantucket.

Jack used his cell phone and called his WBOS team, who by this time was on Nantucket waiting for the steamship to arrive. He filled them in on what had transpired and told them to be at the dock and that there would be police there to apprehend Hinkle.

74

Al Collins received a call at home to get down to the station as quickly as possible—that the chief of the Nantucket police was off island and there had been a development on the murdered DEA agent's case. When he got there, he was told that FBI Agent Blaisdell had called and said that there might be a connection between the DEA drug case murder and the bombing in Boston at Faneuil Hall. He called Blaisdell to get more information, and the agent was clearly excited. He told Al he needed to get a team of officers together immediately to meet the next steamship when it docked.

Blaisdell added that the FBI felt there was a good chance that the terrorist who had caused the explosions that morning was on that boat, and that the man was obviously dangerous and probably armed. Blaisdell said their information was that this man was a passenger on a NEEx truck that was on the ferry with a driver whose name was Hinkle. Blaisdell didn't know how Hinkle was involved, but said Al should arrest both of them. He stressed that no one should be allowed to leave the boat until they had located and apprehended both Cahill and Hinkle. He told Al that they would fax him a picture and description of Cahill. Finally, he told Al that an FBI team was on its way to the island by helicopter but wouldn't be there in time to meet the boat.

"Al, you understand the importance of this, don't you?" he asked at last.

"Yeah, of course I do."

"You're comfortable that you have the right people there to handle this until we arrive? We'll probably get there about an hour after the ferry docks."

Al, somewhat perturbed, said, "I'll take care of it. I'll get all the men I need." After a pause he asked, "What's the connection between this and the DEA murder case?"

Blaisdell told him about the call he'd received from Jack's attorney and about his suspicion that Hinkle was the one who had killed DEA Deputy Director Andrews and probably the other agent. He said he had found out that Jack had apparently been doing some amateur detective work and he was the one who had seen Hinkle together with this other guy, Cahill, after the explosion.

"Incidentally, Al, Jack Kendrick is also on the ferry. He apparently followed Hinkle and his passenger there from Boston. I should tell you that we have expanded our own investigation into Andrews' murder and just this week have identified Hinkle as another suspect. We hadn't told you yet because our investigation isn't complete. In any event, that investigation isn't what's important today. All of the local, state, and federal law enforcement personnel in the area are focused on getting the person or persons responsible for today's bombing."

Al listened to Blaisdell, upset that he had not been informed about these further developments in the DEA murder case. "I wish to hell you'd kept us informed out here on what you've been doing," he said at last. "Are you saying that you don't think Kendrick was involved in the DEA murder?"

"Yeah, it sure looks that way to me now. For Christ's sake, Al, this isn't the time to be discussing the DEA case. Getting your men together, down to the dock, and arresting both of these guys is the only thing that matters. This bombing is really high-profile and has about as much international attention as any event could have. You've got to put the DEA case out of your mind."

"OK, I'll take care of things until you get here."

Just after he hung up, Al's assistant came in and told him a man had gone overboard from the steamship and that the captain wanted to talk with whoever was in charge at the station. "I'll take the call," Al said at once. Picking up the phone, he told the captain that the chief was not on island and that he was in charge. The captain proceeded to explain the events that had taken place, and that he had apprehended Hinkle and wanted to make sure the police would be at the dock.

Al told the captain what he had just learned from the FBI and asked him if knew the name of the man who had gone overboard. The captain replied, "I don't know his name, but he was apparently a passenger in the truck with Hinkle. There's another passenger on the ferry who said he thought the man who went overboard might be the person the FBI is looking for in connection with the bombing. It sounds like that seems to tie in with what the FBI just told you."

"Yeah, well, make sure this guy Hinkle is kept under wraps," Al responded. "I'll be at the dock when you arrive. Also, make sure the other passenger, whose name is probably Kendrick, is also there."

Al then called in five of the officers who were on duty but scattered at different places on the island. He began to make arrangements for meeting the ferry. He looked at his watch and saw that he still had a good hour before the steamship arrived.

75

As the steamship pulled into the pier in Nantucket, the passengers noticed several police cars lined up on the dock and a television crew standing near the exit ramp filming the arrival of the boat. There had been an announcement over the loudspeaker that everyone would have to remain on the ferry for a few minutes until the police came aboard in connection with the man who had gone overboard.

Al Collins and the five uniformed officers stepped onto the ferry as soon as it was secured to the dock, and the captain took them up to the cabin where Hinkle was being held. As soon as Joe saw the officers he said, "The man jumped overboard. I had nothing to do with it."

After listening to the report of the crewman and Kendrick, Al said to Hinkle, "I'm arresting you on suspicion of murder." He then read him his rights, emphasizing that he had the right to remain silent and that anything he said might be used as evidence against him in a court of law. One of the uniformed officers then handcuffed Hinkle and led him off the boat while the WBOS news team captured the event and broadcast it live back to the studio and eventually to networks around the world.

As Al Collins passed by the WBOS team, one of the crew heard him mumble, "Goddamn coincidences, and all on the goddamn ferry."

76

POSTSCRIPT

Ahmed Khalil's body was never found; however, his suitcase was recovered from Hinkle's truck. It contained several forged passports, as well as his legitimate passport with his picture and his legal name, Ahmed Khalil. Under interrogation, Joe Hinkle told the police about the second bag, which was recovered in Alston and found to contain several bomb-making items.

Based on the steamship crewman's testimony, Joe Hinkle was tried and convicted in federal court of murdering Ahmed Khalil, even though he continued to insist that the man had jumped overboard. He was also convicted of the murder of DEA Deputy Director William G. Andrews, based primarily on his fingerprints on a folder in Andrews' car. In addition, he was convicted of conspiracy in connection with the Faneuil Hall bombing and for drug trafficking. He was sentenced to life imprisonment without parole.

Ed Gatious, upon learning of the bombing and the events on the steamship, left Nantucket harbor in a hurry to elude the authorities. He was apprehended by the Coast Guard twenty-five miles northeast of Cape Cod and charged with drug smuggling and being an accessory to the terrorist bombing.

The memorial services for David Mier and Ahmed Khalil were held in Nazareth on successive days, David's with a large crowd of Israeli officials, as well as mourners from the Nazareth community. Only family members and a few friends attended Khalil's memorial service.

Bennie Haas escaped detection because Joe Hinkle refused to give the authorities any information about where he had brought the drugs. He was perhaps more fearful of Haas than he was of the federal authorities.

Al Collins was interviewed repeatedly on national television for several days following the arrest of Hinkle and took personal credit for making the arrests and for breaking the DEA murder case. At no time did he mention the role of either the FBI or Jack Kendrick. He was promoted to assistant chief six months later.

Several of Jack Kendrick's photographs of the events of that Sunday were truly one of a kind. He was the only one to have pictures of Khalil and Hinkle together at the Union Oyster House, and also had the only picture of the altercation between the two men on the steamship. He received more than $100,000 in cash awards in selling them to other media outlets. With the proceeds he and Amy opened their photo studio in Quincy Market and Jack resigned from WBOS.

The nations of Israel and Palestine live in somewhat less turmoil and terror than in the past, although there continue to be frequent demonstrations and occasional violence by the extreme elements on both sides. The terrorist organization in Lebanon, Hezbollah, supported by Iran and Syria, continues to be a threat to Israel and the fragile Middle East peace. The United Nations is successfully administering the city of Jerusalem, and the number and intensity of violent demonstrations there by both Jews and Muslims has gradually subsided following the signing of the peace treaty.